THE IMMORTAL SCALES

GAME OF GODS

BOOK THREE

E. M. LEANDER

First edition
ISBN: 979-8-9904666-0-9

Editing by Ben Gibson and Leonora Stewart
Dust jacket artwork by Salome Totladze
Dust jacket design and typography by Giessel Design
Hardcover design by E. M. Leander
Map illustration by Foreign Worlds Cartography (foreignworlds.net)

To everyone who has read Wren and Aris's story—Thank you.

Polar Ice
The Vault
Abelon Wastes
Abelon City
N
W
S
The Broken Sea
Crescent Islands
Basti
As commissioned by His Majesty
King Leonidas II

Temple of Aenon
The Iron Needle
Soltaire
Chanet Forest
Roallac
Raverra
The Black Strait
Ocron
Estana
Golmere River
School of the
Silver Flame
The Isles
Aclines
Spit

LETTER

FROM KING LEONIDAS III OF OCRON TO NIGHT MAGE VERENA HARKER

My Wren,

I am sorry to hear of your disillusionment. While Ismini has assured me in the past that each Mage-and-Shield pair eventually find their own way, I'll admit, I do not understand how your partnership will work. While Aris is a fearsome Shield, perhaps one of the greatest in their history, he remains at his core a man who lives only for the attention of others, intent on glory above all else. He is a notorious rake, a philanderer, and while you may trust your life to him, please be careful of your heart.

Let me be quite plain. My time here is short. My dearest wish is that you will fly home soon. I can't wait to have you sitting at my side. What a queen you will make.

Yours,
Leo

THE LAW OF THE SHIELDS

First law: Protect your Mage—above country, blood, and all else.

Second law: The bond between you shall be as strong as the roots of the mountains and shall never fail, unto death. A claim shall be unmade only at the express desires of both parties, and then only after careful consideration and approval by the Head Mage.

Third law: Your fellow Shields shall be closer to you than your own flesh and blood. Any evil committed against them is made against Rigrasil himself, for which the penalty shall be swift and severe.

THE GODS

Rigrasil: Father of the gods, and the god of day. He created the First Shield, Odall.

Caladrius: The god of night, often felt to be a balance against the elemental gods.

Aenon: The god of water, patron of Water Mages.

Helene: The goddess of wind, patron of Wind Mages.

Cephus: The god of earth, patron of Earth Mages.

Ignatius: The god of fire, patron of Fire Mages.

PROLOGUE

WREN

A few weeks from now

I wake to a throbbing pain in my temples, bad enough to make my stomach clench and bile rise in my throat.

My eyelids feel sticky and swollen. I've been crying while I slept. The floor jerks again sharply, and my eyes fly open. The world moves by in a dizzying way as the cart creaks along a pitted dirt road. Each time a wheel strikes a rock or hole, I'm tossed around like a rowboat in a storm.

I flip over onto my back, looking for the dark sky above the thick branches. My chest aches. Where my magic was, there is now only a gaping wound, as raw and painful as if I'd taken an arrow to the gut. I call to it out of habit, to any scrap or wisp of night magic I can, but it's no use. There's nothing there, and the effort only makes me more nauseated. Tears leak from my eyes. I don't bother wiping them away.

Overhead, bars of gleaming metal—too bright to be silver—arch and form a roof, just tall enough for me to stand under, if I wanted to. A door is crafted into the side, where I can be let out to relieve myself when we stop—during the day only. They know better than to let me out at night. A lock as thick as my wrist holds it shut. Even if I had something to pick it with—a hairpin or my knife, which they also took—I have no opportunity to.

How has it come to this? I am a bird in a cage, my wings clipped. The silvery metal steals my magic more effectively than the manacles ever did. I am helpless. Trapped. And on my way to be delivered to the Snake Queen.

It's all over. She's won.

I'm sure she'll kill me, eventually. My guards have said as much. But will she first try to use me as leverage against the god of night? She already has the King of Ocron, Leo, in her dungeons. What else could she need me for, except as one more prize to gloat over? I imagine a thousand scenarios in my head as time drags on, each one more gruesome than the last.

And I pray to Caladrius, if my prayers can escape this metal prison—I pray as I've never prayed before. I pray that Aris didn't suffer, that his death was honorable, that he has earned a place among his ancestors at Rigrasil's side.

I can only imagine why I haven't gone gray. Is it because I'm a Night Mage and not an elemental Mage? Or was there something different about our bond that allows me to live when he does not? I have no desire to exist in a world without Aris. There is an injustice in this, in my inability to go gray like the others and end the pain. Mages and Shields bond after they complete training, forming a magical contract, and it results in both their magics becoming stronger. A strong Mage will make a strong Shield even stronger, but I have no way to tell if my own magic has returned to its unbonded state. I scream out my grief, once, twice, as I screamed before into the night, but no green lightning greets me this time, no magic storm, no outlet for my emotions.

Instead, I am only a caged bird, crying into the night.

CHAPTER 1
ARIS

Loren is propped up in bed, the dark red blanket draped carelessly over her hip. I give her a smirk and finish pulling on my pants. The ship rolls on the sea, the last of the daylight streaming in through the windows at the back of her cabin. Being captain has its benefits—her cabin spans the entire width of *The James*, with space enough for a fine bed, if too gaudy for my own taste. The carved headboard is gold-leafed, the bedding silk and embroidered velvet.

Bedding that is currently a mess, gold-tasseled pillows on the floor, the sheets kicked to the side. The rest of the cabin is orderly, her maps and compasses and other implements in neat rows, the few books she keeps stacked together on a shelf. The ship plunges down another wave as I dress, and I sway to accommodate it. Maybe not as effortlessly as Loren, or Stiggur, but close.

"The stamina of a Shield is not exaggerated," she says, her voice husky and low. "Are all as ... gifted as you?"

"No," I say.

I gather up my hair, which has escaped its tie, and bind it back. Loren watches me with dark eyes, her expression composed and carefully blank. Her hair hangs loose, damp at her temples from our time together. It is straight and smooth, like silk threads.

It's hard not to compare it to the riot of curls, bound in a long braid, that I've become so familiar with. I shake my head and snatch my socks from where they landed, on the floor on the far side of the cabin. *Where in the hells did my shirt go?*

"Strange arrangement you have, following that girl around," Loren says, like she's reading my mind. She draws a circle on the blanket with one finger and takes a deep breath that has her full breasts heaving. She meets my eyes, weighing whether she wants to speak her next words. "Man like you, with your strength and talents? Seems like a waste."

I see the look I've seen in so many women's eyes before. A possessiveness, something beyond the simple agreement we had—a satisfaction of our mutual physical needs, nothing more. Invariably this agreement changes; their desires change. And there is no one in this life I want to be claimed by, except one.

"At sea, a man answers to no one," Loren continues. "No country, no flag. He is free."

"Answers to no one but the captain, you mean," I say.

She gives me a smug smile. She isn't giving up. "And would that be so horrible, Dragonslayer?" she asks, her voice as smooth as the silk of her hair. Her finger keeps spinning circles on the blanket, lower, dancing across her flat belly.

Dragonslayer. The word thrums through my head, an endless cadence, as I search for my damn shirt.

If I'd been told as a child that "Dragonslayer" would be the title that followed me, I'd have been puffed up with pride for weeks. Now? It sounds hollow, a haunting reminder more than a badge of honor. I've always prided myself on being an honorable man—though my allegiance is firstly to my Mage, I've never shied away from doing what needs to be done. Once, I disciplined the heir to the Roallacan throne, whatever his name was, after I caught the woman he'd been abusing crying in a palace corridor. I didn't care that he had a crown on his greasy head, or the Roallacan ring on his pale finger. In my mind, it was no more complicated than punishing a man who'd forced himself on a woman—royal or not. I got into a lot of trouble for that one, but I've never once regretted it. But this?

Slaying the dragon wasn't even my doing, not really. I feel like a fraud, taking credit for Dimitra's actions. *She* was the one who shoved me under its great belly, where my blades were able to finally pierce its armored hide. *She* was the one who sacrificed herself—to save us. To save *me.*

Dragonslayer. Dimitra deserves it, not me. The title shames me.

And would it be so bad, really, to stay with Loren and leave all that guilt behind? To break my claim and leave Wren? To chase my own desires freely, rather than those of my family and my Mage?

The thought leaves my head as quickly as it entered. To do so would dishonor the Law of the Shields, and I'd have my name stricken from their records, a fate worse than death.

Not that I need such a threat. I'd sooner fall on my own gladius than betray my Mage.

Besides, I hate boats.

My thoughts no sooner return to Wren than there's a knock on the door, brisk and sharp. *Thank all the gods.* Spending my days tangled up with Loren during this trip has provided a much-needed distraction from my grieving and frustration, but as the sun goes down, and Wren prepares for her evening shift speeding *The James* along, back to Basti, I can feel myself tensing again, my jaw clenching hard enough to ache. Loren likes to speak of the future—one that she clearly sees me in.

Me? I'm barely hanging on to the present moment, and much too entangled with the past.

"Captain?" Stella's voice calls. It's Loren's twin who opens the door, cracking it just enough to peek in. The black silk eyepatch she wears over one eye does nothing to detract from her beauty—and it's the only way I have to tell them apart. Other than the outlandish tricorn hat that Loren insists on wearing when she's on deck, with its large golden feather drooping over one side.

Loren gives me an arch look, misinterpreting my silence.

"Maybe my sister joins us again, hmm?" she purrs, reaching for me.

I am most definitely not entertaining the idea, at least not seriously, when Stella coughs into her hand. The setting sun gutters out at the precise moment she opens the door wider, and the cabin is flooded with green light.

Wren is beside her, a furious expression on her face.

My Mage.

Glowing with green fire, outshining the sun with her brilliance.

CHAPTER 2
WREN

I wake up tonight alone. It takes me a few moments to gather my senses, to remember that I'm in the belly of *The James*, whose rocking motion I'm certain I'll never, ever get used to. My magic is starting to wake up too, the dark orb I see in my center flickering slowly, as if it, too, were stretching and yawning. I look out the porthole at the rushing, white-capped sea. We scale waves like mountains, and my stomach leaps into my throat as the ship pitches down another gray-blue peak.

Fortunately, my stomach is too empty for me to vomit anything up. Bile coats my throat as I tug on my boots and make my way to the head and then the deck.

The fresh wind is infinitely better than the stale, salty air below. I let it whip through my hair for a moment, stray curls streaming out behind me like a banner. I take a deep breath and expel the sourness in my gut. The smell of the sea was ubiquitous in my youth—though I always experienced it from the shore, from the safe confines of my lighthouse. A pang of memory clenches my chest, of my home—the home of my parents and my father's family, going back generations—lying in ruins. Aenon's minion, a great kraken, had been searching for me—and found my home instead. It is nothing but a pile of rubble now. The glass windows at the top, the ones I polished daily for most of my lifetime—gone. The ancient bed with its threadbare quilt—gone. The kitchen floorboards, worn smooth by generations of caretakers—and then gouged deeply by a tiger's claws, stained by his blood. I once worried I'd never be able to get the stains out. It doesn't matter anymore.

All of it, gone.

I look at the quarterdeck, where one of the crew mans the helm, and then forward, but I don't see Aris. I clutch the necklace he gave me. The beautiful green crystal never leaves my neck—I've taken to twirling it around my fingers whenever I think of him. Usually Aris meets me, or he's up here somewhere doing his exercises. Caelus and Rafael stay mostly belowdecks—Caelus praying, and Rafael just ... staring at nothing. I've tried talking to him, bringing him something to eat, but he just stares. I miss his whistling, his bad jokes. I miss having him to talk to—especially about Aris. He'd understand. He'd have something funny to say, some witty, reassuring quip. I think about sharing that bottle of wine with him the last time Aris and I fought—it would take more than a bottle this time, he'd probably say.

But Rafael is lost, caught somewhere in his mind. I can only hope that Caelus has more luck with his prayers than I've had with my efforts.

I run a hand through my wild curls, fighting to tame them back into a braid as my gut continues to churn—not from the tilting of the ship's deck but from growing certainty that I know *exactly* where my Shield is.

"Ah, Night Mage, glad to see you up. You look about as green as an eel, though," a massive red-haired man says, swinging down from the rigging on the mainmast. He lands lightly, at odds with his tall, muscular frame.

"Thanks, Stig," I grumble. Stig—Stiggur—is a Shield, like Aris. His shifted form is a tiger shark—and a massive one. The last time I was on this ship, we were attacked by the kraken—as far as we know, there has only been one—and Stig protected the ship. He'd even hauled my stupid Shield back to us after Aris had thrown himself overboard to land the killing blow.

"Good evening, Night Mage," Stig's companion, Stella, says. She's lean and browned and as smug as Stig, her good eye glinting at me, like she's amused by my state.

I note that I don't see her twin, the captain, anywhere. I feel it like a punch to my already curdled gut.

"Soup's on, if you want to eat," Stella says. I wonder if she's deliberately provoking me.

The idea of food—no doubt something pickled and stinking of fish, in a way that my lighthouse never, ever did—is the final straw, and I have to run to the railing to let loose a mouthful of green bile. I see a seahawk soar by and think of Adriana, wishing I could shift and fly rather than endure this terrible voyage. I think of Delphine, the dragon Shield, and her giant, beautiful feathered wings—I bet she could make the flight from Abelon to Basti in a single night. *Gods, Caladrius, couldn't you have given me wings?* You *have them. Would it have been so hard?*

"Ah, right, then," Stig says, rubbing the back of his neck as I hurl again. "Are you all right to work? T'ain't the morning sickness that you got? My brother—he's with the Ocronian navy—well, his wife swears by gingerroot when she's with child. Cook's got some, if you want."

I hear a thump and then a groan from Stig, and I hope that it's because Stella has kicked him. Hard. Preferably in a delicate part of his anatomy.

Stig can be an utter ass, just like Aris. But he's also not the one paired to a grumpy, seasick Mage who is responsible for Queen Evanthia of Roallac's capture of Leo—King Leonidas, the Ocronian king. Stig's not the one whose heart shattered when he watched his lover die. He's not the one who immediately ran to the first pair of open arms—and open legs—he came across. He's not the one whose face I want to smack nearly as much as I want to kiss.

Morning sickness. What a joke. Though Dimitra's moonberries are still rattling around in the bottom of my pack, there's been no reason to use them. Aris hasn't been interested in touching me—nor I, him. Maybe I was, once. It isn't a feeling I have a lot of experience with. Maybe I felt his presence in my life to be as inevitable as the tides. Maybe I thought that he felt the same way, that I would be more to him than a conquest, that he was someone I could give myself to, body *and* heart. I'd even asked Leo about it—Leo, who's become as close a friend to me through our letters as I've ever had.

Aris had a choice there, in the ice cave. That's the downside of being part of a claimed pair. Sure, when a Shield claims a Mage, both are made stronger, a blessing of the gods—or so Caelus told me. But if I'd known the risks—being paired with a stubborn, philandering asshole *for the rest of my life*, not to mention that if he gets his stupid ass killed, I'll lose my magic and go gray, fade away, lose all will to live until my heart just stops beating—it's a bargain I would never have made.

At the time, when Aris claimed me at the School of the Silver Flame, I thought of him as my champion, someone to guide me through understanding my magic and this world of gods and Shields that I had found myself in. And he was.

And then somehow he became more. Someone I was more physically and emotionally intimate with than I'd been with anyone in my entire life—someone I began to imagine as more than just my Shield. As my partner. My friend. Even my lover someday.

And he sacrificed himself to save Dimitra, choosing her life over mine, knowing that when he died, our bond would kill me too. Bonded partners rarely survive long when one dies. Aris did, after his first Mage was killed. My magic called to him even then, somehow saved him, even before I knew him—like it knew even then I needed him. That bond, that connection, grounded him somehow, gave him a reason to hang on to this life rather than fade. It's the same reason

Rafael didn't go gray after Dimitra died—though he hasn't been looking particularly good lately. He hasn't spoken since her death and has barely eaten—but he isn't gray. Caelus thinks that his bond to Mariana—Caelus's bonded Mage, and a traitorous bitch—as her lover is what kept him from fading. She was at his side, pleading with him to stay alive—just before she betrayed us.

It was only Dimitra's love for Aris that saved him—when she shoved him down, taking the full force of dragon fire herself. She made sure he was able to kill the beast before it harmed anyone else, at the cost of her own life. Noble Dimitra. How I hate her.

And I hate myself for that even more.

Aris took a tooth from the dragon and still carries it with him at all times, his hand straying to it even in his sleep, like a constant reminder of her. Not that he's been sleeping much, from what I can tell. Between his grieving over Dimitra and his ... other activities with Captain Seagraves, I'd be surprised if he was sleeping at all.

The thought of my Shield makes me vomit again. Whether or not he shares my bed, he's still my gods-damned Shield. Isn't it enough that I nearly burn myself out each night, speeding *The James* along so we can get back to the mainland and catch Mariana and the stolen Book of Silver? Must I do it all alone? Where in all the hells *is* my Shield, anyway?

Though the indignant thought echoes in my mind, it's tinged with anger. I know *exactly* where his stupid, perfect ass is. And the rest of him too. I wipe the back of my hand across my mouth, trying to stifle the heaving of my stomach as the ship plunges down another wave.

"Right. I'll bring you something to settle your stomach, then," Stella offers, with more kindness than I would have expected. "Why don't you go on up to the quarterdeck, breathe in that fresh sea air? It'll help, promise."

I nod. "Where's Aris?"

Stella looks at Stig, then back at me, and even in the fading evening sun I can see the flush staining her cheeks.

"Uh, not sure," she says, averting her eyes. "If I see him, I'll send him along."

I sigh. Not so long ago, Verena Harker of Spit would have done as she was told, would have gone and done her job without questions.

But Wren, the Night Mage, the only one of her kind, the chosen of the god of night, Caladrius, himself, she'd burn this ship to ash if she wanted to, and skip her way to shore over the waves. She is *done*.

"Take me to him," I order her.

Stella flinches, the gold hoops in her ears shimmering with the motion.

"Stella. You can take me to your sister's quarters, or I'm going on my own."

I can pretend to be aloof, like seeing Aris practically naked, standing next to an arrogant, rumpled-looking Captain Seagraves—who *is* naked—doesn't bother me, but the gods-damned green glow of my magic will betray me every time. I light up like a star, throwing Aris's features into sharp relief.

The bastard merely raises an eyebrow at me, like *I'm* disturbing *him*.

"Did you need something, Night Mage?" Captain Seagraves is practically purring in the bed behind him, not bothering to cover up. And why should she? She's stunning, all lean muscle and golden tanned skin, just like Dimitra, and nothing like me—short and round and brown. Plain little Wren, just like the bird. Any bravado I managed to talk myself into has vanished, like the sun that's sunken below the horizon.

"If you're done with my Shield, can I have him back? We have work to do," I say, not making eye contact with Aris, definitely *not* noticing the sleek sheen of sweat on his chiseled chest, the satisfied flush on his face, the little curl of black hair damp with sweat and clinging to his neck.

"What work?" Captain Seagraves asks archly. "Need someone to fetch your supper or something? Shine your boots?"

Aris doesn't say anything. His knuckles tighten so hard around the shirt in his hands that I can hear the fabric tearing. But he doesn't say anything. We stare each other down, each waiting for the other to break.

"What *we* do is between us, Captain," I say at last, looking away. "You can have him back when I'm done with him."

The ship pitches hard to the side. I grab the doorframe and *feel* rather than see the lightning strike the sea just inches behind the room's glass rear windows. They rattle in their frames, and I have the satisfaction of seeing the insufferable Captain Seagraves flinch. If Aris even notices, he doesn't let on. I let loose another flash of lightning for good measure, to remind them exactly who I am, who they are meddling with.

And the light is as green as jade, as green as the Sacred Wind—and as green as envy.

I turn on my heel and walk out.

"Night Mage? I don't mean to be ungrateful for the speed, but could you turn down the wind a peg? If those sails tear loose, we won't be no use to no one," Stig says, coming up the ladder to the quarterdeck. In the green glow of my magic, his bushy hair and beard are being blown around wildly, and he has to fight to keep them both away from his eyes. Though he's nearly seven feet tall, with the rippling muscles granted to him by his Shield magic, he's having a hard time standing straight in this gale.

My storm. My lightning, my wind, my waves. Mariana pushed us along with just water magic—but me, the Night Mage? *All* the elements now bend to my whim, and I call them all to me, to push *The James* ever faster. Like a loosed arrow, we fly across the Broken Sea. All around me is light and cool salt air and sea mist—and in the chaos, I find peace. A coil of green light springs from my hands, wrapping around the creaking mast, anchoring it, steadying it. I refuse to let it tear loose. Everything on this ship will do exactly as I command.

Samuel, the one-armed sailor, is the only one brave enough or stupid enough to try to hold the helm while I push *The James* along. I guess he's figured that if he survived a kraken taking his arm, he'd survive a night with the Night Mage. Probably. He has lashed himself to the helm, though.

"Let me up, Stig," another voice says—a voice I'd recognize among thousands, over the roar of a hundred storms.

The wind intensifies, and a bolt of lightning illuminates the sky so close that the instantaneous boom of thunder shakes *The James*, sending vicious tremors through the wood.

I have to hand it to that Black Water Witch. Mariana might be a traitor, but her waterproofing spells on *The James*'s hull are really good. Now that I'm not holding back, I'll have us back to the mainland in half the time that it took us to cross to Abelon.

Stig drops back down the ladder, and Aris climbs up. He's shorter than Stig, his build leaner, though he still towers over me. He leans into the wind, holding tight to the rails, making his way toward me. His lips are moving, but now I can't hear anything over the wind—and I don't want to. I'd sooner pitch him overboard. I hear tigers are good swimmers.

Because Captain Seagraves is right. I *don't* need Aris right now. I might still *want* him—with every fiber of my stupid, traitorous body—but I don't *need* him. Even without his knife lessons, his strategizing, his strength, I am enough. *I* will bring this ship to Basti by night's end, and from there I can make my way back to Aeturnus on my own, and then to the Prasinos Mine, where hopefully I can get a horse or two, I think, pointedly ignoring Aris. Two weeks' hard ride across the plains, and then on to—

Aris lurches across the deck to me with uncharacteristic awkwardness. *The James* topples over another mountainous wave, and he stumbles—catching onto me. My feet are rooted to the deck, rooted like a mighty oak, my magic anchoring into the wood—*I* will not fall.

He wraps his arms tight around my waist, bending his face to my neck, his lips so close to my ear that I can feel the warmth of his breath. He *dares* touch me, with hands that so recently were on ... Gods, I don't even want to *think* about where his hands have been. Where his mouth has been.

But the words he whispers to me aren't in anger. In fact, I can barely hear them. The wind drops by half, the ship groaning in relief, just so I can catch those words.

"You're no good to anyone if you burn yourself out."

The green glow around me intensifies, and Aris ducks his head, shielding his eyes. The wind whips long strands of his hair across his face, salt spray collecting on his lashes. Even like this, he is so beautiful it hurts to look at him. So I don't, and I look instead across the sea in front of us.

"No good to *you*, you mean," I say, resolutely focusing on the black horizon. "Don't worry your pretty head. If I burn out, I have no doubt Captain Seagraves will be more than happy to comfort you."

"If you go gray, I go gray too!" he snaps back, louder this time.

The wind picks back up, and my braid smacks him across the face.

"You survived the death of your last Mage. I'm sure you'll be fine," I say over my shoulder. Going gray is the ultimate risk for any paired gifted person, Mage or Shield.

And it's just so damned typical of Aris. Only thinking about himself. He doesn't care at all if I go gray, only thinking how it would affect *him*. Women wouldn't be half so inclined to glance his way if he went gray.

Gods, maybe it would be worth it.

I raise my hands back into their outstretched position—the sails bell back out, straining at their stays. We are moving so fast now that the water droplets sting my face where they land. Aris adjusts his grip on my waist, his fingers almost painful against my body. It takes him a minute to find his footing.

"I was only fine because of you!" he roars into my ear.

The wind stops. The bowsprit plunges into a wave as the ship utterly stalls, and the men on deck stumble. A wave washes over the quarterdeck before leaving our ship bobbing, rolling like a child's toy in the sea.

Aris whirls me around, gripping my shoulders tightly, like he's afraid the wind is going to pick back up and blow me away from him. His gaze is narrowed, serious, his blue eyes unblinking as they hold mine. His hair has been torn free of its tie, tangled and wild around his face.

The ship begins to move again, lurching forward like it's being tugged on a string as I try to maintain focus.

"Whatever you believe, know that my only goal, ever, is to protect you. So let me protect you. Slow down. We're making good time. It's not worth going gray over. We'll get to Mariana, I promise."

"You LIE!" I roar, wiping streaming tears from my eyes—irritated from the speed of travel and stinging salt, no doubt.

He doesn't so much as flinch—just looks at me calmly, like *I'm* the irrational one here.

"Your only goal is to protect *me*? What would have happened to me if the dragon had killed you? Did you even stop to consider that? If Dimitra hadn't shoved you down? You had a choice—her or me. If you burn Aris, *I burn*. And you—chose—her."

His eyes widen, and I can see white all around the startling blue. Gods, I can see the scene in my mind like it is seared there. The flaming dragon, the guardian of the god of fire, turning its wicked breath toward Aris and Dimitra—and Aris stepping in front, sacrificing himself to protect her.

In his head, I'm his first priority.

But in his heart, it was always Dimitra.

"What are you talking about?" he asks. "When I stepped in front of Dimitra to save her? I would have done the same for Caelus, or Rafael!"

"And I would have *died* if you had," I remind him. "You care nothing for my safety! You chose Dimitra, and your own legacy. Your heroic end. And then you ran right to *Captain Seagraves* for comfort."

"She's dead," he growls, hands clenching at his sides. "Dimitra is dead. And I am left chained to a stubborn, self-centered viper."

His words hit me harder than a blow.

The waves whip higher as I make a half-hearted attempt to keep the ship moving.

"If you burn out, Leo is as good as dead."

The ship stops so suddenly that nearly everyone on board topples again, many now swearing. Aris grabs me, holding me to him, like if I fall, he's going to catch me.

I won't fall. I remain rooted to the deck, my body as immobile as stone. I hope my heart is too.

The sails go slack. Leo. Aris is right. I need to focus on the bigger picture. I need to get to Estana and figure out how to help Leo, how to release him from Queen Evanthia's clutches. She killed the rest of his party and is probably torturing him, just for fun. I can barely bring myself to think about what she's doing to him, what she's done. She killed everyone who traveled with him—all but one single messenger, who carried her letter to us.

Aris is not the enemy. Saving Leo—and therefore Ocron—is the goal. Kind, thoughtful Leo, who works so hard to protect his kingdom—who worked so hard to protect me from the man he knew Aris to be. I know the bond between us is forged by something eternal, some gift of the gods, and I'm not sure if even Head Mage Iraklis can undo it, but I will find someone strong enough to sever this tie, and free me from this man.

But first, I have to fix this mess.

I straighten my spine. I must save my wrath for Evanthia and her Black Water Witches.

"You're right," I say tightly, startling him.

For a long moment, Aris doesn't say anything. Samuel is white, but he's got his hand fixed tightly on the helm, steering us through the night. I hope Captain Seagraves pays him well. The man is brave. I'll give him that.

"When were you going to tell me about Captain Seagraves?" I ask, keeping my tone cool, dispassionate.

Aris is still draped around me. I shrug him off, but he doesn't move far. I consider calling down a lightning bolt to strike him. With his Shield magic, he'd survive it. Probably.

He runs a hand through his wild hair, trying to wrestle it back into a leather tie.

"I don't recall that I need your approval on bedmates," he says. A muscle flickers along his jaw—he's clenching his teeth.

"You don't," I spit back. "You can sleep with whoever you want. It doesn't matter to me."

"Doesn't it?" he asks, like he was hoping it would.

Arrogant peacock.

"Of course not," I say, and I almost believe it myself. "I'm only upset with myself, really—for believing you might have changed, that you might have actually wanted to be with me!"

The last words come out in a rush. I wish I could take them back, but no, it might have been worth it, because Aris looks just as stunned as if I'd actually bested him in his damned knife lessons.

And then Aris does something he's never done, never in all the time we've been together, never once, no matter how much I might irritate him—he grabs me by the neck and *snarls*, his lips pulled back, his teeth elongating as he barely controls his animal shift, as he becomes a man with the roar of a tiger.

And then it's gone, and he's all Aris again, all Shield. He releases me but jabs his finger into my breastbone, hard.

"Nice try," he says, and the words are dripping with scorn, a tone he's never, ever used on me. "For a moment, I almost believed you."

The tears are streaming down my face liberally now, and I make no effort to conceal them, no effort to stop them. My fingers fly to my neck, shaking—he didn't hurt me, but he's scared me. I'm painfully aware of just how strong Aris is, and how he could have snapped my neck, like he did the neck of the Water Mage in Basti, before I could even have thought to defend myself. Not that he would—he'd risk going gray himself, and that is the only comforting thing I can think of at the moment.

"Look," I manage to say, and I take a deep breath, like my heart isn't breaking. "I'm not good at this kind of thing. This ... whatever we have—*had*—I get it, all right? Dimitra told me you couldn't be tamed. I should have believed her. Let's just ... get back to work."

Aris snarls again, pushing me back until my spine hits the helm. Samuel might still be back there somewhere, but he doesn't make a sound. Maybe he's wondering if he'll survive this night after all.

"You have no idea what you're talking about," Aris says, furious.

"Then tell me," I say, and tears are sliding down my cheeks. "What did I do wrong? Were you tired of waiting for me to sleep with you? Is that it?"

"I would wait a thousand lifetimes for you, Wren," he says, the fury leaching from his face. He bows his head and takes a deep breath. "A *thousand*. But to call me a rake, to reach out to your precious Leo, to write to him of your future together while you lie beside me, while your kisses are mine? That is deception on a level that even Nestor couldn't fathom."

My heart plummets. Comparing me to Nestor, his father? The one person he hates above all others in this world? He couldn't have hurt me more if he *had* struck me.

Wait. Leo and I have never written about anything like that.

"What are you talking about?" I ask. The words fall like stones into still water, creating ripples of fear and doubt that spread through my tingling body.

"Don't play innocent with me!" He shouts so loud that my ears ring. "I read the letter!"

"What letter?" I shout back. I think back to every letter Leo has written to me—I burned them all, just in case they ever fell into the wrong hands. Before we realized that Mariana was the traitor in our midst, the six of us—or five of us, at least—had been concerned about the letters Leo and I wrote, despite the fact that they were carried by Shields, of someone reading them, finding out that we were after the Book of Silver, and taking it for themselves. Leo and I had devised a code—a few phrases, anyway—to notify each other if we were worried about a letter's contents being intercepted. We had those letters carried by Adriana personally, to ensure that we were the only two who would read them and know the code. Thank the gods, we did not need it.

Did we?

Aris steps back.

"The letter ..." He braces his hands on his hips and looks back up at me. "The last one. Adriana brought it to me. It had gotten lost—the last one he wrote before Evanthia ..."

My heart stutters, racing so fast I feel dizzy.

"Let me see it," I say, putting out my hand.

Aris hangs his head for a moment, his long black hair hiding the shame on his face.

"I don't have it," he says. "I threw it away after I read it. After I read how he wanted you to 'fly home soon.'" He flicks his wrist.

I close my eyes.

"Of all the Shields in the world, I had to get stuck with the *stupidest*," I mutter. I press my fingers against the spot between my eyes, where a throbbing pain is starting.

"Because I fell for your little innocent act?" he asks, his fangs growing again.

I sigh and open my eyes. Green lightning flashes across the sky, illuminating the deck of the ship as brightly as day for a moment, before plunging us back into darkness.

"Before that, did he write 'let me be plain,' or something like that?"

"You *did* see the letter," he says accusingly.

"What was the last phrase? Fly to him or fly *home*?" I ask, my mind spinning. *Shit.* All this drama and the mess with Captain Seagraves over a *letter*? A letter he destroyed before letting me read it?

My Shield is an imbecile.

"What does it matter?" Aris asks, the volume of his voice rising. "You nag me for being unfaithful, for not choosing *you*, while you are doing the same thing!"

"It's a *code*, you *fucking* idiot!" I yell back.

For the second time in the space of just a few minutes, Aris does something else I've never seen him do before—he looks guilty. His jaw is slack, his eyes wide, unblinking. Then he shakes his head, and the look vanishes.

"No," he says, incredulous, raising a finger, pointing it at me in accusation. "You're not fooling me again."

"Aris," I say, and I put a hand to his chest, like I can push the emotions—the sincerity—from my heart into his. My heart is breaking, but my mind is steady, latching on to the small hope before me, information that could help me save Leo. I take a deep breath, looking into his eyes. The pupils are blown wide, sky blue forming only the thinnest rim around them. "After that last time, when Mariana mentioned my letters could be intercepted, that the Black Water Witches might know our plans, Leo and I devised a *code*. One of the phrases we came up with was that if he was ever compromised, he was going to ask me to fly to him. Now tell me again. Did he say 'fly to me,' meaning Roallac, or 'fly *home*,' meaning he wants us to go to Estana instead?"

CHAPTER 3
ARIS

F*uck. Fuck!*

"Fly home," I mutter. Like I could ever forget those words—the entire fucking letter is burned into my brain, probably for the rest of my life.

Wren sighs, the motion softening her from the stiff-backed hellcat back into the Wren I know, my Wren.

Or at least, the Wren she was, once. *Fuck.*

"Fly home," she repeats, looking up at me. Her eyelashes are wet with tears. Tears that I caused. I have never felt so ... What is this? Shame? Am I ashamed? I hate it.

"Why does he want us to go to Estana? Was there anything else?" she asks, looking down.

I raise my hand, instinctively going to brush back those teardrops, but she flinches, and I withdraw. I feel that flinch in my soul. I have never treated her the way I have tonight, never directed my Shield side toward her—and I never will again.

"So you honestly thought I was writing love letters to Leo this whole time?" she asks quietly.

My silence is answer enough, and she shakes her head.

"I need you to tell me everything," she says. "Every word of the letter. Write it down. Maybe there's something else there that can help me get to Leo."

My heart is racing, pounding with an intensity I've never experienced before. A dull roar blocks all thought from my head.

"You're lucky you're pretty, because the gods sure didn't give you two licks of sense," Stig supplies, unhelpfully, from where he's poking his head back up the ladder, spying on us.

"He's talking about you, not me," Wren mutters, without a hint of a smile on her lips.

Stig nods. "Aye," he agrees, folding his arms over the top rung.

"So rather than *talk* to me about the letter, you ran right to Captain Seagraves's open ... arms?" Wren says.

I wince.

"And Stella's," Stig calls, with a tone of accusation.

"Right. And Stella's," Wren says, crossing her arms, pulling her black robe tight around her.

"Wren, I—"

She holds up a hand, closing her eyes, like even listening to me is hurting her right now.

I swallow hard.

"We need to get back to Basti, as fast as we can," she says. "So I'm getting back to work. I won't burn myself out. I promise."

"And then on to Estana," I say, grateful to be talking about anything else. Work. Let's keep this professional. I *am* a professional, gods damn it. *Gods, how badly did I fuck this up?*

"Go get some rest, Shield. It doesn't look like you slept today," Wren says, dismissing me.

But I don't go, and she doesn't otherwise push. She flicks her hands back out, the green light once more coalescing around them—despite the anguish tearing at my guts, it's still one of the most beautiful things I've ever seen. Then she straightens, takes a deep breath, and the light flares away from her, weaving itself into the wood at our feet, the sails overhead, like a shimmering net. *The James* moves again, but this time, smoothly. As swift as a falcon, the water as smooth as a pond.

Wren doesn't talk to me anymore. I stay by her side as she drives the ship onward with supernatural speed. She's magnificent, steadily using a power that no other Mage can match, and doing it for the rest of the night. I suspect that at least part of this is a show on her part, a stubborn refusal to display any weakness in front of me. And it *is* damn impressive.

Before the dawn breaks, as she promised, we sail into Basti's stinking harbor. The wharf is already swarming with crude dock-workers, and they whistle as Wren stalks by. She ignores them—though I punch one who leers as she passes, and then the rest back off. Wren left the ship with barely a word to anyone—just grabbed her pack from our cabin, and as soon as the plank was lowered, she was on her way.

I look back over my shoulder for a brief moment, catching Loren leaning against the rail, the gaudy plume on her hat bobbing in the breeze, and for a moment only, I'm caught between them. Between two women, between two futures, two lives.

I walk on. Caelus hauls Rafael off the ship after us—Rafael hasn't so much as left his quarters during the entire trip. Caelus looked after him, trying to force him to eat something, to drink, to sleep. He feels responsible, or perhaps that they are like brothers in this, both betrayed by Mariana, lied to by her. Caelus was her Shield—and still is, I guess. He says he can still smell her, the way I can hear where Wren is, so he can track her. Their bond must still be intact. It's a nearly impossible thing to sever.

And Rafael—well, he nearly went gray after Dimitra died. It was Mariana that kept him anchored, somehow. She might be a mean bitch, and I'll gladly run her through the next time we meet, but he loved her, and it was enough to keep him with us. His red robe hangs on his frame like he's made of twigs, though. It's a wonder he's walking at all with the weight he's lost, but Caelus prods him along after us, and somehow he moves.

By the time we get off the docks and catch up to her, Wren is stumbling badly. She's exhausted, and when I try to catch her elbow to keep her from falling, she shrugs me off and, in the predawn darkness, ends up banging her arm on the brick side of a building, hard. She lets out a mumbled string of curses and trudges on.

We make it to the inn and secure a single large room. Caelus and Rafael are still downstairs, negotiating cost and meals, but I need to get Wren to a bed. She's half-dead on her feet, or so I think.

CHAPTER 4
WREN

I whirl on Aris once we reach the room, once we have a few seconds of privacy, and my voice sounds like it belongs to someone else, to some force of nature—the voice of the stars, of the moon, of the night wind. I only have a few moments before the sun rises, and I'll lose this chance to find out the truth. My magic swirls and coils in my core, waiting to be let out. I've only used it like this once, sort of, but I don't falter. Damn the consequences. I thought about it all night, and this is the only way. I'll never be able to trust him again, otherwise.

"*Tell me*, Aris," my voice thunders. "Did you tell me the truth about Dimitra, and Leo's letter?"

His eyes are cold, his lips thinned in displeasure. His hands clench at his sides, but not even Aris Valorius's fearsome strength can resist the compulsion of magic. It is a trait only wielded by the strongest Wind Mages, and then only in dire circumstances, like when their lives are threatened. Saroya tried to use it against us once.

I wield it now against my own Shield, magic connecting us in a thin, invisible line, like a tether. I've only used this spell once before, on Saroya. Never against Aris. It's worse than holding a knife to his throat and demanding the truth—he can't lie now, not even to save his own life.

"At the cave," he says through gritted teeth, each word harsh, like my magic is ripping them through his throat. "I saw that my actions had put my oldest friend in danger, and I moved to protect her, as I would have done for any one of our group."

His eyes close for a moment, and when they open again, his brows drawn tight, I can see the depth of his pain. He cannot believe I am doing this to him, betraying him, and it pisses him off to no end, but there's nothing he can do about it. I grab a tighter hold of my magic, silently urging him for the rest. I cannot stop now. I need to know. And then, I need to know if he sought out Captain Seagraves because of me, because of Leo's letter, or if there was something else. Something deeper.

"My last thoughts were of you," he says, glaring at me. "I prayed to Rigrasil that you would not go gray, that you would survive me. That I wished I could have told you ..."

He turns his head, looking out the window as the first rays of dawn break over the mountains east of Basti.

My magic flickers, and I feel the hold I have on him break, the end like a whip, snapping across my chest. I stumble and nearly fall. When I stand straight again, Aris is still glaring at me. He closes the distance between us, and for the second time in a single day, I am afraid of him. I grab at my magic, but like a misbehaving pet, it eludes my grasp. It is day, and I am defenseless. He practically throws me against the wall behind me, one big hand on my collarbone, pinning me there. He's trembling all over, and I feel like he's desperately trying not to hit me.

I raise my head, meeting his furious gaze. I *dare* him.

"I would rather break our claim and remain a disgrace for the rest of my life than spend it tethered to a Mage who doesn't trust me," he growls.

I swear his teeth look longer than usual, like he wants to tear my throat out. I grab at his arm, but he is as immovable as stone.

"If you *ever* fucking use your magic against me again, I will leave you. Do you understand?" he shouts.

I can feel the heat of his breath across my face, and the tremor in his arm intensifies. I stare him down.

"Then don't give me a reason to," I throw back, carefully annunciating each word.

His upper lip curls, and he snarls at me, his jaws an inch away.

My heart is hammering against my chest like a frightened bird. I wonder if he can feel it, if he can tell it belies the anger on my face.

He pushes away from me, the force knocking me back against the wall, my skull smacking it with a dull thud. He turns his back on me and walks away without another word, without turning back, without any kind of farewell at all.

Gods, what have I done?

CHAPTER 5
CAELUS

I am the lowest of Shields. Rigrasil should have made me a cockroach shifter for all the honor I have in this world.

How could I have truly believed that anyone as beautiful and talented as Mariana would choose to be with me? I told myself it was to save face—as third pick at her games, she was already humiliated.

After Eudoros told me he wanted to dissolve our claim, I thought Mariana would be my redemption, a way for me to regain honor among my brothers.

I was wrong.

When she volunteered so readily to accompany Wren and Aris west at the request of the king, I thought it was a way for her to try to get Aris back. And now I look after her lover—not Aris but rather Rafael, a man caught between life and death, not yet gray, not wholly alive. It is my penance, my duty to tend to him. *Take care of them,* she said to Wren. Somewhere in that frozen heart of hers, she cared for both of us in her way.

And now I am failing Rafael too. He grows thinner day by day despite my efforts to get him to eat. He doesn't talk, barely sleeps—he just stares at the ceiling, hour after hour. His cheeks grow hollow, and a sparse blond beard is trying to grow, like lichen. He lost his Shield, as I lost my Mage. I wish he were able to discuss it with me. He has an agile mind, a quick wit, and a ready laugh. I value our conversations, the way he can see to the heart of a matter in a blink. I miss them more than I can say.

I put my head in my hands, raking my fingers hard through the tangles in my hair. What have I done in my life to deserve a fate such as this? Abandoned by two Mages, and now not even able to keep my brother-in-arms alive.

If I were a wolf now, I'd be able to howl out my grief, my shame.

Instead, I sit by Rafael and read my books, looking for answers. And I pray.

May Rigrasil forgive me, for whatever I have done to offend him.

CHAPTER 6
ARIS

I come back after a few tense minutes pacing the halls. Wren is curled up in her bed, her back toward me. She's shaking, or crying, or something. My hands are shaking too—whether from a side effect of her using her magic on me or just from the effort of holding back my anger, I'm not really sure. The way she dragged those words out of me hurt in a way I've never experienced before. She might as well have stuck a knife in my chest. Honestly, I would have preferred the knife—that kind of wound would have healed, barely leaving a mark, because of my own magic. But being betrayed by my Mage? *Fuck.* It's not something any Shield should ever have to endure. It might not have left a visible mark, but that wound will hurt the rest of my life.

Even if, a small, stupid part of me argues, I deserved it. I thought she had chosen Leo, and I lashed out in the only way I know how. Gods forbid I actually *talk* to her about *feelings*. Maybe I should even have asked her to do it, honestly—asked her to use her magic on me, so she'd know I am sincere. At least now she knows the truth. Well, thank the gods the sun came up when it did, or I'd have said something *really* stupid.

After a while, Wren's shaking stills, and when I stand to tuck another blanket around her, her eyes are closed. Her eyebrows are drawn tight, like she's still mad, even in sleep. Well, that's fair. I deserve her anger. I'm not sure how I can make things right between us, but I swear to Rigrasil that I'll spend the rest of my life figuring it out.

Rafael is sitting on another of the thin mattresses, staring blankly at the window, as still as a statue. He hasn't said a word since Dimitra died. He's lost, somewhere in his mind. I imagine it's how I felt when Stefan died—but then, I had Wren. Mariana betrayed him too. Gods, I imagine he'd probably rather be gray. I know I would in his place. Ignatius, god of fire, better have something damn important in store for him, to keep him living in such agony. At least, that's what Caelus says. "Mysterious are the ways of the gods," he says. He seems to find comfort in that phrase, as he repeats it a *lot*.

Caelus sees me watching Rafael and motions me toward the door. We make our way downstairs and work on our plan over bowls of undercooked oats and mugs of steaming tea. The tea, at least, is decent. And the innkeeper's wife—the one who assumed I was the one leaving bruises on Wren the last time we were here—eyes me with distrust as she serves us. I give her my best smile—the one that has literally charmed the pants off many a woman—but she only harrumphs and turns away, her cats following her, their tails held high. I wonder if I am losing my touch. Eager to avoid *that* admission, I change the subject.

"We should find a messenger, get word to Estana and the school and, gods, everyone else you can think of. Have them keep a lookout for Mariana. Maybe they can catch her before she reaches Roallac."

"She's landed north of us," Caelus says, his gaze a little unfocused. He breathes in deeply through his nose and exhales slowly. "My guess is that the mountains will delay her a bit, and then she'll stay on the northern coast until she reaches the Black Strait. With a good horse, it will take her ten days, maybe two weeks."

"You can track Mariana? She must be a hundred miles or more from here by now," I say around the spoonfuls of oats I am shoveling into my mouth. They might be bland and chewy, but they're still better than anything on *The James*. We don't really know how Mariana got off Abelon. Was there a ship waiting for her on the coast? Or could she really walk on water, the way she bragged? The distance from Abelon to the closest spot on the Ocronian coast takes a good ship *days*. Mariana is strong, but is she *that* strong, to keep that kind of magic up for so long? Caelus isn't gray, so we know she's alive and not burned out, at least.

And Caelus is a good Shield—he nearly bested me in the arena, which is no small feat. He's also turned out to be a damned decent man, even if he is a stuffy, pious prick sometimes. None of us blame him for what Mariana did. She fooled us all. Still, I have no doubt he's been self-flagellating ever since, and sometimes literally. He's starting to grow a shaggy brown beard, too, not that he was ever one to care much about his appearance. Now that Mariana is gone, he doesn't seem to care at all about anything—except getting back to her.

"I can smell her, like snow on the winter wind. My wolf nose can find her."

My face must have betrayed my skepticism, because he adds, "Why, you don't think you could track Wren across the continent? Across the world?"

Good point.

"Across the world," I agree.

We finish our meal. Caelus drums his fingers against the table, restless. I know what he wants to ask me—and I hate what it means. "So, Mariana hasn't broken the claim?"

"Not yet," he says, wincing. "It's no easy feat. Head Mage Saroya could do it, could break a claim between Shield and Mage. Usually it's the Wind Mages who have that gift, along with their ... persuasion."

I think back to how Darius used a wind gag to quiet Wren when he first brought her to the School of the Silver Flame, and how Saroya tried—and failed—to get Wren to stop after she'd kidnapped her. Wren was briefly able to control that gift as well that night. I guess I could be thankful that the Roallacan Mages were primarily Water Mages and had an innate prejudice against the other elements, including Shields.

"There are Wind Mages from the Isles who might ally with Queen Evanthia," Caelus says. "I have no doubt Mariana will try to avail herself of this at her first opportunity, so I must be quick."

I can see the guilt in his strange yellow eyes.

"Go on," I tell him, before he musters up the words. "Go get her. I'll take Wren and Rafael back to Estana."

"I can't leave you with both of them. Rafael's practically useless—and you'll need me if you run into trouble in the tunnels," Caelus argues, though it's clear he wants to take my offer.

Shit. I'd forgotten about the tunnels—those claustrophobic, panic-inducing spaces that were barely large enough to be called tunnels. More like crawl spaces. A crypt. An endless maze of holes honeycombing through the mountain. One wrong turn, one rock-slide, and a man could be lost forever. He might not even be found for years, when his body had already turned to dust, and ...

"I just have to go back the way we came," I say, squaring my shoulders. "Pretty much a straight shot through to Aeturnus. I'll have Tekton take us on from there."

Caelus drums his fingers again on the table. The innkeeper's wife brings us another round of tea—watered-down leaves but also a heaping mound of ash mixed in, a Shield's preferred way to gain nutrients. It is like a mother's milk to us, and even Caelus can't hide his pleasure at downing it.

I give the woman another smile, and this time she flat out glares at me. *Damn.*

Caelus lets out a breath. "I have a better chance of reaching her if I shift," he says, looking me in the eyes.

I understand what he's not saying. Every Shield has a shifted form, a shape they can take at will. While it is an awesome magic and one that has saved my ass more times than I can count, it also has its risks, as I well know. And if Caelus shifts now, he'll have to leave behind everything—his clothing, his shield, his gladiuses. He'll have to run as a wolf for days to weeks before he'll be able to shift back.

But he might just be able to catch Mariana before she delivers the Book of Silver to the Snake-Bitch Queen. As a wolf, he can run for days without stopping. He might just be able to stop whatever she's planning.

If he doesn't go wild first. Spending that long in a shifted form is not without its risks. Rumors are always swirling about Shields "going wild." After Stefan died, I nearly considered it myself. To let all the grief and pain of being a man simply *go*.

Caelus is still looking at me, his strange yellow eyes steady.

I nod.

He reaches up and unstraps the leather harness holding the twin swords across his back. His hands tremble the slightest bit as they caress the worn leather scabbards—maybe for the last time. He pushes them across the table to me. I ignore the way the yellow in his eyes glimmers.

Next comes his round shield, nearly indistinguishable from mine, save for the patterns of scratches and gouges in the wood. How I'm going to carry two shields and four swords, I have no idea—but I'll manage. One Shield giving another his weapons and shield is an honor, usually reserved for close kin.

I guess I'll have to do.

"I'll send those messages you wanted before I head out," he says. His eyes stay on his weapons, like he's memorizing every scratch and worn spot. "And I've asked the innkeeper to send my books by messenger back to Aeturnus. I left the dragon one in Rafael's bag."

"Send word when you find her," I tell him. I take his weapons, resting my hand on his shield. "I'll take care of these for you."

Caelus nods and swallows hard. He looks away, and he looks

older now than his thirty-odd years. I don't just mean his hair, which is wild and streaked with gray already, but in the way his lean frame sags into his chair. I remember that when I fought him at the arena, at the games where Shields fight to gain the honor of claiming the strongest Mages, those were his second games too. His first Mage had decided that he'd rather not be part of a Mage-Shield pair, that he'd missed his true calling as a cleric. Caelus may be the single most devout person I've ever met—which, honestly, isn't saying all that much—but he is still a Shield first.

And to have his second chance, his second Mage, betray not just him but the entire country? It is a shame that he'll likely never live down. If he ever hopes to regain his honor, if he hopes to someday stand proud before Rigrasil in the afterlife and proclaim to him, "Yes, I did my duty," then he'd better get moving. Now.

He extends his hand, and I take it.

"Good hunting, brother," he says.

"Good hunting, brother" I return. "*Fac fortia et patere.*" My real brothers are assholes, and he knows that.

Caelus is a better man and a better Shield than all of them combined.

I drop off Caelus's things in the room, then go back downstairs and ask the innkeeper for a bath.

"Bathhouse is open," he reminds me.

I fight back a wince. The last time I was there—*Gods*—I practically deflowered Wren right there in the damn water. And she'd come to me, trusted me. Stood before me, naked and glorious in the water, glowing like a star.

There is no one like her in all the history of the world.

And of course, I fucked it up. Because that's what I do.

"Just a bucket of water. And some soap," I grunt.

He shrugs but brings me what I ask.

"You can use the room by the kitchen," he says, nodding toward the door. "Leave it clean, or I'll charge you for double."

This time of day, there's no line to use the small room. Most of the inn's patrons are just leaving for the day, so I have the room to myself. It's drafty but warm enough, kept so by the proximity to the roaring kitchen fires. It will do.

I put down the bucket of water and look into the surface. There's a pair of lanterns in here, and in their dim light, I can just make out my reflection in the dark stillness.

The face that stares back at me sickens me.

It's not a new feeling—revulsion. It's just I don't often feel it when looking at *myself*.

I look at my shield and gladiuses, resting in the corner. They're as much a part of me as an arm or a leg—I know every dent in the steel border of my shield, every slash in the heartwood it's made from. I've honed my swords to an edge sharp enough to shave with.

It is I who am the unknown now. I don't like the person looking back at me.

When I claimed Wren, I was the one taking a gamble. I was the renowned—if tarnished—warrior, the undefeated Shield, and she was no one. Now she is the Night Mage, with magic that makes mountains shake and the sea reverse its tides—and I'm the asshole she's stuck with, the one that keeps letting her down. The one who's been feeling sorry for himself, while she's been carrying the burden of this quest. She deserves better. *I will be better.*

I pick up my knife. It's a small one, one I usually reserve for shaving my face. Tulliano made it for me a few years ago, and it's been with me ever since. Tulliano is a Fire Mage, and also the best weaponsmith that the School of the Silver Flame has. I sharpen the blade out of habit, but it doesn't really need it.

Shaving with a knife isn't the easiest thing, but it is effective.

Besides, Shields heal quickly, so any cuts are soon smoothed away, often not even leaving a scar.

I splash water over my head, tasting salt as it streams down my face.

I unsheathe my knife and, with steady hands, raise it to my neck.

CHAPTER 7
RAFAEL

When Dimitra died, I *felt* our bond break.

I could feel her pain. The flames, melting the flesh from her bones—and then ... a crack of thunder, inside my head, and a feeling like my sternum was fracturing into a dozen pieces.

And then nothing. Stillness. Silence. All the light, all the color in the world, gone.

The grayness beckons, tempting me to numb the pain.

I can't fight it anymore.

CHAPTER 8
WREN

There is a stranger in my room.

I wake up slowly, disoriented. I expect to be in the stuffy cabin on *The James*, but I'm not. Instead, I'm in a normal bed, not a bunk. The floor is not moving—*Thank the gods.* The pillow smells of soap instead of fish, and someone's tucked a soft blanket around me. Afternoon sunlight streams through a large glass window.

I sit up, rubbing salt and sleep from my eyes and stretching. I feel about a thousand years old, like all my bones and joints are stiff. Plus, I'm absolutely *starving.* I hope breakfast—or dinner, or whatever as long as it is edible—is nearby. I try not to think about Aris, about what I said to him this morning. About what I did to him. *He deserved it.*

My movement wakes Rafael on the bed across from me. He opens his brown eyes blearily. They don't focus on me. They don't focus on anything. He just lets out a sigh and closes them again.

The other man in the room is in a bed just past Rafael's. I remember coming in this morning, and there was no one else here then.

The man stirs. My eyes flick to the window—the sun is still up, so no magic powers—and then my hand slips under my pillow, where I stashed the small knife I usually wear in my boot, the one Aris has been training me with. This man hasn't shown any aggression, but I figure it would be best not to take chances. He seems to be fairly large, judging by the bulk under the blanket. Physically, he could probably overpower me quite easily. I guess the sting of my last trip here in Basti hasn't left me yet—I was pursued by two Shields and their traitorous Water Mages, intent on kidnapping me and selling me off to Queen Evanthia of Roallac.

Where is Aris? Have I managed to piss him off so much that he's abandoned me to the mercy of strangers?

The man's breathing pauses. He's heard me move. *Shit.* I grip my knife handle, though it is still sheathed in my lap.

He rolls over, eyes closed, and I get a look at his face.

That's when I realize it's not a stranger there at all.

It's Aris.

And he's shaved his gods-damned head.

I can't hold in a snort of laughter. His eyes fly open and his body stills. Without his long black hair hiding his face, he looks somehow sharper, even more like a predator than usual, like the softness of his hair was the only thing soft about him, the rest of his face all angles and planes. His eyes seem to glow with a light of their own, as blue as a flame.

"Good morning, princess," he says with a feline smirk. His hand goes reflexively to his scalp, to run his long fingers through the thick strands—but he finds nothing and pauses for a second.

"What did you *do*, Aris Valorius?" I ask, still fighting back a giggle. I wonder if it is hunger or exhaustion making me a little delirious. He looks fearsome like this, with just a hint of black stubble on his scalp—and yet I am not afraid of him, not even after our fight this morning. I bet it would be soft, like velvet.

He rubs his scalp absently, then sits up, stretching out his long, muscular frame. I can admire his body, the fluid, catlike grace he possesses, and still be mad.

Right?

"Caelus says that great magic requires sacrifice," he says, bending and reaching for his boots. "The gods gave men magic, and the divine books, and in return had to leave the mortal plane. Consider this"—he gestures at his scalp—"a new beginning. A fresh start."

"But ... your *hair*! You great, preening peacock—what were you thinking?"

This elicits a sly smile from him, and damn it all if my heart doesn't flip over in my chest.

"Penance, princess. Penance."

"You think that if you shave your head, I'll forgive you?" I ask. "You're an idiot."

Rafael has fully woken up now and sits up, wobbling a little. He's grown a bit of a blond beard, like his own vanity left him when Mariana did.

"I thought it might be a start," Aris says, still looking at me. Tension sizzles between us, like a storm just before lightning strikes. "I forgive you, you know, for using your magic on me. I should have offered to do that."

I look down and attend to my own boots. I consider throwing one at Aris rather than saying I forgive him for sleeping with Captain Seagraves and withholding Leo's letter ... because truthfully, I don't, and I don't think I will for a long, long time.

He sighs, stands, and gets Rafael up.

We make our way downstairs to where the inn has started serving the evening meal. Caelus, Aris tells me, has moved on, in an attempt to overtake Mariana before she can reach Roallac. I can barely pay attention to him over the growling of my stomach.

Magic takes an enormous toll on my body, and I down three portions of stew and bread while Rafael only picks at his. Aris just sips on his ash water. I'm wiping up the dregs from my last bowl with a crust of thick bread when I finally slow down enough to talk.

"So, are we heading out tonight?" I ask, stuffing the last bit of bread into my mouth. Aris refills my mug of water and pushes it across the table, careful not to let our fingers touch. Something in my chest cracks a bit, like the ice around my heart is trying to both thaw and hold its ground at the same time.

"We might as well," Aris says, glancing briefly toward Rafael. "Up to traveling?"

Rafael doesn't answer.

Aris sighs, running a hand absently over his scalp. "You're slowing us down, Raf," he says bluntly.

I kick his leg under the table. Rafael is grieving the loss of his Shield *and* his lover. It's nothing short of a miracle that he hasn't gone gray. Rafael winces a little at Aris's attack but otherwise doesn't say anything. He just turns his head, looking into the fire.

"We can leave him at Prasinos," I offer. It's a large town, and there will be caravans going back to Estana regularly. We can make sure he gets back, and we can go on our own much faster than if we're coddling Rafael the whole way. The idea of leaving him behind makes my stomach churn, but what choice do we have? He *is* slowing us.

Still, the idea of being alone in the wilderness with Aris for weeks doesn't thrill me the way it might have once. Instead, the thought coils in my stomach, tying into tight, frozen knots. I think I might vomit up all that stew I just ate.

"What about Aeturnus?" Aris offers. "We can leave him at the temple. He and Tekton got on well enough, and it would get us on our way sooner. We may need Tekton to get us back through the tunnels to Prasinos, too."

"It would be a day out of our way to drop him off and then make it back to the tunnels," I say, considering our options. We can't leave him in Basti, and I'm sure as all the hells not putting him back on a ship alone. "Unless we can find someone in town who can take him, maybe a guide too."

Aris sighs, leaning back. He crosses his legs, resting a knee against the table.

"It's a shame you can't fly," he says.

I raise an eyebrow.

"Like Saroya. Some of the more powerful Wind Mages can fly, apparently. Not a long distance, but Saroya made it from the school to Estana pretty quickly that way once. You're stronger—I bet you could go farther. I could shift and follow you."

I snort. "I've never tried it."

Saroya was an incredibly strong Wind Mage—and she had years of experience. While I might be able to figure some of this out on my own, like the truth-telling, I doubt I could figure out how to make myself fly like a bird.

"Even if I figure it out, I don't think I can go across the entire continent."

Rafael sits up. He's still staring into the flames, but something has finally gotten his attention. Something has made his gaze sharpen, for the first time in days.

"Take me to Aeturnus," he says. His voice breaks, rusty from disuse. He clears his throat.

"It will slow us down too much," I protest, though inwardly I'm thrilled that he's spoken. "Prasinos is the better option."

"I won't slow you down," Rafael says. And with renewed strength in his voice, I almost believe him. "Besides, I have an idea."

CHAPTER 9
ARIS

Oh, Rafael has an idea. Rafael *always* has ideas.

"Remember the time you wanted to go check out the salamanders? *That* was a crazy idea. This is a *terrible* one," I say.

He grins at the memory. "Yeah. That was fun, wasn't it? Took weeks for your eyebrows to grow back."

CHAPTER 10
WREN

"It's a crazy idea, but maybe not a terrible one," I mutter.

We've packed up, gathered some supplies, and headed back to the tunnel entrance outside town. We're the only ones starting this journey so late in the day, but underground, the time doesn't really matter so much, and I'd rather be awake at night, when I can use my powers if needed. The last time we went into these tunnels, we came across a trio of mountain trolls, the favored creatures of the god of earth, Cephus. If we are going to have trouble again, I want to be able to fight.

I wonder if my green lightning can strike underground. I guess I'll find out.

"All the best ideas seem crazy at first," Rafael calls over his shoulder. His eyes are clear now, and his energy has picked up substantially. He practically bounds on ahead of us, holding a spelled lantern to light the way. He still looks like a ghost of his former self, but at least he's talking again. He even ate a little before we left the inn.

"And you're going to do what? Just run through the tunnels by yourself?" I ask Aris.

He visibly flinches at that. He doesn't like being underground. Gods, he can barely stand being indoors.

He doesn't answer me.

We walk behind Rafael. The tunnel to Aeturnus is an easy one, with no major turns or forks. We'll get there in two days, probably. Or nights, I guess, since we're traveling at night. I only know this because I can feel my magic kindling inside me, my core coming awake. We walk on in silence mostly. Aris hasn't come out and actually said he is sorry for what he did, what he assumed—but he is coming with me, helping me. I still can't believe he cut off his hair, though the look is growing on me. He looks less like the "pretty boy" Zale called him at the Shield games, and somehow ... fiercer.

"You're staring again," he teases.

I look away, focusing on the back of Rafael's red robe, the way the lantern light flickers on the smooth stone walls. *Just keep walking.*

And once we get to Estana, what then? Leo's message was cryptic, something about queens, and unfortunately, Aris tossed it away. By the time we get to Estana, all of Ocron will know about Queen Evanthia's treachery. They'll know she has their king held hostage. Aleka and Ismini are probably already convening a war council and planning his rescue, maybe even sending some Shields and Mages after Mariana. I wish there were an easier way to communicate than the King's Messengers.

Aris has written out what he remembers of Leo's letter, and my fingers turn it over and over in my pocket as my mind searches desperately for clues. So Leo knew he was in trouble—and he needed my help. I wonder if he managed to get letters to anyone else before ... *Gods, my chest aches.* I try not to think too much about what kind of torment he must be in, knowing everyone with him is dead, not being able to communicate with anyone in Ocron now, feeling all alone ...

And we're a continent away.

I walk faster.

We make decent time. Rafael and I take a brief nap in the

morning while Aris keeps watch. I'm careful to keep my back to him. I'm worried that I'll betray something, that I'll cry again in my sleep, and I'm not ready to forgive him. *I'd wait a thousand lifetimes for you.* These words play over in my head as I drift off to sleep, and I can almost imagine hearing him say them again, whispering them to me in the dark. He said he has forgiven me for using my magic against him—I feel like saying that was like trying to strike a bargain, like we both screwed up and so let's just forget both things ever happened.

If only I could.

We reach Aeturnus just after midnight the next day and make our way across the town to the temple. The massive stone staircase that winds up the mountain is difficult even in daytime, and Rafael and I have to stop several times to rest before we reach the top. Between his lantern and my green glow, though, we can see well enough. I suspect Aris shifts his eyes to a tiger's vision a few times to scout the way.

To my surprise, Tekton is waiting for us.

"I'm surprised to see you awake," Aris says by way of greeting, grasping Tekton's hand tightly in his own. Though Tekton is a Shield without shifting abilities, he's just as large as Aris and returns the grip.

"A little bird told me you'd be here soon," he says, and I don't miss the flicker of red that stains his cheeks.

Aris rolls his eyes with a groan. Adriana, his little sister, is a hawk shifter—and apparently, she's got Tekton's attention. Meeting someone when you're stark naked after shifting does tend to leave an impression.

"Come in, friends, come in," Tekton says, ushering us into the Temple of the God of Night. The black stone shines in the firelight.

We pass through the portico and into the main hall, where the massive statue of Caladrius stands, astride his horse, Obsidian. I can't help the sigh that escapes me—coming here feels welcoming, familiar, like coming home. *Gods, I wish Obsidian were still here.* Part of me wishes I could just stay here, in this temple so far from the drama unfolding in the east. Just stay here and forget about everything. Hide from it all.

Aris would never be able to live with himself if we stayed. And, I realize, I couldn't either.

Still, the temptation is there.

We relay everything to Tekton, from our trip to Abelon to Mariana's betrayal and Dimitra's sacrifice. He sits us in the dining hall and serves us a hot meal he and Delphine prepared earlier in the day for us, gods bless them. We then tell him our plan, and that part takes a bit of convincing.

"It's a good plan," he eventually admits, running a hand over his tired face.

"Told you," Rafael says, elbowing Aris, who grunts in agreement.

"Doesn't mean I like it, though," Tekton says, trying to smile.

As the sun comes up, streaming in through the hall's high windows, Delphine comes out to greet us, still rubbing sleep from her dark eyes. She's still a child, barely fourteen, a slighter, more skittish shadow of her giant uncle. Her brown hair hangs in tangles around her pale face, her feet bare on the stone floor. She sits by Aris, swinging her legs on the bench.

"You're still wearing the bracelet I gave you," she says shyly, nodding at the braided leather on his wrist.

Aris nods solemnly.

Delphine smiles and shows him the identical bracelet on her own pale arm, though hers is decorated with bits of polished obsidian.

"Where's everyone else?" Delphine asks, looking around the room like the others might materialize.

I bite my lip. "It's just us," I tell her.

Her eyes snap to mine, wide and a little wild.

"Dimitra died when we got the Book of Silver," I explain. "And Mariana and Caelus ..." I can't finish. How do I explain Mariana's betrayal?

"Oh," Delphine says, slumping a little in her chair. "I'm sorry. I really liked them."

She chews on her bottom lip, trying to process this without crying. We all pretend not to notice her swiping at her cheek as a single stray tear escapes.

"Mariana didn't die," Rafael says gently, putting a hand on her arm. "She betrayed us, all of us, and left. Caelus went after her."

"All right," she says, her voice only wobbling a little. "So you have it, then? The Book of Silver?"

"No," Rafael admits with a groan, crossing one foot over his other knee. He is surprisingly calm, his voice steady, when he continues. "Mariana took it. Caelus hopes to catch her before she can give the book to the Snake Queen."

"We need to get the Book of Silver back, and find the Book of Gold," Aris says.

I notice he doesn't mention the fact that he killed a dragon.

Delphine leans her head against Aris's shoulder for comfort, letting out a deep breath.

"About that," Tekton says, raising a finger. "I've been doing some research and corresponding with Panos back east. I sent him my copy of the Book of Silver to read. I ... couldn't interpret all of it." He rubs the back of his neck. "There are so many translations to some of the words, and he's one of the only ones who can really read it, besides Caelus. I hope he has more luck than I did."

"I'm sure you did the best you could," I say, patting his arm. "You've been invaluable, to all of us."

Tekton flushes before clearing his throat and continuing.

"Panos doesn't think that just having the three divine books is enough. The conditions will have to be perfect for Evanthia to call Aenon back into our realm—the three books, a 'great sacrifice,' and some kind of celestial timing. He thinks that's why she mentioned the winter solstice in her letter. It's the shortest day of the year, when Rigrasil's power will be at its weakest. There must be some significance in that. And she already has the Book of Bronze."

"Do you think she intends to use King Leonidas as the sacrifice?" I ask, wringing my hands on the table in front of me.

"Maybe," Aris says, spinning his mug in his big hands. "Or maybe he's just bait. There's no way she can get all three books in time by herself, otherwise."

"What's Estana up to, then?" Rafael asks. "Has Panos said?"

"Preparing for an assault on Roallac. They're mobilizing the army, and the navy is patrolling the Black Strait at either end. They're worried about the swamp, though. Panos says Evanthia's power is immense, that the water itself there seems alive." Tekton clears his throat. "Ismini and her Earth Mages are talking about building a bridge across the strait, but it's taking time."

"Time we don't have," I muse.

Rafael nods.

"Speaking of," Tekton says, turning to look at Delphine. His dark eyes are shining. "Delphine, the Night Mage has a favor to ask of you." His voice is level and calm.

Delphine perks up. "Anything," she says, already nodding.

Aris puts a hand on her arm, and she instantly stills.

"Listen to the whole plan before you agree," Aris says. "You can say no, and no one will be angry with you. It's big, what we're asking."

"I want to do it, whatever it is," Delphine says, raising her chin.

Aris chuckles, then gestures for me to continue.

I take a bracing breath. "Delphine, we have to get back to Estana, and quickly," I tell her. "King Leonidas has left us a message, and we're on a quest to retrieve the Book of Gold before Queen Evanthia can get it. We want to take you east with us and deliver you to the Shields, where you can start your training."

I exchange a glance with Aris—his gaze is guarded, but he nods for me to continue.

"And we want you to fly us there."

The words fall around us like stones into water. The ringing silence after makes my skin prickle, like I've made a terrible mistake by even suggesting it. She's only a *child*, after all.

Delphine might be a Shield—and a rather small one at that—but she *is* also a dragon shifter, the first of her kind. During our first stay here, Tekton kept her shifting a secret. Delphine has been here for years, practicing her flight at night, staying away from people until she could learn to control her fire-breathing—which, come to think of it, we haven't yet asked if she has under control.

"All of you?" Delphine asks, narrowing her eyes and looking us over. "I've never carried more than just Tekton."

"Just me and Rafael," I tell her. I'm small, and Rafael has lost a lot of weight—between the two of us, we shouldn't be much heavier combined than Tekton.

"And what about you?" she asks, looking up at Aris with something like worship in her eyes. To her, he's a hero—and I suppose he is.

"I'll shift too and run," he says, patting her arm with something like fondness. "Don't worry. I can keep up."

"Through the tunnels?" she asks, her brows knitting.

He cringes. "Over them," he says, holding up his hands. "Tiger paws are good on the snow. We'll fly at night so you're less likely to be seen, and camp during the day."

"She's never flown so far before," Tekton warns. "A few hours, maybe—but all night, for days?"

"I can do it," Delphine says stubbornly. "I want to. I want to help."

"And you'll keep her safe?" Tekton asks. His arms are crossed, his biceps flexing against his shirt.

I'd have sworn this man didn't have an aggressive bone in his body, but for his niece? I can tell he'd take on Aris without hesitation.

"I swear it," Aris says.

Delphine's eyes shine as she looks up at him. "When do we leave?"

"I *will* get her to Commander Markos for her training," Aris tells Tekton as we leave the hall.

Delphine trails after them, soaking up every word. She's been in this isolated temple for so long—and she is just a girl. If there were another way to get us to Estana at speed, I would gladly take it. Guilt gnaws at my gut—but what choice do we have?

"You'll see to it that she's kept safe, and not exploited, not bullied," Tekton continues.

Aris nods his assurance.

"I swear," he says again. "Shields take care of their own. She will be given the same protection—and the same training—as anyone else. Markos is a good man. He'll watch out for her the way he watched out for me. It is the best place for her—the *only* place for her to learn the skills she'll need."

"For the life you want for her, you mean," Tekton says, frowning.

"The life all Shields should have the chance to live," Aris says, with more empathy than I thought he possessed.

Tekton can't shift—magic in our world is changing, and he and I are just two examples of those changes. I imagine he's been as much an outcast as I have, as much alone. While Tekton has had Delphine, they have been two of a kind, two mismatched Shields. They are each other's family. When Delphine leaves, it'll just be Tekton and his temple, left alone in the middle of the mountains.

We're asking an awful lot, of both of them, but I have to credit Tekton. He does his best to help us prepare for the flight without asking for any sympathy, without making Delphine feel guilty at all. He is proud of her and wants to give her a chance to truly fly. He guides us to the library, where he and Rafael pore over maps, plotting out the fastest routes, what towns to avoid, and the best places to stop for breaks.

Delphine has scampered off somewhere to pack her things.

Rafael traces his finger over the map. “She can make it to here. There’s good cover. And then we can turn south to follow the Great Western Road ...”

“Why don’t you get some rest?” Aris’s voice is far too close to my ear, his breath warm on the back of my neck, and I can’t help the shiver it sends down my spine. “We won’t leave until tomorrow night. Get some sleep.”

“You should as well,” Tekton says, not lifting his gaze from the map. “You won’t be sleeping much while trying to keep up with Delphine.”

“And clean up too,” Rafael says, also not tearing his eyes away from a piece of paper he’s scribbling notes on. “You stink. Both of you. Honestly, why do you think I stayed so far ahead of you in the tunnels?”

While I appreciate that Rafael’s sense of humor is returning, I do not enjoy being his target. But he does have a point. I can’t wait to scrub off the grime of our travels.

“Come on,” Aris says, heading out of the library, leaving me little choice but to follow.

It feels almost natural, walking these halls, headed back toward the room we used last time, even though everything has changed. We walk in silence.

The rooms are as comfortable and cozy as I remember. The darkly furnished sitting room has a steady fire going, casting a cheery glow. The bedroom is dominated by the large bed, neatly made up with dark blankets and soft sheets. Spelled candles glow along the walls. Tekton’s even laid out soap and towels, and dried fruit and water. *Welcome home.* I can practically hear Caladrius’s voice echoing through the temple.

“Go ahead and bathe,” Aris tells me, breaking my reverie. “I’ll unpack. We need to travel as light as possible so Delphine doesn’t have to carry extra weight, and we’ll need to make some room for Caelus’s things.”

He dumps out my pack onto the bed. Belatedly I realize that the little bag of moonberries is still in the bottom—the bag lands on the top of the heap, and the drawstring falls open. A few small ones roll down the blanket, looking like little dried blueberries.

Aris stares at them for a moment, and I feel heat rush to my face. I rush for them, stuffing the berries back into their bag, but Aris has caught one and rolls it thoughtfully between his fingers.

"Where did you get these?" he asks, meeting my eyes.

"Um," I stammer. I go to grab the berry from him, but he whips his hand back, out of my reach, toying with me. His mouth turns up in a smirk. I kick him in the shin.

"Give it back!" I say.

He grins and lifts his hand higher. "Come and get it," he taunts.

I huff and cross my arms, glaring at him.

"Where did you get these?" he asks again.

"Um," I say again. "Dimitra. The last time we were ... here. In case ... well, she thought I might need them."

"I see," he says, and he lowers his hand.

He tosses the berry back to me, and I shove it into the bag and draw the string tight.

Taken once a month, moonberries are one way that women can prevent pregnancy. Dimitra's words are as caustic in my mind today as they were on that last trip—*Do not burden Aris with an unwanted child.*

When I look up from the bag, I see that Aris has taken a step closer. I could back up—I could back down—but I don't. I lift my chin and glare at him, and hope that the dim lighting hides the flush on my face.

"And have you taken them?" he asks.

Gods, his voice is low now, a whisper, a growl. I grind my teeth. *I am mad at him. I am mad at him.* The phrase runs through my mind, though it gets harder to focus when I look up at him.

"There is no need," I counter. It does not come out as acidic as I meant it to.

He comes closer. Prowls closer.

"What do you know of *need*, little Firefly?" he asks, and I can't tell if it sounds more like a question or a confession or ... and something deep within me catches fire. Ignites. *I* am glowing, green light suffusing the air around us.

And then his lips are on mine, gently, like he's asking permission —and I can't think of anything except the feel of his strong, warm back under my fingers, and the softness of his short hair, like velvet beneath my touch.

"I'm still mad at you," I moan, pulling myself up on my toes to meet his mouth better, to pull him closer. To taste the apology on his tongue.

"I know," he says, his lips moving on mine. "I know."

He pulls back, running his hands down my arms, dipping his head until his forehead touches mine. Shivers run down my spine, and I feel his grip tighten.

"Back there," he says. Then he clears his throat and tries again. "On the boat. You said you thought I cared for you too."

My heart hammers in my chest. So he was paying attention.

"You are mine, as I am yours," he says, giving me another soft, sweet kiss. "And I will spend the rest of my life trying to prove it to you."

"You still haven't said you're sorry," I mutter.

"Haven't I?" he asks, kissing the side of my neck, my throat. His hands travel down my waist, landing on my hips, pulling me tight against him.

"No," I say, but there's no malice in it, no reproach. Gods, he's like the force of the moon on the tides, and I'm helpless against him.

He pulls back from me, taking my chin in his fingers, raising my face to his.

"I'm sorry," he says. He holds my gaze, unblinking. "For everything. And I will never doubt you again."

The green light around me sputters and then flares brilliantly, casting shadows. I am a star, flooding the room with jade-colored fire. Aris closes his eyes.

"What happened?" Aris asks, not moving away.

I smile and kiss him. He keeps his eyes closed.

"I glow when my emotions are ... intense. And they are very, very intense right now."

He rewards me with a smile that would stop the very stars in their paths.

That night, and into the next day, I sleep more deeply and soundly than I have in ages. Aris sleeps on a sofa by the fireplace in the other room, his feet stretched toward the flames. I make a mental note to have Rafael teach me how to put a warming spell on his boots and socks. I think he'd like that.

If Rafael notices anything different about us, that perhaps we've started mending the rift between us, he has the good sense not to comment. And Tekton is too concerned about Delphine to pay much attention to anything else.

"I'll be fine, Uncle," she reassures him, hugging him tightly. "I'll send a message as soon as I'm settled. And I wrote a note to Hector—the baker, not the logger—to make sure you stay fed."

Tekton laughs and ruffles Delphine's hair. She's still just wearing her short dress and no shoes, but it hardly matters. In a few moments, she'll shift, and we've packed the necessary warm clothing for her trip in our pack.

Aris straps his swords to my back. They are large, and I feel clumsy. When he adds the round shield to the harness, I nearly fall over. I feel like a turtle.

"Just don't fall off, all right?" he says, and he flicks the tip of my nose with his finger.

"Just keep up, all right?" I counter.

He grins and steps back, stretching his arms and legs, readying himself for the journey. I'm nervous about being away from him—potentially miles and miles away if Delphine is as fast as she says. What if we land and get into trouble, and he's not there? I'll have to rely on Rafael and myself to keep us safe. I'll have to make sure we land before dawn, so I can use my magic if needed. I've grown so accustomed to having my arrogant bodyguard around. He makes me feel safe, body and ... well, not my heart, obviously, but... maybe. Someday.

He catches me staring at him and raises an eyebrow. I smile and shake my head, studying the gleaming obsidian tiles on the floor as we walk. I've missed this place. I wish we could stay longer.

We'll have to camp in the mountains tonight, back to sleeping in musty bedrolls instead of comfortable beds, but at least Tekton knows a cave where we should be able to stop the first night. And the cave is not far—we should be there in just a few hours. We're going to take it slow until we see how Delphine does, and Aris will meet us there. Easy. Just a little flight on a dragon's back, nothing to it.

We make our way out to the front of the temple. The night is moonless and calm. No one will be able to see us. The weather is perfect, with just a light easterly wind, like Caladrius himself is blessing our passage.

Tekton gives Delphine one last hug, sweeping her up in his big arms until she squeals with laughter.

And then she shifts. A moment and a whisper of wind, and instead of a thin, pale girl, there stands a dragon.

And she is *magnificent*. Taller than Aris at her shoulder, and probably close to thirty feet long. Her scales are shiny black jewels, and they flash with glimpses of scarlet. Her wings are feathered, and she stretches them out over our heads like a glorious canopy, tossing her head with delight. For a girl who has been kept a secret for so long, she is absolutely reveling in this small freedom, in shifting for us.

She folds her wings across her back and tosses her head again, snorting a little cloud of smoke. *Come on*, she seems to say. *What are we waiting for?*

Tekton straps a thick leather harness around her shoulders and forearms, latching it with a buckle. It's reinforced with steel wire where it rubs against the ridges of her neck, to prevent the leather from fraying against her razor-sharp scales. It's not a saddle so much as a handhold. I walk around Delphine, and she settles herself down, lowering her belly to the ground. This close, she smells of leather and sulfur and smoke. Her scales shine under my fingers like living gemstones. I have never really been jealous of Shields, but to be something as extraordinary as this? I might reconsider.

Aris grabs my waist and helps me up. Rafael climbs up behind me, and Tekton tosses up our packs. We have to be careful to sit on a thick woolen blanket and not Delphine's scales—otherwise, if we shift or rub against them the wrong way, we could end up with some really nasty cuts on our legs.

Rafael has Caelus's weapons and shield strapped to his back. I'm sure we make quite the awkward pair, two turtles on top of a dragon. Delphine stands, and I'm reminded of the mammoths we rode back in Abelon. She is narrower across the shoulders, though, and it feels a little like I am back on a ship as she walks around the entrance, stretching a bit, settling us until she feels comfortable. Her scales feel like hardened leather, flexible, rather than brittle like the glass shards they resemble. She snorts another puff of smoke. I grab the handhold so hard that my knuckles go white.

"I'll meet you at the cave," Aris says, holding my eyes. "If you have to stop early, stop. I can always find you through our bond."

"Be safe," I blurt out.

He gives me a smirk. "Don't worry about me, Firefly. I'll see you soon."

He gives Delphine one final pat on her shoulder, and then he shifts. In the darkness, his white fur glows like moonlight. He is a massive tiger, sleek and fierce, as deadly and beautiful in this form as he is as a man. He stretches, his claws scratching the stone. Tekton rolls his eyes and scuffs his boot across the marks and then tosses me up Aris's clothes. I loop his wolf tooth around my neck along with my green pendant and stash the dragon tooth and Delphine's bracelet in a pocket. I see Delphine's eye catch on the tooth, and she snorts again, this time with enough smoke to obscure Tekton's feet for a second. Her scarlet eyes are narrowed, looking at the place I stored the tooth of the Abelonian dragon. Then she tosses her head, like it's of no consequence, and butts Tekton affectionately. In a few more moments, we are all ready to go.

Delphine walks to the top of the stairs, prancing like a nervous horse. Rafael has his arms around me and tightens them, trying not to fall. The hilts of Aris's swords smack the back of my head as we wobble, the straps pulling at my braid. It takes us all a second to settle.

"It'll be all right." Tekton soothes Delphine, stroking her nose.

Little curls of smoke issue forth from her nostrils, but she listens and quiets.

He murmurs something to her and then steps back. She arches her long glittering neck, shaking out the last of her nerves. Her great black wings extend some twenty feet to either side of us—and then she's running and pitching herself off the edge of the stairs.

For one terrible moment, we are falling. My stomach lodges in my throat, and I squeeze my eyes tightly. Frigid air rushes past us, stinging my cheeks. I picture our bodies lying broken and mangled on the ground at the base of the stairs, and I feel like I might vomit.

Then there's a mighty pull, a snap of wings, and Delphine is gliding, soaring over the log homes and buildings of Aeturnus, and I'm jammed back against Rafael. We tremble for a moment, adjusting our grips on the harness. Then Delphine veers sharply left and heads out for the path between the mountains we've mapped.

For a moment, I have to just stop—my mind is so overwhelmed with sensation that I can't think of anything but the rush of cold air past my face, the speed at which we are going. Flying like this is pure joy, pure exhilaration. And Delphine has been able to do this for years and been cooped up in her temple? I understand Tekton's hesitation, his need to protect her, but gods, this is the greatest thing I've ever done. No wonder she was jealous of Adriana, envied her freedom to fly across the continent at whim.

Her great black wings stretch out forever. Briefly I'm reminded of Caladrius's wings, so similar—sometimes, at least—in color and shape. Overhead, only the faintest hint of the green Sacred Wind dances in the sky, like Caladrius is with us, like he approves of the journey we're undertaking. Without one of the books to help me communicate with him—or unless he can come to me in a dream again, however he did that—I'll never know.

I look down and think I see a streak of white and black below, leaving the town and racing through the pine trees. I wonder for a second if anyone saw him. I have to grin at the idea, at someone looking out their window and wondering if they're hallucinating or if there really is a *tiger* running past their home.

We're going too fast for me to talk, so I just hold on as best I can. My nose is freezing, and I'm glad Tekton gave me thick gloves to wear, even if they make it hard to grip the leather before me. Even Rafael must feel the cold—I hear him mutter a few words, and feel his body behind me warming. If I have to have someone with me, I'm glad it is a Fire Mage. I'll have to get him to show me that trick. Soon I'm contentedly toasty and settle in to marvel at the landscape as we fly.

The Dragon's Spine mountains have been deemed impassable for generations. Also, all kinds of things prowl here, including trolls—which is why the Earth Mages decided on their elaborate tunnel system, to transport goods and people through to the coast. We pass no towns, no settlements—just miles of snow-covered peaks and valleys, towering pines, frozen streams. It is breathtakingly beautiful, and when Delphine banks sharply to the right, gliding neatly down to a snowy ledge, I'm almost disappointed that this part of the trip is over. I don't really have a concept of how far we've come, but it's far.

I haven't seen Aris in hours, which makes me uneasy. He'll be able to find me using our bond, which he says he can hear like a bell.

Any of the gods' creatures could be out here, waiting for us—maybe Cephus's trolls again, or one of Helene's manticores. But I see no tracks out here, nothing disturbing the snow for miles around. If there's a trap here, it's well hidden.

Rafael and I slide off, and Delphine shifts. The leather harness falls around her bare feet, and Rafael immediately slides his red robe around her shoulders. She wraps it around herself gladly. Her cheeks are pink from the cold, but her eyes are shining.

"How are you feeling? Tired?" I ask, digging in the packs for her clothing.

"That was amazing!" she yells, and her voice echoes off the cave walls behind us.

Rafael chuckles, and I look around at our campsite.

It is too smooth to be a purely natural cave. I suspect an Earth Mage passed through here at some point and made it into a convenient stopping point. They've even left a stack of wood, kept dry from the snow at the back of the cave, though it is splintering with age.

Rafael gets a nice little fire going in the cave, and soon we are warm, dry, and preparing some food. Delphine is dressed and wrapped up with a bedroll around her shoulders, like a little chipmunk in a nest. She looks tired, but she's smiling to herself as she gazes into the fire.

All in all, this first flight has gone better than I could have expected, and we're making excellent time. I worried over every aspect of the flight—whether we'd be too heavy or awkward for Delphine to carry, whether she'd tire quickly, whether the weather itself would delay us. I expect our trip across the flat grasslands of Ocron will take us a matter of days instead of weeks at this rate, and I feel a little flicker of hope in my stomach. We will beat Mariana to the eastern coast at this rate—we can get to Estana and the Book of Gold before she can get the Book of Silver to her queen in Roallac. And maybe we'll stand a chance of ending this nightmare.

Aris leaps into the cave with a roar, breaking my thoughts. He's breathing a little hard, puffs of warm air forming little clouds from his nose as his sides heave, but otherwise, he seems all right. Ice has formed on his fur, especially around his chin and whiskers, and I lean down to brush them off.

A whisper of wind, and Aris has shifted back too. He grabs me up in a hug, burying his freezing cold nose and face into my shoulder. I squeal at the attack, pushing uselessly at his massive—and naked—shoulders.

"You're so nice and warm," he purrs, rubbing his arms inside my robe.

Gods, his fingers are like ice, and I struggle uselessly to get away from them.

"Either get me some clothes, or take yours off," he says, and he takes a nip at my earlobe.

"I was trying to get them before you pounced on me!" I huff, though I can't help laughing, and when Aris goes to open his mouth again, Rafael hurls his pants at him, followed by the rest of his clothing.

"The boots are next," Rafael warns, cocking his arm back.

Aris snorts out a laugh but gets dressed. His skin is flushed with exertion and the cold, and he grabs me again once he's dressed, plunking us both down next to the fire, and holds me close while he thaws out. He buries his cold nose in my neck again, and I can feel his breath skittering across my skin, warming me through and through. Rafael shoots me a glance, raising one eyebrow with a grin, before returning his attention to cooking.

"Any trouble?" Aris asks, looking up at Delphine.

The girl is grinning broadly, looking more animated than I've ever seen her. She's practically vibrating with energy, nearly bursting from holding in her words.

"None! And the air currents were amazing! You should have seen me—I could have gone higher, but I didn't want to miss the cave! And ..." She continues on for a few more minutes while we eat and stretch and get ourselves ready for the night.

As Aris warms up, he starts to unfold and eventually stretches his long legs out, letting his feet warm up by the fire. Delphine is asleep the moment her head hits the ground, a smile on her pale face.

This time, when we lay out our bedrolls, Aris looks at me and raises an arm. *Come here*, he's saying.

I don't argue. And I can't say I need his body heat this time either, because Rafael has our little cave snug and warm and dry. I just need to be near Aris.

We snuggle between the bedrolls, Aris's back to the fire, his arm draped over my waist, holding me against his chest. He is asleep in a moment too, worn out from the day's travels—and as I lie there in the flickering firelight, Aris purring in my ear, I wish I could freeze this moment and live in it forever.

CHAPTER 11
ARIS

I like running. Always have. It gives me time to clear my head. Back at the School of the Silver Flame, I used to run ten miles in the morning with the other Shields before classes started. Sometimes Dimitra and I would race.

Gods, I miss her.

At night, across the expanses of white snow that reflect the moonlight, I can barely make out Delphine's shape most of the time. I can always hear Wren, though, if I listen. I can and will always know what direction she is in. My paws on the snow are swift and sure, and the miles fall away behind me. I don't pass many people—there are only a few scattered log dwellings as we reach the foothills. I wonder what they'll make of tiger prints, so I do my best to stay away from them. Tigers aren't found here—generally, they're found in the southwestern part of Ocron, and even there they are rare. We pass quickly through the Dragon's Spine mountains and on into the broad plains of central Ocron.

Usually by the time I catch up, they've set up camp, and there's a fire going and food being prepared. After a long night of running, it's a glad sight. Even nicer to find Wren waiting for me, a shy smile on her face. Though I sometimes stay awake during the day—I am a Shield, after all, and don't need sleep the way she does—I still spend the time near her, holding her close under the bedroll.

And if our hands wander, well, we do our best to stay quiet.

One day, when we stop in a small wooded area, I can't sleep at all. I'm restless, and my tossing and turning is keeping Wren awake. I get up and make my way outside the camp to sit on a fallen pine log. The needles layer the ground, and the air smells nice.

My ears prick at the sound of footsteps over the pine needles behind me, of feet moving softly, slowly, trying not to be heard. Trying to sneak up on a tiger.

"Put your toes down first, Delphine, not your heel," I say.

The sound stops. Overhead, a breeze ruffles the pines, and a couple of birds sing. They come down to our camp and flitter around Wren's sleeping form for a bit before taking off again.

Delphine comes from behind me and sits on the log at my side.

"Can't sleep?" I ask.

She shakes her head, her hair falling like a curtain, partly hiding her face. She pulls her feet onto the log and wraps her arms around her knees.

"How'd you know it was me?" she asks.

I raise an eyebrow, and she lets out a huff.

"Tell me the story about the salamanders," she says.

"A bedtime story? Rafael tells it with much more flair," I say. Not to mention embellishments.

"Well, tell me another one, then," she says. "Did you ever fight in Roallac?"

"Never in Roallac, but close. Along the Black Strait once," I say, thinking. "Stefan and I were part of a phalanx sent north. There was rumor of pirates raiding the villages there, on the Ocronian side. We hid in one of the villages, and when they landed, we attacked. Turned out they were actually Roallacan men, scouting for weaknesses along the border. Evanthia denied the whole thing, of course, but it caused a big scandal for a while. Roallacan delegates weren't welcomed in Estana after that."

"Were you ever scared?" she asks.

I lean back on my hands and give her a grin. "Never. As Rafael says, I have an ego is as big as my muscles. Nothing scares me."

"Really?" she asks, and it takes a second for me to register that maybe *she's* the one who's scared, out here in the middle of the country when she's been hidden away in a tower for years, away from the only family she's ever known.

I loop an arm around her shoulders and pull her close. "We're all scared sometimes," I tell her. "That's why your training is so important. I want you to be able to face whatever life throws your way."

She leans against me, and we watch the pines dapple the sunlight across the ground. A pair of brave rabbits come over to Wren but hesitate when they see us, and then bound away again.

"I need to ask you something," Delphine says after a moment.

I wait.

She pushes the hair back from her face, staring absently at something far away—not looking at me.

"Ask me anything," I prompt. I have two younger sisters—I'm decent at talking to teenage girls.

If she starts asking about clothes or boys or something, though, I'm out.

"Did you kill that dragon?" she asks quietly. Her eyes dart to mine, then away again just as fast.

Fuck. Should have seen that one coming.

"I did," I say. I reach into my coat and pull out the dragon's tooth. It's so big my hand won't wrap entirely around the base. It's rounded and a little blunt—meant to be wielded by strong jaws that can crush bone.

Delphine's hand shakes a little as she takes it from me, turning it over in her palms.

"It's bigger than mine are," she says, frowning, and hands it back.

"It was only a dragon," I say. "*You* are a Shield."

It was a tool of the gods, the same as the trolls and the kraken and the manticore. Caelus took the claw of the manticore to protect us on our journey. Mariana said it was the smell that kept other trouble away from us the rest of our trip west; Caelus said it was the goddess Helene's magic, still somehow potent, that protected us. Maybe, in some way, I took the tooth for the same reason, a good-luck token. Ignatius, god of fire, isn't the worst of the gods, though he probably didn't appreciate me killing his pet.

I tuck the tooth back into its pocket and then knock my shoulder against Delphine's.

"How did you kill it?" she asks. She's finally looking at me now, a mixture of emotions on her face I can't quite place. Fear? Anger?

"It had us cornered, actually—Dimitra and me. We were all trying to distract it so Wren could get to the book," I say, leaning back on my hands. Gods, I can still smell the dragon flame. "It was breathing its flame—we need to work on yours, by the way—and I stepped between it and Dimitra."

"Then what?" Delphine breathes, her eyes wide.

I hesitate.

"Then ... Dimitra shoved me," I say, and I swallow before continuing. "She got me underneath it, where my swords could penetrate its scales. She saved me—saved all of us, really—and sacrificed herself."

I have to stop and look away from Delphine's piercing gaze. We sit quietly for a moment, Delphine folding her hands over her stomach, like she's guarding it.

"Would Wren's robe stop dragon flame, do you think? She told me it was spelled to protect her from all kinds of things."

"Ismini and Panos are two of the strongest Mages in Ocron," I tell her. "They personally imbued that robe with every protective spell they could think of."

I think back—it's protected her from more than just skinned knees and broken bones. She was dropped by one of Helene's beasts from high in the air and somehow survived. I don't know if I'd want to put it to the test against Delphine's flames, but I'd wager it would withstand them. Knowing Panos and Ismini, it would withstand the flames of Ignatius himself. Mage robes are something special, the magic practically woven into the cloth they're made of.

"You should have had them spell your clothes too," Delphine says.

I agree, though I'm sure if it were possible, they would have done so. It probably has something to do with the fact that we lose our clothes when we shift, so it isn't worth the immense effort of putting those long-acting spells on them in the first place.

"I'd rather they spell my socks to stay dry," I joke, grinning at her. She was clearly worried about us. I can only imagine what she went through, not knowing if she'd see any of us again, or maybe if she'd ever leave her tower.

She chews on a fingernail for a minute.

"You think your friend who made your swords can make me some armor? For my dragon form?" she asks.

"Tulliano? Probably," I muse. "You don't need it, though. There's not much in this world that can take down a dragon."

"You did," she says quietly. But she doesn't pull away from me.

Caelus's dragon book says that dragon fire is hot enough to melt nearly anything, including steel. Not to mention dragon scales are extremely hard and sharp. I bet they'd cut through most metal fairly easily. I'm not sure what Tulliano could do for dragon armor, but I'm sure he'd welcome the challenge. I'm glad Tekton thought to reinforce Delphine's harness with steel wire—I have to wonder if he figured out her scales would cut through plain leather the hard way.

"I'll ask Tulliano next time I see him," I promise. I like Delphine. She's smart and tough. In a few years, she'll be a Shield I'd be proud to fight alongside, dragon form or not. "And I'll make sure you're trained up before you start at the school. Markos is good at finding ways to tailor training to your strengths and weaknesses. The Mages will be falling all over themselves to be claimed by you."

"Thanks," she says. She tucks a strand of hair back behind her ear, biting her lip nervously. "I just ... I wanted you to know I'm not mad that you killed a dragon. It's weird that you carry its tooth around, just so you know, but I'm not angry. I'm glad, actually, since it killed Dimitra. I liked her."

I sigh, and we look out into the forest together, soaking up the weak sunlight.

"So did I."

CHAPTER 12
WREN

Flying begins to take a toll on us all. Delphine never complains, but she looks paler each day. Rafael has to coax her to eat, and whenever I try to get her to land earlier, to make the flights shorter, she snorts, just as she does in dragon form—though with less smoke—and ignores me.

"I'm a Shield," she says.

"And even Shields need to know their limits," Aris says. He doesn't like the pallor in her cheeks either.

"I'm fine. When I'm not, I'll tell *you*, not the other way around."

"She's feisty," Rafael comments, unable to keep the smile from his face. They get on well, spending a lot of time discussing her fire-breathing and ways to optimize her aim, temperature, and so forth.

The next night, though, Delphine is flagging. By the time we land, Aris is already waiting at our campsite. I dismount from Delphine, sliding down from her considerable height and landing on wobbly legs. Aris shifts and catches me up against his bare chest before I pitch forward and crumple.

He sets me down gently, but as soon as my feet touch the ground, the soreness in my thighs and back makes itself known, and I can't help the groan that escapes my lips.

"Gods," I mumble. I sit and bend forward to touch my toes, feeling the pull down the backs of my legs, and the kinks on my back start to unbend a little. Riding a dragon is *nothing* like riding a horse, or even a mammoth. Years of hard work have given me calluses and strength enough—but even after a long day of hauling oil up a lighthouse, my back *never* hurt like this. I feel suddenly as old as Panos, and a pang of wistfulness goes through me at the thought. Missing him and Ismini feels like a throb in my chest—not unlike the throb in my back, which is tightening up again. Aris pulls on his clothes while Rafael bullies Delphine into eating something. It's a good thing we're close now—I'm not sure any of us want to keep this up for much longer. Maybe one more day. Two, at most.

"Sore?" Aris asks, far too cheerfully.

With his gifts of strength and healing, I bet he feels perfectly fine. He probably wants to go out for another ten-mile run now or something and then do his calisthenics. I just want to sit down on the cold ground until my legs go numb.

"No," I say, standing and self-consciously straightening up. "You?"

He snorts, like this is funny, and hands me my pack.

After we eat, Delphine settles down to sleep. Rafael stares absently into the fire. I'm not sure I'll ever get used to this, the quiet, pensive version of Rafael. I wish he'd sing again.

"Come on," Aris says, extending a hand. "Time for lessons."

I groan but take his hand, letting his strength help my wobbly legs. *Gods.* Sitting still for even a moment has got me in knots. Aris walks a short distance away from the campfire, a knife glittering in either hand. In the dusky predawn light, his eyes are supernaturally bright and fixed on me with a predatory gaze that belies the ease in his stance. I stumble out to him and wordlessly take my knife from my boot.

"Guard," he warns me—a split second before his knife comes down in a slashing attack from the right.

I bring up my knife quickly—too quickly, as it turns out, because the movement cranks something in my back, and when his blade hits mine, the vibration in my hand shoots up my arm like a lightning bolt.

The knife falls from my hand, and I fall with it.

The knife hits the ground point-first, sticking in the cold earth at my feet.

I am caught by Aris's hand under my arm. He hauls me up, and I prepare my ears for a verbal lashing—*Don't ever let go of your knife*, maybe, or *You should listen to me when I tell you to stretch more.* That one seems to be his favorite lately.

However, this time he surprises me.

"Are you all right?" he asks.

I wince but retrieve my knife and stand back up. "Yes."

"Good. Don't ever let go of your knife," he reminds me. Again.

I sigh and try not to roll my eyes at him.

"You should really stretch more," he continues.

This time I do roll my eyes, and when I do, I just catch the movement of his knife on the left this time, a flicker of firelight over the flashing blade. I raise my right arm, intending to block—but my back seizes, and my body twists from the sudden pain.

Even Aris can't react to my motion that fast, and the tip of his knife glances across my shoulder, tearing a slice into my coat.

"What in the *hells*, Wren?" he asks, sheathing his knife and then grabbing for mine.

I am bent double, my palms against my thighs, trying to breathe through the stabbing pain in my side.

"I just ... need to stretch," I get out.

"Obviously," he says.

Then I'm being grabbed, bundled up unceremoniously, and deposited on a nearby boulder. The stone is freezing, and the cold seeps through my pants almost instantly. I remind myself to have

Rafael teach me how he keeps himself warm for our next lesson—he wants me to focus on control, but right now, heat seems like a better idea. I go to stand, but Aris puts a hand on my shoulder, pushing me back down.

"Sit," he orders.

"It's cold," I argue.

He sighs but brings me his bedroll, spreading it out over the boulder like it's a coverlet on a bed. I scoot over to it and give him a smile of thanks—my legs are warmer now, at least.

"Good. Now take off your coat," he says.

"But it's *cold*," I remind him.

"Yes," he says. He hands me a small sewing kit—little more than a leather envelope holding a thick curved needle and some coarse thread. I swallow hard—clearly, this is intended for sewing skin and flesh rather than cloth, but it will have to do. "Fix that," he says, pointing to the tear in my coat. "Or you'll be even colder."

I grudgingly agree that he has a point. Besides, he's brought my bedroll too and drapes it over my shoulders once I take the coat off. Considerate of him. He checks over my shirt, making sure his knife didn't cut me.

I *feel* rather than hear Aris move behind me. The skin on the back of my neck prickles in anticipation—and when his touch comes, it is the warm, firm pressure of his hands, his fingers working into the knots in my neck, systematically working outward, kneading each knot until he feels it ease.

He takes his task very seriously. I feel myself start to relax along with my tense muscles, and I almost can't help leaning back into him as he continues his work. The needle and coat drift from my hands, completely forgotten.

He clears his throat. "Take your boots off," he says abruptly.

"What?" I ask. I turn to look at him over my shoulder, but he's staring at my feet.

"Boots. Off."

I comply.

Once Aris has deemed my neck and shoulders sufficiently unknotted, he moves to my feet. Watching him crouch there, intent on his massage, his dark head bent, I feel suddenly flushed, suddenly self-conscious. My feet are sweaty and probably stink after being stuffed into boots all day—not to mention on the back of a dragon—and I pull them away, tucking them under the blanket with me.

Aris crouches there, looking amused—and a little concerned.

"Did I hurt you?" he asks.

I shake my head, unable to give voice to whatever it is I am feeling. Something warm and strange. Shame?

Or something else?

"I won't touch you unless you want me to," he reminds me, and he extends a hand, gesturing toward my feet. "But this will help. I promise."

I consider, then gingerly extend one foot to him.

He goes to work, massaging the instep, the back of my ankle, my calf. And he's right—it feels *so* good. It's so strange, how a simple touch can make me feel so much. When I think about it, I might have gone months, even a year, without actually touching another human being while I lived back in Spit. Animals, sure. But people? They stayed away from me, never venturing closer than they absolutely had to, to drop off payment or supplies. The touch, the care that Aris is showing my aching muscles—it does something to me. Unlocks something. Somehow it's different from when our hands drift over each other when we are tucked up in our bedrolls, eyes closed and close to dreaming. And I like it. I like it a lot.

"Even Shields get sore sometimes," Aris says, entirely for my benefit, to keep my mind off whatever magic he's working on my sore legs. "Massage is a great way to loosen the muscles back up. And stretching, of course." He smirks.

"Of course," I echo.

I swallow hard. He's moved on to my other foot, my other ankle, my other calf, slowly working his way up. I think about him massaging other Shields, or being massaged—probably by Dimitra

—and I'm suddenly glad that Rafael *did* make me focus on control. Otherwise, I'd be glowing green and causing all sorts of havoc on the weather. Probably hail.

Aris pauses at my knees, and I realize belatedly—he's kneeling between them.

"How does this feel?" he asks, cocking his head to the side. There's a double meaning there, and it leaves me flustered.

"Fine. Great," I mumble. "Much better, thank you."

He rests a hand on either knee, moving them up to my thighs. My heart flips in my chest—*Don't stop,* it screams.

"Do you want me to keep going?" he asks. His eyes glow like the blue heart of a flame.

Yes.

"No. I'm good now, thanks," I say. I pull my feet away and busy myself with retying my boots, feeling suddenly very warm despite the cold air.

He stands, brushing off his pants, and extends a hand to help me up. My shoulders and legs feel infinitely better, and I being to really, *really* wish I'd let him keep going. How far would I let him go?

He doesn't let go of my hand.

"I can work on your lower back, if you'll lie down," he says, eyes glowing. "I won't even try to seduce you, I promise. I just don't want you to be in pain."

I shake my head, looking at the fire, at the sun breaking the horizon—at anything but him.

He takes my chin gently in his fingers, turning my face back to him.

"Don't you trust me?" he asks—and I realize I've wounded him a little. He sees my own nervousness—how can I compare to the other women he's known, with my inexperience?—as a rejection of him somehow.

"I don't trust myself," I admit. And it's true—heat flares up my neck, across my cheeks.

Aris looks a little relieved, and a lot mischievous. His thumb moves from its place on my chin to my lower lip, dragging slowly across it.

"I can be patient, Firefly," he says, bending to kiss me.

It's soft and sweet—chaste, even—and despite the cold night, I'm aflame. I've been so starved for touch, so starved for affection—and now that it is before me, I can't have enough.

"There is no one else but you," he murmurs against my lips. "If you'll have me."

I throw my arms around his strong chest, burying my head against him. The words stick in my throat. I want to say them. I do.

But I don't.

Aris lets out a long, shuddery breath. He holds me for a long time, one hand rubbing gently across my back. And then he picks me up, the bedroll still wrapped across my shoulders, and deposits me gently back by the fire.

"Here," he says, handing me the coat and sewing kit again.

I chuckle and thread the needle, my cheeks flaming.

"After you fix it, you're going to stretch again."

CHAPTER 13
RAFAEL

I've never thought about being a teacher—Dimitra was always too preoccupied with being a Shield, leading her phalanx, maybe even being Commander one day.

Fate, it turns out, had other plans.

Working with Delphine has given me a new sense of purpose as we go about our quest. I find myself thinking about her training while we fly, how we can work on her control, how to temper her flames. Tekton, gods bless him, was so worried about keeping her *safe*. So it seems her instruction is up to me, if I don't want her to burn the whole country down.

"Tell me again why you can't stop breathing fire once you start," I say, sitting cross-legged with her by our campfire.

"I *told* you," she says, rolling her eyes dramatically. "I *don't know*. I just *can't*."

Teaching Delphine forces me to relive the day that Dimitra died. I don't like it. That dragon, that ancient creature of Lord Ignatius, spewed a liquid flame that burned and burned, never stopping until Aris killed it.

And then Mariana betrayed us all.

Whatever in the hells she'd been up to, well, what was between us was real. And it was Mariana who saved me from going gray, whose feelings—dare I say love?—for me kept her at my side, pleading with me to stay, when Dimitra died. It was a candle flickering in the dark, and I leaped for it. Her last words to Wren were "Take care of Rafael and Caelus for me." Mariana might be a traitor, but I know, deep in that frozen heart of hers, that she cares.

I shake my head, returning to the issue at hand. Anytime I think about Mariana too long, I can sense the gray shadows at the edge of my vision closing in, tempting me to join them, to just let all the pain go.

Thank the gods for Delphine. She's given me something to think about outside myself. Dimitra and Mariana might be gone from my life, but fire is one thing that can never be taken from me.

And I've been thinking a lot about it—dragon fire—and why it has to just burn until Delphine runs out of it. I bet it has to do with the accelerant sacs in her throat. Caelus left his book about dragons with me, and I've read it cover to cover several times over. There isn't much, mostly myths and a lot of stuff about the uses of dragon scales.

Examining a dragon—even a relatively small one like Delphine—is not easy. I had to put my entire head inside her mouth—which smelled putrid—to get a good look. I could feel the saliva dripping from her fangs onto my neck. There, in the back of her throat, were the openings of two small glands. Once I removed my face from her mouth, I was able to palpate them along the outside of her neck.

"Do you ever try just closing your mouth when you're breathing fire? Suffocate the flames?"

"Now why didn't I think of that?" Delphine says, tapping a finger against her cheek playfully. "Maybe because then the accelerant pours down my throat, choking me until I vomit the flames back up. My insides might be as fireproof as your robe, but that doesn't mean it feels good."

"You're a Shield. Your body will do what you tell it to, once we figure it out," I say, trying to be reassuring. In truth, I have no idea. There's never been a dragon Shield.

She huffs. "You should just let me shift, and I'll show you that *it won't work.*"

I raise an eyebrow in disbelief. "We're in the middle of a plain full of dried grass, and we haven't had rain in days. Tell me, oh knowledgeable one, do you really think that's a good idea?"

She frowns, kicking the dirt in front of her.

"Fire is the most beautiful and powerful of all the elements," I tell her.

"I *know*—"

"Don't interrupt," I say, wagging a finger at her. "I wasn't done. It's also the most demanding."

She crosses her arms, glaring at me. She's tired, and she's frustrated, and I'm being obnoxious. Time to change tactics. In truth, I'm not sure I could contain her fire if she did get out of control. She's not as large as the dragon we faced in Abelon, though I'm not sure that matters. Wren could help, but still, I'd feel better if we were near a large body of water. Or in one.

"You want to hear about how I got my scars?" I ask.

She perks up, torn between being a sulky teenager and being genuinely interested in the story.

I've seen her eyeing them. It's hard not to notice them—my hands are covered in thick, waxy scars that extend up my arms, across my shoulders, down my back, and up my neck, a pale contrast against the tan of my skin. Even with the help of a Water Mage's healing magic, it took months to recover, and the range of motion in my fingers has never been good enough to play the lyre again.

"Fine," she says.

Not as enthusiastic as I hoped, but I'll take it. I splay my fingers, tracking the way the flesh on the back of them was melted, warped. I'd never known pain like that before.

"I was at the school," I say. It's been years, and I can still smell my charred skin. "It's a … competitive place. There were five Fire

Mages in my year, and I was the best. It's a lot of pressure, as you'll find out."

"You were there with Aris? And Dimitra and Stefan?"

"I was," I say.

Aris and Wren are off somewhere, presumably at a nearby farm to see if they can buy some food for us, but more likely just sneaking some time for themselves. Gods, I've known Aris forever—and we've had our differences. Dimitra never would fully admit how much she liked him, but I could tell. Hells, I was half in love with Aris myself at one point. But seeing him with Wren? I can only hope to Ignatius that someday someone looks at me like that.

"Anyway," I say, taking a deep breath. "There are lots of chances for us to show off. There's this big celebration in the winter, where all the students get dressed up, and the Mages have a chance to kind of showcase their magic. It's our chance to impress the Shields, and I knew I had to do something damn impressive if I wanted Dimitra to notice me."

"How did you know you wanted Dimitra to claim you?" Delphine interrupts.

"Long story," I say, smiling fondly. "Another time. Anyway, I had this crazy idea to basically make myself wings of fire, like Ignatius."

"So you burned yourself?" she asks.

"Patience, Sparks. I made light without heat—it's something that's pretty tricky, the way we make our spelled candles and such, but on a much larger scale. And I wanted big, *big* wings. And then, as one does at these parties, I had ... a little too much to drink."

Delphine rolls her eyes, but she's listening intently, so I ignore it.

"Fire only behaves as long as you do," I tell her, holding her brown eyes with mine. "The spell started to slip, to flicker, and then —when I saw Dimitra talking to a Wind Mage, one I *knew* I was competing with for her attention—I lost control. I wanted my wings bigger, and *bigger*. The spell got out of hand, because of my pride. I thought I was strong enough to handle it. And I was wrong."

"So you burned," Delphine says, though the words are quiet this time, like a whisper.

"And so did everyone around me," I say. "The Mages were mostly all right—some singed hair and whatnot. Our robes are fireproofed, among other things, to protect us from the magic we wield. The Shield standing next to me had no such protection, and the fire leaped for him. I took my own robe off and threw it over him, smothering it—then the flames came for me instead."

"You talk about fire like it has a soul," Delphine says quietly. "Like it is alive."

"It is," I say. For a moment, I am lost in memories, in the way Battos's leathers curled and burned, in the screams of pain as his hair caught fire. He healed quickly, being a Shield, but he never spoke to me again.

"It took the other Fire Mages and me only a few minutes to get the blaze under control, but the damage was done—to my reputation, and to my body. After that, I did everything I could to learn about control. I never tried to show off again."

"And Dimitra still picked you?"

"She did," I say, smiling. "And it was the best day of my life." She was a friend, a partner like I'd never imagined. She was quiet and fierce and honorable, loyal to a fault, and as strong as Odall himself. She would have been Commander one day, and I would have gladly stood at her side. We talked about it a few times. Shield Commanders don't often have Mages, but to Dimitra, our bond was sacred, and she never would have broken our claim.

"Why?" Delphine asks. "Why did Dimitra still pick you?"

It's a reasonable question. I asked myself that all the time our first year together. After that, I couldn't imagine us ever being apart. Even now, my chest aches where I could feel our bond break, like a wound that will never heal.

"Because being the best isn't always about being the strongest," I say. "It's about being the smartest. You can be both, Sparks."

CHAPTER 14
ARIS

The weather is colder than usual today. Thick gray clouds cover the sky, and the dawning sun gives only weak color and light. It's probably going to snow. We found cover in an old barn, and though the hay is moldy and the roof has fallen in on one side, it is otherwise pretty stable and will keep the worst of the weather off us.

Time has reclaimed this farm. Thick carpets of long-stemmed grasses rise higher than the rotted fence posts, and there is no sign of anyone living here except a family of mice—who, of course, immediately ran to Wren and snuggled into her coat pocket, poking their little twitching noses out every so often.

For a tiger, they'd make a delicious little snack.

"I thought you were a vegetarian," Delphine says, watching me side-eye the mice.

I don't like eating rodents, never have.

Still, the primal urge between a cat and a mouse ...

"Only in Shield form," I mutter.

"We don't eat our friends, Aris," Wren says, putting a hand over her pocket, like that would keep me from them.

"They're not more than a mouthful, anyway," Delphine says cheerily. "Do we have time for some knife lessons before bed?"

"Better you than me," Wren mutters.

I grin. "Both of you," I say, drawing my knives as they both draw theirs. "Let's go."

Delphine's getting better by the day. I'd expect nothing less. She applies herself to each movement I show her with determination and masters it in moments.

Wren ... well, not so much.

"You're still better than you once were," I tell her when we've finished.

She huffs. "Not by much."

"Delphine's a Shield. You can't compare yourself to her," I remind her.

"I'm not, not really," she says, but she's pouting.

I pull her in, planting a kiss on her head. "You've got me, Firefly. I'll be your thorns, remember?"

"I remember," she whispers back, hugging me, burying her face against my chest.

"Do you think your babies will be Shields or Mages?" Delphine asks suddenly, looking at us.

Wren chokes on a laugh and disentangles herself from me.

"What?" we both ask.

"Well, children of Shields are Shields. Children of Mages are Mages. If the mother is one and the father is the other, the child generally follows the mother, right? So would your kids be Night Mages too? Or maybe other kinds of Mages, since you're kind of special."

Rafael grabs Delphine in a playful headlock and ruffles her hair. She's strong, and a Shield, but still just a teen, still gangly, and Rafael has several inches of height on her.

"Leave them alone, Sparks," he says, dragging her to the other side of the barn.

She flails, laughing, and finally gets away. She punches him on the arm as they walk. It's Rafael's turn to teach her—she gets frustrated because he won't let her shift and breathe fire. He shared his own story with her a few days ago, and she's been more patient since, but only a little.

Tonight, as they sit by the fire, I can see him demonstrating his breathing techniques, filling his lungs from the bottom, using his own breath as a way to channel his magic, to make the fire do what he wants it to do. She tries to imitate him.

I run a hand across my scalp. Wren's flushed, probably more from Delphine's comment than our knife practice.

"So ... heard from Caladrius recently?" I ask, desperate to change the subject. Not because I don't like kids, don't want them—I do. Tigers might be solitary, but I was raised with five siblings in a culture where legacy is everything. I've always assumed I'll have them someday. But Wren?

Wren crosses her arms, shielding herself from me, watching Rafael and Delphine laugh by the fire.

"Not since I touched the book," she says quietly. "Do you think we'd know if Queen Evanthia had it?"

I step closer and wrap my arms around her back, until the top of her head is tucked beneath my chin and her hands unwrap themselves and grab me instead. Gods, I see no future for me except with Wren by my side.

"I don't know," I say. "We'll have to trust Caelus to get to the Book of Silver, and we'll go after the Book of Gold. We get to Estana and figure out what the plan is to get Leo back, and then we go do whatever we need to, to help."

"You make it sound so simple." Wren sighs but she leans into me, letting me support her.

"I'm a simple man," I say, kissing the top of her head.

She grins, looking up at me with a suspicious glance. "You are *not* simple, Aris Valorius. I've never met anyone who complicates my life quite like you."

But then she kisses me, and I think, *It really* is *simple.*

I would burn down this world for her.

CHAPTER 15
LEO

I pray a lot.

There's not much else to do. The cell that Evanthia keeps me in is open and airy, with high windows to let in some light. There's a mattress and blanket, and even a small bathroom in the back with running water. There are no doors, of course, in case I decide to drown myself. The guards are my constant companions, silent as death. As much as they pretend otherwise, that I am a guest in their country, a cage is still a cage.

The guards tell me nothing, and Evanthia has not come to visit other than on the first day. The guards feed me at change of shift, but still I get no news. I wonder if they are mute. They don't even speak to each other.

I repeat the names of all those who traveled here with me—all except one of the messengers, a young boy whose name, to my chagrin, I never learned. I pray to Rigrasil a thousand times a day, hoping that they've earned a place of honor in the afterlife.

"Idas, Nikandros, Rubita, Iason," I chant. The names of the Mages who came with me.

The guards roll their eyes at me.

"Vitruvia, Keti, Zale, Ionna." The Shields who were with me. All of them, dead. The Roallacan people harbor some long-held animosity toward Shields—an ancient grudge, since no Shields have ever been born in Roallac.

They were the first to die. All of them, thrown into Evanthia's pit of vipers.

I hear their screams in my dreams, see their faces when I close my eyes.

Next came the ungifted. They are not treated well in Roallac, their status felt to be somehow lesser than Mages and Shields. They work only the most menial jobs here, a prejudice Evanthia was not keen on giving up if our countries were joined.

Michaelis, my personal guard and friend since childhood, defended me to his last breath, trying in vain to give me a chance to escape.

I don't sleep much.

I pace my cell, and I pray.

Nineteen good men and women are dead because of me. Because I insisted on going to Roallac as a show of confidence in our countries' budding friendship. Because I turned down Evanthia's offer of marriage.

She offered amnesty to Iason, the Water Mage who'd come with us, if he'd agree to break the claim with his Shield, a panther shifter named Keti. He refused.

And now they are both dead.

I should have expected it, I suppose. Evanthia has never married. She wants the blessing of the Book of Gold to extend to Roallac in the way it now extends into Aclines, making their fields and animals more fertile. It was a reasonable offer, a way to ally our two countries. Roallac suffers in comparison to Ocron, with its swamps and lack of tillable soil. It depends on the sea for much of its economy.

But when Evanthia told me, a feverish gleam in her eyes, how she planned to bring Aenon back into our realm, I refused her. The god of water, unchecked, with the countries of Roallac and Ocron to do his bidding? He was never one of the kinder gods—he is too volatile. He is the god of the gentle spring rains but also the storms.

"But he'd be working *with* us," Evanthia argued. "Don't you see?"

"You think you can control a god?" I asked.

She didn't like that at all.

"I'm going to do this, with or without you," she said, her jaw set firmly. "Your country can profit from this, or be destroyed. The choice is up to you."

I wonder if Wren got my letter, if she's found the Book of Silver. I miss her. She was a breath of fresh air in the capital. She was so smart, devising our written code. I have full confidence in my messengers' ability to guard my letters, so I never bothered before. I wonder what Markos and Iraklis are up to, whether they are coming to fight Evanthia. Of course they are—without me, Ocron will wither. I am a fool a thousand-times over for making this trip, for not taking the 'making an heir' part of my job more seriously. Without me, the blessing of the Book of Gold will fade. And I am under no delusions that Evanthia will let me live when Iraklis and Markos do get here—the only reason I imagine she's kept me alive at all is that she hopes I will change my mind before then.

Gods. A thousand times a day I find myself wondering what will happen if I say yes.

Do I marry her, the Snake Queen, who killed nineteen citizens of Ocron, as my punishment? Do I have any doubts that she would kill me, immediately, in the event that we ever had a child?

It will soon be the solstice. Evanthia plans to bring Aenon back to our realm anyway—whether or not I marry her, the entire world is now at risk. I think part of the reason she's kept me alive is so that I can witness it.

I shudder to think of any other possible reason.

I eye the windows of my cell—they are glass, and too high for me to reach. I harbor some small hope that perhaps one of my messengers will fly by and spot me, so I spend as much time as possible in the middle of the room, where I'm more likely to be visible.

And I get on my knees. And I pray.

CHAPTER 16
WREN

We reach Estana near dawn. It is as glorious as I remember—in the rising sun, the golden stone of the city wall gleams, the pennants with Estana's golden sun on a red background snapping out in the morning breeze. It feels so wrong, being here when Leo is not.

We land in the dark, not very far from The Golden Crown, where Aris and I stayed so many nights ago. I dismount—legs rubbery, but maybe I'm getting used to this a little, because they're no longer sore—and rummage in the pack for Delphine's clothing. She's just finished shifting and getting dressed when Aris arrives, padding through the fallen pine needles on silent tiger paws. I am starkly reminded of the first time I saw him—nothing but glowing blue eyes regarding me from the dark. A pang grips my heart—how very far we've all come since then.

We walk toward Estana with a caravan of farmers bringing their goods in to the market.

We've barely started when a group of soldiers comes thundering down the road on great warhorses, Shields and Mages with them.

Some of the Shields have already shifted—there is a large black wolf leading the way, and a scarred brown bear by a red-haired Mage in green at the back.

Aris steps in front of us, though there is no need. This group is on some kind of mission and largely ignores us. It passes us by—all except the bear and the Earth Mage, who drop their pace, leaving the group without anyone else noticing.

The bear lumbers up to Aris, roaring, and rears back on her hind legs, towering above my Shield, her teeth bigger than my hand. She is a fearsome creature, with huge black claws and brown fur criss-crossed with shiny white scars. Delphine shrieks and grabs my robe in fright. The bear throws its massive paws wide—

And envelops Aris in a crushing hug.

Ismini, the Mage in green, leaps down from her horse, and I fly into her open arms. Rafael stands back with Delphine, one hand on her shoulder.

"Oh, I've missed you two," Ismini coos, holding me tightly.

I am surprised by the tears that spring to my eyes. Ismini smells of earth and grass, and I bury my face in her shoulder. She doesn't let me go until I let go first, and a kind smile spreads on her freckled face as she surreptitiously wipes away my tears.

"I don't suppose you've seen a dragon on your way this morning, have you?" she asks. "There's a rumor out west, another creature loosed on us by the gods. It's got the capital in an uproar." She glances over at Aris, who is pinned to the ground by a laughing Aleka —at least, I think she's laughing. It's hard to tell on a bear. Aris is laughing, anyway, and futilely trying to shove her off him.

Rafael remains quiet, though Ismini greets him kindly.

I look back at Delphine, who looks a little awestruck. She's looking between the four of us with wide dark eyes, and I realize that, despite our little group, she really hasn't met many other Shields, and she certainly hasn't seen them in shifted form. And Aleka *is* fairly terrifying.

Aris finally taps the ground with his free hand, signaling that he gives up the fight—he can't say the words, because he's laughing too hard. The bear grunts and rolls off him, and he sits up, grass all over him and dirt on his face, mussed and laughing.

This is a side of him I don't often see, and I like it. *We've come home*, I realize, and that tightening in my chest eases a tiny bit.

"Delphine," I say, gesturing for the girl to join me. She shuffles over and allows me to put an arm around her thin shoulders. "Meet Ismini, my mentor and one of the strongest Earth Mages on the continent. And Aleka, her Shield." I ruffle the bear's fur as she comes over.

To Delphine's credit, the girl stands stock-still as the bear sniffs her over, up and down, her breath blowing back the loose strands of her hair. The bear looks over at Aris, and he runs a hand through the stubble of his hair.

"Yeah, Aleka, this is Delphine," he says with a lopsided grin. "Delphine, meet Aleka, captain of the city guard. No doubt she'll ask you to call her Auntie Aleka soon. She has a habit of adopting orphaned Shields." The bear shoves her shoulder into him, and he nearly stumbles, though he grins and slaps her shoulder back.

"An orphaned Shield?" Ismini asks.

"She's been living with her uncle at the Temple of the God of Night. We ... offered to bring her east with us to train," Aris says.

Aleka grunts, and Delphine flinches at the sound.

"I'm ... happy to meet you," Delphine says, though she looks anything but. She dips her head, letting her long brown hair hide her face.

I tighten my arm around her shoulders. "You can trust them," I tell her. I don't divulge her secret—it is hers to tell, and hers alone, if she wants to.

Delphine looks up at me and back at Aris, who nods, one hand still on Aleka's broad, furry back. Ismini shares a glance with me, one eyebrow arched over her grass-green eyes. Delphine takes a deep breath, standing up a little straighter. We've finally gotten her to agree to wear clothing beyond her ragged shift, and for the first time, I truly see her as a Shield and not as a child. When she speaks, it is with a strength and authority I haven't seen much of in her, and Aris fairly glows with pride.

"I'm Delphine Kalla. And *I* am the dragon."

For a moment nobody speaks.

"Well then," Ismini says, hands on hips like this is nothing extraordinary, her mothering instincts taking over. "We're happy to meet you. Commander Markos isn't here, I'm afraid. He's already gone north, to Roallac, along with most of the other Mages and Shields we can spare."

We thought he probably wouldn't be here—but still, Delphine's face falls a little. She's been looking forward to finally meeting the man even Aris admires.

"We have a lot to tell you," Aris says.

Delphine nods, torn between wanting to go to Aris for comfort and being wary of Aleka, standing at his side.

"She won't bite," he whispers to her.

Aleka lets out a *whuff* of air and lets Delphine approach her.

"You must all be exhausted," Ismini says. "Come on. Let's get you cleaned up and fed. I'll assemble what's left of the palace council, and we can get to work." She keeps one arm around my shoulders and takes Delphine with her other as she walks back to Estana.

Rafael drifts behind us like a red-robed ghost. I catch Ismini glancing worriedly at him.

"We got a message from Caelus about Dimitra and Mariana," she whispers to me.

I wince.

"We have a lot to catch you up on," I say. Mariana betrayed us. Caelus is chasing after her, but we haven't heard from him in days. And Dimitra's death still feels fresh in my mind—I can still smell the dragon's fire that incinerated her, leaving nothing behind but ash and charred bits of metal. I can't even imagine how Rafael is feeling or what he's going through, how he's managed not only to not turn gray, but somehow, in some small way, to keep on going.

Ismini shakes her head, her red hair not budging an inch from her braided crown. "So it appears," she says, squeezing us harder around the shoulders, like that alone can protect us. It feels good.

"Be a dear and bring poor Ludus along with you," Ismini calls over her shoulder to Aris.

He snorts but grabs the horse's reins and walks behind us, chatting one-sidedly with Aleka as we go, responding to her grunts and headshakes as if talking to a bear were a perfectly normal thing for him—I suppose they must have had these kinds of conversations before.

As we walk, Ismini tells me what's been going on in the capital—since Aleka is captain of the city guard and Ismini is mostly an academic now, they were left behind while their fellow Shields and Mages went on to Roallac.

"Someone's got to guard the capital, I suppose," she says, sparing a glance back at Aleka. "It chafes her, though."

"Has anyone heard from King Leonidas? Is he all right?" I ask.

"No one knows," Ismini says, sighing. "Although if he'd died, we'd know it. *Ocron* would know it. The country will not flourish without a descendant of his line alive. The Book of Gold requires it."

"About that," I say, looking back at Aris, who is watching me with his predator eyes.

He gives me a nod.

"Has Queen Evanthia said anything about wanting the book? Has she made any demands?" I ask.

Ismini nods, her lips tight. "Even if we knew where it was, I'm not sure the council would agree to send it off to that snake witch," she says, with as much venom as I've ever heard from her.

"We don't need to send it off," I say, and I tell her quickly what we've learned of the books and how they can be used to communicate with the gods. Whether by his own will or whether he has lost the ability to reach me, I haven't heard from Caladrius since I held the Book of Silver. I *have* to find that book and make him answer me. I have to find the strength to defeat Evanthia, to get Leo back to Estana. To make right all the strange things that have been going on with magic. This is *my* quest—*our* quest—I think, looking back at Aris again. What we were always destined to do. To bring the books together, to bring *balance* back to magic and to our world. We can use the Book of Gold, return it to its hiding place, and then ... well, we'll figure it out.

"Well, that's all well and good," Ismini says, chewing on her lower lip. "But we still don't have the book."

"Yes." I sigh. "King Leonidas mentioned he had some people working on it, some librarians and some spies, or something."

"You'd be surprised how often those two professions overlap," she says with a wry smile. "Come on. Before this poor girl collapses. Food, baths, and I think perhaps a nap. I'll take care of everything else."

Eventually, we put Delphine on Ismini's horse. She *is* exhausted, but her eyes are wide as we approach the capital. We make our way down the main street—this early, a few shops are opening, but not many people are about yet. Smoke curls from red-shingled rooftops, and the smells of fresh bread and fires soon overwhelm the fresh grass smell of the plains. The cobblestones clip along under Ludus's hooves. He is entirely unperturbed by Aleka padding alongside him.

We pass shops and small businesses, and the golden statues of King Mathaios and Queen Yanna in the city center. Delphine loves these, fascinated by the giant size and gleaming gold, and starts asking questions about whether they are solid gold or just painted that way. Rafael, gods bless him, tries to keep up with her questions, though it isn't easy.

We cross the moat and the wide bridge before coming up on Estana's palace, that ethereal stone building that is like a city unto itself. We pass the manicured gardens and cypress trees and hand off Ludus to a waiting attendant.

We're greeted by Tolis at the gates. He's as sprightly and energetic as ever, his short white hair sticking nearly straight up and bobbing with his movements. He wears the impeccable red-and-gold livery of Ocron, and a gold badge that marks him as the steward of the palace. I expect this is a position he's had for many years, judging by his age, and he loves his work, judging by his exuberance. Despite the somber mood of the palace, he greets us cheerily and escorts us to a suite not unlike the one Aris and I initially shared, but with two additional rooms on the side of the sitting room, for Delphine and Rafael. They each claim one wordlessly and throw themselves onto the soft beds.

Ismini and Aleka leave us to gather their council, and I am left alone with Aris.

I am starkly reminded of the last time we were in a room like this, here in Estana. I had just woken from a days-long slumber after battling Saroya—and Aris and I kissed for the first time. I can feel my face flaming, and make myself busy with hauling my pack into the closest room. I roll my shoulders once I drop it onto the lavish bed, trying to work out the kinks that riding a dragon has knotted into them, and catch Aris watching me. He raises an eyebrow.

"Need another massage, Firefly?" he asks.

I look down, at the plush coverlet on the bed, at the dirt on my boots, at anything but his piercing gaze.

"I was thinking about a bath," I mumble. I sneak a glance at him and see him smirking—I realize I'm holding my folded robe before me like a shield.

"Good idea," he says, and he prowls closer, plucking the robe from my hands. "Mind if I join you?"

This close, he smells like leather and metal—and it's all I can do not to ignite. I bite my lower lip, looking up at him—my Aris, my Shield, my protector.

All mine. And all alone at last.

Surely the council can wait a few minutes. Is it the tension in the air that is making my heart race, the knowledge that we have only a moment before we're returned to the pressures of reality? War with the gods or not, all I can think of right now is Aris.

I raise a hand to his neck and pull him down for a gentle kiss.

"Give me a few minutes first," I say, and my voice sounds breathy even to my ears. We are so close I can see his pupils dilate as the breath leaves his chest. I turn before I lose my nerve, and walk into our private bathroom.

Gods, if there is one thing I missed about Estana, it's the baths. This room is tiled in creamy marble, and there's a freestanding tub with a golden faucet. I don't really care what magic is involved in making sure that steaming water is ready at the mere turn of a faucet—I'm so layered in dirt and grime that honestly I'd jump in even if it were freezing. I peel off my traveling clothes—I have rings of dirt around my ankles from my socks—and unravel my braid. My scalp *itches*, and it feels so good to have my hair free. I kick my dirty clothes to the side, and once I've relieved myself and given myself a mental pep talk in the mirror—trying not to notice how bedraggled I look and instead trying to see myself as Aris sees me—I slip into the massive bath, now full of scented bubbles. I can't help but sigh as I dunk myself under, momentarily weightless in the massive tub. I break the surface with a splash, which is the exact moment Aris chooses to walk in.

I wipe the water back from my eyes and smooth my hair, now hanging heavy down my back. He's smirking again, and I swear he's never reminded me so much of a stalking wildcat as he does now. He locks eyes with me—I've sunk down so the bubbles provide me some small amount of modesty—and removes his shirt in one swift motion, casting it aside by my discarded clothes. Gods, he's magnificent—and he knows it. My eyes snag on the scar on his left shoulder, the one I stitched up what feels like ages ago—the only indication that he might actually be mortal and not something from a dream.

Aris moves behind me, kneeling on the tile.

"Move your hair, Firefly," he says.

I gather the long strands and pull them over my shoulder—and feel Aris's warm hands settle there instead.

"Relax," he whispers, and his fingers begin working their magic on the knots in my shoulders, like he's massaged them before. I try to busy myself with washing my hair, dunking under again to remove the suds—the water is turning muddy but then clears again. I may not be thrilled with Aenon these days, but whatever water magic this is, I'm loving it.

Aris works patiently on my shoulders, moving to my neck. The tension floats from me as easily as the dirt of the road does, and I lean back into his touch, groaning as he works on the base of my scalp. He inhales sharply but doesn't say anything. In this quiet sanctuary, we are more alone than we have been in weeks—and I am melting, my defenses, my excuses, crumbling, winnowed away from me like the dirt from my body.

His hands travel forward to my collarbones, lightly, like he's asking permission. I lean my head back, meeting his eyes—neither of us missing the fact that arching my back like this exposes my breasts from the bubbles. I have no coy words, no flirtatious phrases or seductive glances in my repertoire, but I don't need them. A glance is all it takes between us—my permission, given. His fingers travel lower, down my sternum, before tracing the space under my breasts and then giving them as much careful attention as he's given my shoulders and neck. Heat coils low in my abdomen, which has nothing to do with the heat of the water, and my breathing becomes shallow.

His hand slips lower, beneath the bubbles. A thrill runs through me that has nothing to do with magic—and I don't stop him. He pulls me back against him so he can position me the way he wants me, my wet back against his bare chest.

I feel … like floating. Like I'm a bubble on the water's surface myself, iridescent. For one glorious moment, we are all there is in the world. When I open my eyes, I see Aris above me, a smug grin on his handsome face, eyes glittering. I reach back and grab the back of his neck, where the hair is still short and soft, and bring his lips down to mine—and pull the rest of him down into the water with me.

CHAPTER 17
ARIS

By the time Rafael bangs on the door to tell us to hurry up and get ready, there's as much water on the floor as there is in the tub. My pants are still on, and my skin is chafed where I pulled Wren to straddle my lap. She hides her face against my neck now, glowing and panting, nothing between us but a single infuriating layer of cloth.

Rafael knocks again, harder, and I snarl at him.

"Fine! But Panos will be coming in next, so you might want to put some clothes on!"

I sigh, brushing hair out of Wren's face. Her lips are swollen and her cheeks are flushed—she is the most beautiful thing I've ever seen, and I steal one last kiss before she's scrambling for a towel.

I peel my pants off—still seated in the tub—and rinse off as best I can, running a little more water to scrub my scalp. I never thought I'd say this, but I don't miss having long hair. When I stand, Wren has a towel for me and holds it out with a crooked smile, her eyes still glassy and dazed. She looks me over boldly, for the first time, from head to toe as I dry off. Maybe I flex and pose a little for her. She rolls her eyes but can't keep a smile from her face. She uses her foot to mop our wet, dirty clothing along the floor, sopping up a little of the mess.

We find some clothing in the bedroom's wardrobe—a plain dress with a corseted back I have to tie up for Wren, and some standard black Shield gear for me. She's so much less guarded right now—though she still turns her back to me when she dresses. When she reaches up to brush her hair, I snag her around the waist, growling against her ear.

"Will this meeting take long, do you think?" I ask.

She shivers—then smacks me with her hairbrush.

"Behave," she warns. I growl.

"Are you decent?" Rafael calls from the hallway.

"Rarely," I shout back. "But I'm wearing pants, if that's what you're asking."

Wren rolls her eyes, opening the door from the bedroom to the sitting room. Rafael cackles. Leaning heavily on his arm is Panos, chuckling as well.

I grab Wren's hand, pulling her back a bit. I kiss her soundly, bending her back in a dramatic pose, taking advantage while I still can. She squeaks a little, one hand slapping my chest, but the other small, warm hand wraps around the back of my neck, holding my lips to hers. She narrows her eyes at me, disentangling herself with as much dignity as she can summon, her cheeks crimson.

"Mage Wren. I am so pleased to have you safely returned to us," Panos says with a wheeze, giving me a crooked grin. Somehow he's aged a decade since we saw him last. His eyes are rheumy and his posture more stooped. He raises one bushy white eyebrow at me with a cough.

"You too, Shield Aris," he wheezes.

Wren gives him a warm hug. Ismini and Aleka follow soon after, and an army of servants bringing food and drink. Delphine stumbles out of her room, wiping sleep from her eyes, which widen like a startled deer's when she sees all of us gathered.

"I'll help you bathe and dress, miss," one of the servants offers. She's carrying a set of black clothes—Shield clothes—for her.

Delphine's mouth drops, and she looks at me, nearly bouncing on her toes with excitement.

"Go on," I tell her.

She races after the servant to the bathing room. Thank the gods Wren had the forethought to clean up after our interlude.

"Well," Aleka says, sitting down in an overstuffed chair and propping her feet up on a footstool. "Tell us everything."

"Everything" takes a while. At some point, Delphine reemerges. Her hair is neatly braided—like Wren's—but her close-fitting black clothes are all Shield. She is thin and small, almost birdlike. She's lost weight on our trip east, and she didn't have much to spare in the first place. My sister Rea would snap her like a twig in the arena. I've got some work to do to get her caught up. Ismini is eyeing her too, already planning a feast, I'm sure. For now, she just loads up a plate with a thick wedge of cheese, bread, and a half-dozen fruit tarts, and she fills a goblet with ash water.

"Don't look at me like that—the girl needs to eat," Ismini scolds me, shoving the food at Delphine.

I raise my hands in surrender.

Now we can get down to business—how we're going to find the Book of Gold, rescue the king, kill the Snake Queen, and keep the god of water in his immortal prison. Nothing to it.

"Head Mage Iraklis and Shield Commander Markos have crossed the Black Strait and move on western Roallac with half our forces," Aleka says, pointing to the narrowest crossing between our countries. "The rest are spread along our northeastern coast. We've also called in some favors to old allies in the Isles, and their ships are keeping Roallac from going too far south. Not sure how long they'll hold on, though." She rubs the back of her neck. "Rumor is Evanthia is offering to spare them, given their water magic, if they'll join her. I expect we'll see a number of defections within the week."

"What is the size of the Roallacan forces? Just Mages?" I ask.

"Unclear," Ismini says, pursing her lips. "They don't claim Shields, don't believe they need them." She huffs. "So we're pretty sure it's just Mages and infantry. No room for horses in that swampy place."

"Their numbers are less easy to define," Panos says, coughing again. "They don't attack in force but with stealth, melting and disappearing like mist. Some of them are able to wield the swamp gases, making great deadly fogs that can smother a whole camp. Their Mages are well trained."

"That's insane," Wren says, turning pale.

"Our Wind Mages have found ways to fight it," Ismini says. "Once we blow that fog back on them a few times, they won't dare try it anymore."

"Has *anyone* heard from King Leonidas?" Wren asks.

Ismini shakes her head, and Aleka snorts.

"Not a damned word, other than Evanthia's. She swears he's still alive—and will be, as long as we hand over the Book of Gold by the winter solstice. We are ... working with Rigrasil's priests, trying to figure out how the country will survive, should anything happen to the king. There's a distant cousin who would be the next king. He's not a direct descendant, but it's all we have. They hope it will be enough to continue to secure the god's continued blessing on Ocron."

Wren fidgets a little in her seat, pondering what Aleka said. I grab her hand and give it a squeeze.

"Sorry," she says to me quietly. "Of course you'd have a plan in place in case Leo ... in case something happened to him. It doesn't mean you've given up on him." She looks at Aleka head-on, unblinking, like she dares Aleka to challenge her.

Aleka huffs, amused at the thought that Wren would try to intimidate her.

"Of course not," Ismini says, patting Aleka's arm. "But we do need someone here to run things, since King Leonidas is ... otherwise occupied. Alexandros is a good man, and he's working hard, communicating with Iraklis and Commander Markos daily."

"What's with the solstice thing, anyway?" I ask. "Tekton said he'd been talking to you." I look at Panos.

"Yes," he says, "and he was kind enough to send me the copy of the Book of Silver from the library at Aeturnus."

I'd nearly forgotten about it—Tekton and Caelus started translating it while we were there, but Tekton said he couldn't complete the rest without help.

"Was there anything in the book?" Wren asks, at the same time Rafael does. They exchange an excited grin.

"I hate to disappoint you," Panos says gently, shaking his head. "Though there was an entry about using the books to bring the gods back to our realm—the magic that they gave us has to be willingly returned."

"Evanthia will remove magic from our world, to bring Aenon back?" Aleka asks, frowning.

Panos shrugs. "I think it is the sacrifice of the magic of a single individual that she needs," he says, a bit of spittle collecting at the corner of his mouth as he talks. "More important than that is the timing. That's why she needs the solstice—the veil between worlds thins. It is the only time of the year when Queen Evanthia can summon Lord Aenon. And even more importantly"—he looks Wren straight in the eyes—"it is the time when the power of Caladrius is at its strongest. It may be that only you, my dear Wren, can stop Aenon, should he cross over."

She sits back in her chair, reeling a little. I put a hand on her thigh, squeezing gently. *Wren, battle a god?* The idea makes me fume, remembering how Caladrius just *speaking* to her ruptured her eardrums, how turning his godly gaze on her burned her skin. And that was in dreams and visions.

"It won't come to that," I say to her softly. "Evanthia doesn't even have two of the books yet."

"She must have a lot of confidence that she *will*," Aleka grunts. "And from there, the destruction of our world is inevitable."

Ismini rolls her eyes.

Delphine has stopped midmotion, a fruit tart halfway to her mouth. A raspberry falls off and lands on her plate. "What?" she asks, breathless.

"The people of Roallac are … historically prejudiced against Shields and ungifted people," Ismini explains gently. "Even Mages without water magic aren't welcome there. With the god of water on their side, we worry that their bigotry would spread."

"Genocide, she means," Aleka says.

This time, Ismini glares at her Shield. "Not helping," she hisses.

Aleka ignores her.

"So we just keep the Book of Gold from Evanthia, and she can't call Aenon," Rafael says.

"But then she'll kill King Leonidas, and Ocron will suffer," Ismini reminds him.

If Leo dies, as he has no heirs, Ocron will lose the magic of the Book of Gold. Crops will fail. Birth rates will drop. Plagues and pestilence will ruin the land. Perhaps Evanthia has found a way to transfer this blessing to her own, swampy country.

"She'll probably kill the king anyway," Aleka retorts, "and if she uses the books, undoubtedly Ocron will suffer."

"Caladrius mentioned that the magic of the Book of Gold wasn't as tied to the king's line as we think," Wren says, frowning.

"What did he say? Specifically?" Panos asks intently, his bushy white eyebrows raised. "There's not much in the Book of Silver, and Rigrasil's priests haven't been able to tell us for sure one way or the other."

"He said that the magic would live on if King Leonidas died," Wren says, twirling her green pendant around her fingers as she thinks. "That the blessing would not end with our king."

"And you believe him?" Aleka asks. She's got one of her many knives out and is balancing it point-first on the tip of one calloused finger, much to Delphine's delight.

"He wants me to use the books to bring *him* to our realm instead of Aenon," Wren says. "He says he can restore the balance of magic here."

"The balance was probably only thrown off in the first place because Evanthia had the Book of Bronze," Panos muses. "Who knows what she's capable of, with years of unlimited access to the gods?"

"Well, I don't trust Caladrius. I bet he was just saying that so you'd focus less on saving the king and more on getting the books for him," Aleka says, flipping her knife over. She grabs it in midair and flings it. It sticks deeply into the far wall.

Delphine's mouth has fallen open.

It's a simple trick, one she showed me long ago. I can't stifle a smile at the memory—I ruined a lot of nice knives against the stone walls at the school that way.

"There are too many differing stories," Panos says, shaking his head. "We need to use the book to talk to the gods ourselves, and see if we can sort this out."

"Which ... do you have?" Delphine asks. "The Book of Gold? You have it, right?" She's leaning forward, eyes glittering.

"Not ... not exactly, no," Ismini says, looking at Panos.

"Not at all, she means," Aleka says, frowning.

Ismini rolls her eyes. "No, we just don't know *exactly* where it is. But it must be in Ocron somewhere, or Evanthia would have already won."

"Already killed us all, she means," Aleka says.

Aleka never did know how to pull her punches. It's one of the things I've always admired about her.

"You're *not helping*," Ismini hisses again, glaring at her Shield.

Aleka shrugs, unfazed.

"All right, well, that's a start," Wren says, looking at me.

"It's a fucking big continent," I say. "Could be anywhere. Could be in some ditch somewhere, for all we know."

"King Leonidas told us to come here," Wren says. "It *has* to be here."

"King Leonidas has had his entire spy network—the King's Librarians—looking for it," Ismini says.

"Real librarians?" Delphine asks, confused.

"Of course. Keepers of knowledge," Panos says, without a hint of sarcasm.

Great. Our fate is in the hands of academics.

"So we should ask them, then, right?" Wren asks.

"I spoke with one of their leaders yesterday," Ismini says quietly. "He said they didn't have any clues"

"And if the king knows where the book is, he can't tell us," Rafael says.

He's been so quiet I almost forgot he was there. He's staring into the fire, absently twirling his fingers, making small animal shapes out of the flames, which chase each other and leap over the logs.

"Well, if the king knows, someone else knows—the spy who told him," Wren argues.

"And spies are so easy to find," I groan. "You sure he didn't say anything about the book in those letters you burned?"

Wren glares at me. Then her eyes widen.

"Not in my letters. In yours."

Ismini makes me write out, again, word for word, *exactly* what Leo's last letter to Wren said, since Wren's copy is now illegible from being read a thousand times already on our trip east. Each scratch of the pen has me wanting to tear my eyes out, but I manage to get it down at last.

. . .

My Wren,

I am sorry to hear of your disillusionment. While Ismini has assured me in the past that each Mage-and-Shield pair eventually find their own way, I'll admit, I do not understand how your partnership will work. While Aris is a fearsome Shield, perhaps one of the greatest in their history, he remains at his core a man who lives only for the attention of others, intent on glory above all else. He is a notorious rake, a philanderer, and while you may trust your life to him, please be careful of your heart.

Let me be quite plain. My time here is short. My dearest wish is that you will fly home soon. I can't wait to have you sitting at my side. What a queen you will make.

Yours,

Leo

"It's a code?" Rafael says, turning the paper upside down. "Maybe there was something concealed in the lines, the alignment of the words? In the paper itself? Are you sure you remember it precisely?"

"I remember enough," I growl.

Wren comes to my side and slips her arm around my waist.

"It should only be the words after 'Let me be quite plain.' The code King Leonidas and I decided on was based on him using anything describing a bird—flight, a nest, that kind of thing. 'Fly home' has to mean come back to Estana. So the book has to be here, somewhere." She kindly ignores the first half of the message, where Leo warns Wren that I'm an attention-seeking peacock driven by my ... passion. Which, honestly, is fair.

"And the rest? He intends for you to be his queen?" Panos asks, looking from me to Wren and back again.

Wren shakes her head, and I hold her against me more tightly.

"No, I never agreed to that," Wren says.

"It's got to be part of the code," I say.

"He asked you, though?" Ismini presses.

I let out a growl, my canines aching as they try to grow, to start a shift into my animal side. Like I'd let anyone take Wren from me.

"Only in jest," Wren says, glancing at the paper.

Despite her words, spots of pink start to appear on her cheeks. I'm really wishing I hadn't thrown away that ring I got her in Basti—then they'd know, then the *world* would know that Wren is mine, and mine alone. Who knows where it is now? On the bottom of Aenon's sea somewhere.

"Wait," Rafael says, straightening. His eyes have that hazy, unfocused look they get whenever he has a crazy idea. "Read me the last line again."

Ismini obliges.

Rafael leaps from his chair, a grin on his thin face.

"Follow me!" he shouts, and he races from the room.

"Hold on now," Panos grumbles.

Ismini stops to help him rise, but Aleka, Wren, Delphine, and I are already out the door. We see Rafael's red robe disappear around a corner, and give chase through the palace's halls, ignoring the pointed looks of the few people who are still here.

He finally comes to a stop before the throne room. The room is massive, and empty. The last time I was here, it felt smaller, packed as it was with supplicants. Now our footsteps echo as we enter.

Sunlight filters in from above, cunning windows carved into the soaring stonework. And on the dais at the end is the throne of Ocron, gilded wood with a sun on top. The rays shoot out from the throne several feet, thin bars of glittering gold.

"See?" Rafael says, pointing.

We look at him—Ismini and Panos haven't made it yet, but we can hear them coming.

"I see a big gold chair, but no book," I say.

Rafael huffs. "Yes! One chair!"

"No chair for a queen?" Delphine asks.

Awareness dawns on me.

"No chair for the queen to sit beside her king," Wren says, the same realization hitting her. "Aleka, the last queen, did she have a throne? Was it stored somewhere?"

"No," Aleka says, the grin spreading on her face making her look positively feral. "Traditionally, the king's seat is the seat of politics, in the palace. The queen's throne is the symbolic seat of religion, in the Temple of Rigrasil. *That* is where we'll find the Book of Gold."

CHAPTER 18
WREN

We enter a wide stone plaza in disrepair. The cobblestones are large and made of fine golden sandstone, but broken and uneven. On the far side of the plaza is a building that dwarfs the shops, a single spire above the pediment, rising five or six stories into the sky, as if to pierce it. The temple is made of the same glimmering golden stone as the city wall and palace, but it hasn't been maintained. The figures sculpted into the pediment—it is clear they represent the gods, each with their element in their outstretched hands—are weather-worn and chipped.

Aleka, Ismini, and Rafael accompany us. Delphine we managed to convince—with great difficulty—to stay at the palace. Aris is anticipating some kind of trouble here. We aren't the only ones looking for the golden book. I can only hope that no one else has found it first. I think my horse feels my nervous energy, as he prances a little underneath me.

To the left of this building are two smaller temples. The paint on their main doors is faded, and one of the doors is falling off its hinges. One door is red and the other yellow. The doors of the two smaller temples flanking the right of the main building are blue and green. Each is under some level of repair—except the blue one, the Temple of Aenon. I even spy scorch marks on the marble columns of this temple, and the pediment has been completely erased.

"Welcome to the Temple District," Panos says, his voice creaking like a glacier, booming through this open space.

We walk our horses toward the central, largest building. A shiver goes through me, and I look back over my shoulder. To the far back of the plaza is another temple, this one hidden in the shadows, though it must be as large as the golden central temple before me. The spire has been broken off; there are no doors, just a gaping black maw of an entrance. I feel myself drawn to it, like I could fall into whatever dark space is inside there, like a whirlpool. The Temple of Caladrius calls to me.

A sound breaks the spell, and I turn around to see a squadron of soldiers carrying supplies into the square—carts full of golden stone and all kinds of tools. The sound comes again, and I realize it must be a hammer on stone, over and over again. The soldiers move in and out of the golden temple before me, where Panos is leading us. He manages to dismount his horse with a surprisingly effortless grace despite his enormous, flapping robe, and he ties his mare to a post. We do the same.

I look back over my shoulder at the Temple of Caladrius. I want to go to it.

"Later," Aris says, following my gaze. "If we don't find what we're looking for here, we'll go see Caladrius's temple."

"Didn't Caelus say the temples were built where the veil between our realms was thinnest? Like at Aeturnus?"

"That's right," Panos says, taking the reins of my own horse.

I dismount, only snagging my robe for a moment on the stirrup, and look back at the dark temple again.

"I haven't heard from Caladrius," I whisper. "Maybe there I can hear him, like I could at Aeturnus, at his statue."

Aris frowns and looks at the temple too. "Book first. Then I'll take you to talk to your god, all right?" He puts an arm around my shoulders.

It's still hard for me to tear my eyes away from it, back to the golden temple before us.

"All right," I agree. Book of Gold first.

We walk up the stairs to the wide columns of the temple. It's built like the one at Aeturnus, with two rings of columns, though this one appears to have just one large central room, not the maze of tunnels that runs under Aeturnus's temple.

"This is the Temple of Rigrasil," Aris says, and he sounds almost reverent.

I guess he's been here before—he moves confidently, not looking about wide-eyed like I am. This is a place of great importance to him, the final resting place of the Shields. His shoulders are squared, head high—he does not shrink before his god. I wonder if his mother is buried here.

Dimitra should have been. And Zale, and all the other Shields who went north with Leo. My chest constricts painfully with the thought of all those who have died already for these books—and my gut tells me that the death toll is far from complete.

I shake off my gloomy thoughts, trying to focus instead on the Book of Gold, on finding the throne of the queen, and on getting Leo back. We follow Panos up the wide, shallow steps and enter the temple.

The inside is a single large room, with rows of benches flanking a central walkway. At the front is an altar or something, now covered in white cloth. This is done, apparently, to protect whatever is underneath from the clouds of stone dust that is being kicked up as repairs are being made. There's not a lot of people in here, and the temple is in poor shape, so I expect it will take them a long time. Years, maybe. The benches are relatively new, though, the golden wood still smelling faintly of the forest. Above us, open holes to either side let in sunshine and let out dust, though I expect windows once covered them. Behind the altar, a massive, splintered window glows with the afternoon light. The panes were in shades of orange, yellow, and red, spread like the rays of the sun, now fractured, casting only sputtering images of color on the floor.

"As you can see, renovations are underway here," Panos says, showing me around. "Even with the war. People look to the gods for answers, for help."

"Why had they fallen into such disrepair, then?" I ask.

"The importance of the gods has … diminished, with time," Panos says. "Ever since people realized their prayers were going unanswered. As you can imagine, it costs quite a bit to keep these temples. King Leonidas's father preferred to spend the coin on Ocron's infrastructure—did you know, I was there when he planned the Great Western Road?"

"Another time, Panos," Aleka says, moving past him. "This temple has always been sacred to the Shields. *We* have kept our part of Rigrasil's temple intact."

It's hot in here, and I remove my heavy outer cloak to keep cool—and in a moment, I see the reason why. A Fire Mage, a squat man in a flame-red robe, is trailing a finger along a broken pane of stained glass. As we watch, the metal flares cherry red, and oozes into its proper place. It's a beautiful use of magic—to create art. It reminds me of the ball here, a lifetime ago, where all the Mages were wearing decorations made from their magic—a dress of shimmering leaves, elaborate jewelry made of ice. I miss Leo with a pang in my heart—we flirted, but I think deep down we both knew that I was destined for Aris. I shake my head, dispersing the memories. The man making the stained-glass windows waves at Panos, who nods in return.

"All of this King Leonidas is trying to restore to its former glory," he says, sweeping an arm around the room.

Aris is uncharacteristically silent, his hands stuffed into his pockets. He's watching a group of men in the far corner, men who I realize are as tall and broad as he is, though something about them seems … grayer. Broken. Something that makes me feel like whatever they once were, they've now cracked, and something vital has leaked out.

They don't speak, don't make eye contact with anyone. They just move stiffly, automatically, moving heavy materials around for the stonemasons with no emotion at all on their faces. I shudder, returning my attention to Panos.

"Are the other temples being restored too?" Rafael asks, wide-eyed.

"The others too," Panos says. "As you can imagine, though, support hasn't been great for Lord Aenon in recent months. Lord Caladrius is starting to gain some popularity." He glances at me. "I've had a number of requests to channel more resources into his temple, from those hoping to gain his favor. And yours."

Panos sighs. "Such beauty and history should not be forgotten, or looted. I consider study of the gods as a ... sort of hobby of mine, a pursuit in my dotage," he says, frowning at the stained-glass window at the front of the building.

I frown too—I've never had much time for hobbies. They're for rich people without jobs, and with too much spare time on their hands.

I look around, like I'm going to find an answer written somewhere, hidden under a layer of dust or behind a broken beam, but there's nothing. Just wood and stone and the sound of gray men moving boulders. A steady stream of workers file in and out of the temple, stacking tools and wooden planks for scaffolds in a corner. They look at us curiously, some of them blatantly stopping to watch.

"There's no throne," Rafael notes, nodding toward the front of the room.

I've noted that too but haven't given voice to it, afraid to dash the fragile hope that has been kindling in my chest.

"We moved it below, to the crypts, so it wouldn't be damaged during the renovations," Panos says, wheezing more heavily now. He leans on his cane for a moment before making his slow way down the temple aisle. Am I hoping that the book will simply be hidden inside the throne? Perhaps in a secret drawer in the back. Or maybe stashed beneath the seat cushion, the way I used to hide sweets from my father back home.

Gods, I miss my lighthouse. When I had those mirrors polished, the beam of light would have outshone even *this* glorious place.

Aleka and Ismini converse quietly behind us. Panos speaks to a few workers along the way as we make our way toward the rear of the temple.

"Just paying our respects," Panos tells a Shield standing guard at the end. There is a doorway at the end, behind the altar, with words above carved in a deep relief.

VIRES, HONOS, FIDES.

The Shield guarding the entrance is a tall, muscular woman with sharp black eyes, her shield and gladiuses worn on her back. She nods to Panos, Aris, and Aleka but largely ignores the rest of us.

"Good to see you, Aris," she says as he passes, putting a hand on his shoulder. "I heard about Dimitra. I am sorry."

His jaw clenches, and his hand goes reflexively to his jacket pocket, where he still keeps the dragon tooth.

"A stele has been ordered and will be erected here in a place of honor," the woman continues.

Aris nods and walks on. To anyone else, it might look like he doesn't care, like the news means nothing to him. I can tell, though, in the set of his shoulders, in the way he let out a relieved breath when she spoke. He cares, and he cares very deeply. A stele—the stone marker afforded to each Shield buried here—will still tell the world that Dimitra Gataki was here, and that she sacrificed her life, even if her body could not be buried here. Caelus said that she'd reach Lord Rigrasil's presence and be able to stand tall before him, that she'd earned a place of honor in the afterlife with her actions.

Aris never talks much about the afterlife—but he found comfort in Caelus's words then, and now in the words of this guard.

I'm not sure how I feel. Will I have to face Caladrius when I die? The thought chills me to my bones.

The air through the doorway is cold and still and damp, and it seems to cling to my very bones as we descend. The stairs go down in a spiral for several floors. Periodically a long hallway branches off, down which I can see tombs to either side. The hallways are lit by spelled lanterns. Some of the tombs have men and women kneeling before them, praying or simply paying their respects.

By the time we get to the bottom of the stairs, Panos is wheezing heavily and leans on Aris for support.

"At the end, there," he says, pointing.

There's a door at the end of this hallway, through which I cannot see. Aris leads Panos first. The older man moves slowly, which gives me plenty of time to read the inscriptions on the tombs as we pass. They are stacked two and three high, shelves into which stone coffins or urns have been placed. As Aleka said, at least this part of the temple is well kept, clean, and in good condition. In front of each tomb, there is a stele marked with the Shield's name and a few lines about them.

Alexis Stylianou
Wolf
Captain of King Leonidas I's personal guard
Claimed of Stephanos Politilis, Wind Mage
Mother of three Shields

Arkadios Boulas
Eagle
King's Messenger

. . .

Skyllar Belos
Snow Leopard
Librarian
Father of one Shield

They continue on in much the same manner—name, animal shift, job. A few mention children—having Shield offspring seems to be held in the same regard as the highest military honor. Again I wonder if Aris's mother is here, somewhere—having had six children herself, all Shields, she surely earned her resting place here. Aris keeps his gaze straight ahead, his steps slow to accommodate Panos but otherwise steady, purposely not looking at the inscriptions we pass. I wonder how many of these house his friends.

I wonder if Stefan has his own tomb, somewhere. The Hall of Shields does not house Mages—but I've never heard of a similar setup for Mages. Perhaps Stefan is buried under the Temple of Helene, goddess of wind. I should find out and pay my respects to the man who was like a brother to Aris—better than, actually, if the rest of his brothers are anything like Spyridon.

We reach the end of the hallway in silence. Panos leans on the doorframe but gestures us inside.

It is a large space hewn out of the rock. On one wall hang dozens of gladiuses, their blades looking as bright and polished as Aris's, though the leather grips show their age. On the far wall are two blades that appear to have been dipped in gold, bound to a shield that is also gold.

"Odall," Aris whispers, the word falling reverently from his mouth.

I look to him, but his gaze is transfixed by the golden weapons.

God's Light and Sun Fury, Delphine said. Even in the dark, in the unwavering light of the spelled lanterns around us, they glow.

"When Odall died, his weapons turned to gold," Panos wheezes, one hand on his chest. "A blessing from Rigrasil of the highest honor."

Aleka and Aris also touch their chests in reverence.

The rest of us look at what rests below those golden weapons—a chair that is a delicate replica of the one in the palace, with carved sunrays around the top, and a golden cushion on the seat.

Aleka goes to it directly, ignoring Odall's weapons and the rest of the treasure on the walls, and systematically starts looking it over, her slim fingers tracing every inch of the carvings, looking for some kind of secret notch or panel. Aris and Ismini join her. My heart is pounding in my chest, my hands clammy from the cold and damp. Aleka tosses me the cushion. It is heavy, so I start looking for a way to remove the golden velvet from it, thinking perhaps the book is hidden inside. As I fiddle with the tassels, Rafael lets out a crow of triumph, his long fingers pressing a button near where the queen's feet would have been—and a long panel opens.

We crowd him, even Panos. Rafael's scarred fingers shake as he removes a cloth-wrapped bundle from the throne—it's the right size and shape.

"We can't tell anyone," Ismini whispers. "There will be riots, people demanding we turn it over in exchange for King Leonidas's life, those who want to keep Lord Rigrasil's promise of prosperity in Ocron intact with his bloodline's survival."

Rafael peels back the fabric, just enough to reveal the corner of the object he's holding. Even in the dim light, it glimmers. Solid gold, the same strangely glowing shade as Odall's swords. He covers it back up hastily.

"So what now?" Aris asks, frowning. "We've got the book. We can't turn it over, or Evanthia will use it to destroy us."

"*We* use it," I say. "Let me speak to Caladrius, see if he can help us."

"Let *me* use it," Panos wheezes. "Lord Aenon is *my* god. As a Water Mage, maybe I can talk some sense into him."

The idea of Panos berating the god of water, like a grandfather disciplining an errant child, makes me smile.

"Lord Cephus and Lord Aenon have long been rivals," Ismini says thoughtfully. "Perhaps we can enlist the god of earth."

"It's a *book*," Rafael says. "Why don't we just read it?"

We all look at him like he's suddenly grown three heads.

Aleka bursts out laughing. Rafael flushes, his lips downturned.

"It's written in the language of the gods," Panos says gently. "There are few of us left who can still read it. It would take me some time to decipher it alone."

"Where's Caelus when you need him?" Aris mutters, running a hand over his scalp.

"All right, so we know it's here," Rafael says. "Do we just put it back? We never speak of it again, keep it safe until the solstice has passed?"

"Are we sure it's actually the real one and not another copy?" Aleka says, frowning. "I heard the one in the vault at the palace was fake. Perhaps this one was planted too."

"Then why would the king lead me to it?" I ask. "Give it to me, Rafael. I'm the only one here who's used one of the books before. Caladrius can tell us what to do."

There's a collective shrug from the group, as if they all agree that doing *something* is better than standing around here doing nothing. Rafael extends the book to me.

A boom shakes the room, dust shuddering free overhead and drifting down on us like snow. Ismini sneezes, then wipes her hand through the air, and the dust immediately clears.

"What was that?" Aleka and Aris ask at the same time.

Aris growls and draws his swords.

"Come on," Aleka says, following suit. "Stay behind us. Did any of you tell someone where you were going?"

"Only Delphine," I say. "And she'd never tell. She knows how important this is."

"Unless they got to her first," Ismini whispers, and fear clutches at my chest. If something happens to Delphine, I'll never forgive myself.

"She's a dragon, Wren," Aris reminds me. "There's not much they'll be able to do that might harm her."

"Right," I say, swallowing down the panic threatening to burst from my throat. Gods, I hope she's all right. I hope she kept her knives on her, like Aris told her to.

"Here," Rafael says, thrusting the book at me. "Sounds like I'm going to need my hands free."

Another boom resounds overhead, and even here, at the bottom of the stairs, we hear a great shout.

"Let's go!" Aris says, leaping forward, Aleka close on his heels.

They race down the hallway with the speed gifted to them by the god of day, reaching the stairs in seconds, and take them in leaps and bounds until they disappear out of sight.

Rafael and Ismini are close behind, their magic ready and swirling around their fingertips.

I bring up the rear with Panos. Powerful his magic might be, but he is old and slow, and he leans heavily on my shoulder for support. And I have no magic now, and no time to use the book to speak to Caladrius. I free my knife from my boot and shift the book to my left arm as we make our way to the stairs.

When we reach the base, I can hear the clashing sounds of metal on metal, and Aris's roar of anger.

"Hurry!" Ismini's voice rings down to us. "Panos, we're going to need you!"

"Come on," I say, ducking under Panos's arm to bear the brunt of his weight.

"Thank you," Panos wheezes into my ear.

I don't like how hard he's breathing.

Despite his voluminous blue robe, he's nothing but twiggy

bones, and we make decent progress up the winding stairs, only stopping once to rest. Sweat is pouring down my face, and soon I'm breathing as hard as Panos. It's no different from hoisting a barrel of oil up the steps of my lighthouse, I tell myself. I might not be a Shield, but I'm tough. And determined to help my friends, however I can. I distantly hear Aris, hear the rage in his voice as he roars. I *have* to do something.

As we round the final turn in the stairs, our way is blocked by a body.

It's the guard, the tall woman. Her eyes are glassy, and water trickles from her gaping mouth, making the stone steps slick.

Panos's face hardens. "Come on," he says, stepping around her as best he can, summoning his frail strength.

I follow, clutching the book tightly to my chest, trying to conceal it under my robe. My foot falters when I accidentally step on the guard's ankle instead of the step.

"Sorry," I murmur.

Of course, she does not reply.

Panos pauses in the doorway, one shaking hand grabbing at the frame, one clutching his chest. I peek over his shoulder.

The temple is in shambles. Some of the soldiers who were unloading construction supplies appear to have taken up arms against the Fire Mages working on restoring the stained glass. Bolts of fire fly across the room, scorching the golden stone where they hit. In the aisle, Aris and Aleka fight back-to-back, their swords flying faster than my eyes can follow. A flood of people surrounds them, climbing over the wooden benches, eager to get at them. Blood flows freely from a cut on Aleka's temple, and Aris is splashed with it, though I can't tell from here if it is his own blood or someone else's.

Ismini has a pair of men wrapped in green vines that have sprouted through the floor, the thick leaves stuffed into their mouths to keep them from talking. Water Mages, judging by the puddles at their feet. Ismini has them immobilized with one hand, and with the other she sends pebbles, like arrows, whizzing through the crowd, cracking the skulls of the mob surrounding her Shield.

Rafael is locked in battle with another Water Mage. They duck behind the columns, each trying to outmaneuver the other. The gray men and women I noted earlier don't even try to move, don't speak—when one is hit by an errant spear of ice and falls, impaled through the chest, the others don't even blink. *That* is the kind of fate that awaits me if Aris falls.

Gods damn it! I have to do something! There are too many.

Panos turns, gripping my shoulder tightly. "Give me the book," he wheezes, gesturing to the bundle in my arms. "There's something I need to do."

I hand it over, curious. We know the books are ways to communicate with the gods—is he going to try to ask for help?

A sigh of veneration escapes his thin lips. "I have been waiting for this moment for a lifetime," he whispers, peeling back the fabric, exposing a glimpse of glowing gold. He covers it again, closing his eyes, one hand resting on the cover. "And for this, little Wren, I am truly sorry."

He opens his rheumy eyes, a pained look on his face, and utters a single word.

"*Push.*"

CHAPTER 19
CAELUS

The mind of a wolf is comfortable, almost too much so. As a wolf, my priorities start to waver after days of running, from finding Mariana to finding a den, and hunting. To my wolf, life is simple. I feel his presence more strongly hour by hour, minute by minute, as our paws eat up miles and miles of the northern coast. No one would blame me for going wild—and after a while, I wouldn't care anymore. I would simply ... stop existing. Almost like going gray. It is tempting.

But I am no untrained boy. I am a Shield, blessed by Rigrasil with the strength to protect my country and my Mage. And so I shove my inner wolf down, deep inside.

I keep running.

CHAPTER 20
DELPHINE

They leave me in a *library*.

Forget the fact that I single-handedly flew them across the entire continent, forget that Tekton and I are also directly involved in this whole magical mess. *They* get to run off to look for the Book of Gold, and leave me here, doing nothing. I cross my arms, swinging my legs over the edge of the table I'm sitting on, and wait for something interesting to happen.

I was bored a lot in Aeturnus. We didn't get a lot of visitors, and I wasn't allowed to tell them my secret, anyway. I was a ghost, haunting the temple, until Aris and Wren arrived.

And now? They get to have all the fun, go on all the adventures.

I knew it was coming. I'd agreed to it—I'd fly them to Estana, far quicker than they could get here on horseback, so that I could come here to start training.

Except Commander Markos is in Roallac, fighting the war. Hells, I've even heard they took students up from the School of the Silver Flame, since their regular soldiers were getting so bogged down in the swamps up there. Meaning there is no one here to help me start my training, except Aleka, who is—surprise—off finding the Book of Gold.

I pout, jump off the table, and go to the nearest stack of books. I read through Tekton's little library a hundred times—maybe I can at least find something interesting to read, if I can't be helpful. I wonder if there are dirty books here. Tekton's were dry and boring, mostly texts on the gods.

The library in Estana dwarfs our entire temple—it has multiple stories of books, and in the large atrium, a glass or crystal chandelier. It's a gorgeous, decadent, sparkly monstrosity covered in spelled candles, and it's bigger than my entire bedroom back home. I love it. The floors are marble, polished to a reflective shine, and the chandelier casts little glittering rainbows over it. The place is mostly empty —there are tons of big, soft red chairs scattered around, but I've seen no one else except Tolis, the steward, who went prancing off a few minutes ago.

"Delphine Kalla?" someone asks.

I turn, startled to hear my name called out loud.

It's a man with red hair and bright hazel eyes, wearing plain, worn brown clothing and boots. He looks strong, and he's a few years older than I am, maybe around Aris's age.

"Yes?" I ask, looking at him askance. I don't know this man, which means I shouldn't trust him. He's not as tall as Aris, but something in the way he moves reminds me of him. Maybe he's a Shield.

"I'm Remiel. One of the ... librarians," he says. His voice is nice. I bet he's a good singer.

"How do you know my name?" I ask.

"Tolis," he says, offering a hint of a smile. He's rather stone-faced, this Remiel.

"You don't look like a librarian," I say.

"What do librarians look like?" he counters.

"I don't know. I've never met one," I admit. "Old, maybe. Hunched over. Glasses hanging off their noses."

"I'm a Shield," he tells me. "Like you are."

I knew it!

"How do you know who I am?" I ask.

"When you've met enough Shields, we're easy to spot," he says.

That makes sense.

"You've heard of the King's Messengers? Adriana Valorius told me she met you."

"Yes," I say.

He doesn't try to come any closer, just stands a few feet away, watching me carefully. I like Adriana—she's pretty, and she can fly, and she does pretty much whatever she wants. I want to be her someday.

"I'm with the King's Librarians. We're a network of Shields spread across the continent. We gather information."

"You're spies?" I ask. Ismini mentioned the librarian-spies.

He nods, again without smiling.

Huh. That's ... kinda neat, actually.

"So that's how you know my name."

"I know a lot about you," he says. "You *are* one of a kind."

"Yeah," I say, scratching the back of my neck. "It's not as much fun as it sounds."

"Is there something I can help you find here?" he asks, gesturing at the shelves.

"So you're an actual librarian too? Not just a spy?" I ask.

He nods.

"Is the Book of Gold here somewhere?" I ask. If anyone's going to know, it's him. I could find out if Aris and Wren are on the right path, or maybe I could find it myself. That would show them. I'm not just a convenient transport, a winged steed—I'm a *Shield*.

"It is not," Remiel says, frowning a little.

I pout.

"We do have a blank replica that we bring out for special occasions, the king's coronation and such. Would you like to see it?"

"Sure," I say, trying not to betray my excitement.

"We keep it in the vault. Come on," he says, turning and wagging a finger at me to follow, so I do. Aris said to stay in the *palace*. He didn't say anything about leaving the library.

"Are there jewels in the vault?" I ask.

"Yes," Remiel answers, leading me from the library into the main hall. A few of the guards nod to him, like they did to Aris, which reassures me that I'm following one of the king's trusted Shields around and not some random lunatic.

I've always liked sparkly things. Crystals, glass, shiny stones, and metals. I think it's the dragon in me.

And Remiel is going to show me a shiny gold book *and* the king's treasure trove? Now this I've *got* to see.

CHAPTER 21
ARIS

Aleka and I break from the crypt in Rigrasil's temple, stumbling over the body of Phoibe, the tall Shield who was guarding it. We push back the pair of idiots who are trying to force their way in.

Phoibe was a few years ahead of me at the school, but we fought together before. She was a fierce Shield, and I have no doubt she is greeting Rigrasil in the afterlife with her head held high.

I will mourn her later.

Aleka and I have no problem sending the rabid-looking men before us to meet their own god. With their blood dripping from our swords, we look over the chaos before us.

The Fire Mage we saw repairing stained glass is fighting two Water Mages, and the battle is not going in his favor. He may have trained at the School of the Silver Flame with the rest of them, but he is no battle Mage. He throws up shields of flame, deflecting the torrents being directed at him, turning them to steam, but he is losing ground.

A phalanx of soldiers bursts into the temple, ripping off their work clothing and even some Ocronian garb to reveal the uniform of Roallac—a black snake eating its own tail on a field of ivory.

Aleka is breathing hard from exertion, her blades flashing in the filtered light. She's exchanging blows with two soldiers, two idiots who ran straight toward her, thinking that because she's slightly built and a woman, she'd be an easier target than me.

Their heads hit the floor with a grisly plop a few moments before their bodies do.

The rest of the soldiers hang back a bit. I'm not sure they have a clear leader, just an agenda—to get through us to the book.

And like all the hells is *that* going to happen. I look back over my shoulder and see Wren and Panos emerge from the crypt.

I make my way back over to them, Aleka at my back, slashing at anyone stupid enough to come near us. Eventually, the mob decides to rush us, and they all break at once, coming at us like a wave.

A ripple of rock goes flying past us, and most of the first row of men and women stumble, some of them directly onto our blades. Pebbles and bits of stony debris are embedded deep into their bodies. Ismini also has two of their Mages wrapped in vines—tightly, by the shade of purple they are turning—and with her other hand, she blasts wave after wave of stones at the oncoming Roallacan soldiers. Rafael and another Water Mage race around the periphery, exchanging blasts. Rafael is powerful, but against water he is at a disadvantage. Soon clouds of vapor all but conceal the two of them.

We finally make it to Panos. I don't see Wren anymore.

"She's safe! I sent her below!" Panos yells into my ear, his hoarse voice barely audible over the clash of battle around us. He's leaning on his cane, watching the battle from the crypt entrance and throwing weak bolts of ice at the Black Water goons. "There's a tunnel below that leads outside the palace. It should seal shut behind her. She'll be waiting at the Golden Crown."

Wren is *alone*, in the crypt below, making her way through some tunnel under the city? And to an inn, where there aren't guards or anything? Gods, what was Panos thinking? I look back through the temple, at the chaos—well, maybe we don't have a choice. To the inn, then. Even up here, my chest constricts at the thought of being underground again. The crypts were bad enough—I kept seeing trolls out of the corner of my eye, just waiting to pounce on us.

"You get to Wren," Aleka shouts. "Keep her and the book safe. I'll get the rest of us to the palace and send you a message when it's safe to come back."

"You can't handle this crowd on your own," I snarl, whipping a blade across the abdomen of a soldier who lunges at me. I dodge him easily enough, and after my blade pierces his skin, he falls back, howling, and another takes his place. And another. Blood is making my sword grips slick.

"Aleka is not alone," Panos says. "But Wren is, and *she* is your priority. Now go!"

He pushes his hand out, uttering a few words, and the first row of Black Water soldiers stops, their feet frozen to the floor. Aleka cuts them down like so many blades of wheat. Her short blond hair is dark with sweat and blood, and I expect she'll have a few new scars after today, but she never falters. There's a reason Leo made her captain of his city guard.

The soldiers waver, forming a circle around us, a seething ring of metal and crazed zealots.

"Go!" Aleka shouts at me. "That's an order."

I'm not sure that as captain of Estana's guard, Aleka has any actual authority over me, but I table that argument for another day. I'd sooner eat my own socks than admit that I actually fear the tiny woman.

I think for a moment—I'll go faster as a tiger, but then I'd reach Wren without my weapons, and I'd be more use with them—so I push through the ring of soldiers, Aleka at my back, Panos and Ismini thinning the ranks around us as best they can. Honestly, Panos is pretty useless, but Ismini might actually just tear the whole place down on her own. Blood seeps into the golden stone at our feet, dishonoring the Temple of Rigrasil.

I swear here, under the eye of Rigrasil himself, that Evanthia will pay for all she has done.

I don't even bother killing the last few, just maim them enough to get past them, until I reach the front of the temple. Like all the hells am I going through the tunnels under the crypt—I'll go above and meet her at the inn. I don't recall an entrance to the tunnels there, but then, I never had much chance or inclination to explore them. So I run on.

The courtyard outside is awash with Ocronian and Roallacan soldiers. How did so many Black Water sympathizers get inside our palace walls? How long has this been planned? The Ocronian soldiers have formed a barrier with some carts and overturned tables and are making a stand here, in front of the temple. The Roallacan soldiers are disorganized, but they scream and seethe like water crashing on the rocky shores of Spit—breaking against the wooden barricade and threatening to break through.

There's no time to think about that now. I race around the edge of the courtyard, exchanging blows when I need to. My feet fly across the broken cobblestones, past the Temple of Caladrius, and out onto the main road of Estana.

There's fighting here too, though much less, and the citizens of Estana are not about to let some Black Water bitches push them around. The few snake-wearing soldiers I do see—perhaps attempting to loot the shops—are being detained or beaten by crowds of angry shopkeepers and shoppers. I see Rose—Rosanna?—a woman I met one night at a tavern, tying a thick rope around a soldier's hands as he's held down by two others. I see a little old lady smacking another restrained soldier with her straw broom. I pass Shields who were caught out here when the chaos started, gamely holding their own, taking down as many Roallacan soldiers as they can. Out here, at least, the fight seems to be going in Estana's favor.

I make it to the wall. There are few guards here, armed with javelins, and they do little more than nod at me as I pass. I'm glad, because I don't need to lose any more time. Wren is alone.

I sheathe my swords and race toward the Golden Crown, putting all my strength and energy into my legs, going faster than I've ever gone before. The main road has taken me around to the northern gate, so I have several miles to go before reaching the rebuilt inn. There is no one out here on the grasslands but me, no enemy army. I wonder how long Roallac has been concealing its soldiers inside Estana, hiding them in plain sight, waiting for one of us to return, or to lead them to the book, hoping their queen would reward them for it. I have to keep it from them.

The inn comes into view, the newly painted sign once more glittering with golden paint. I push past the others making their leisurely way toward the door, ignoring their shouts, barreling through and to the innkeeper without slowing my stride.

"The fuck do you want?" he asks, putting his beefy hands down on the counter. His face is red with anger at my intrusion.

I can hear the people behind me, the ones I probably knocked over, cursing.

"Wren. Where is she?" I ask, taking deep breaths to steady myself.

"Who?" he asks. "Last customer of the day checked out hours ago. Now go on, Shield. You're scaring people away!"

I do not have time for his games.

I put a hand on the counter and leap over, grabbing the innkeeper by the shirt collar and hauling him off the floor. He's a shorter man than me, but stocky, and it requires no small amount of muscle on my part to dangle his toes off the ground.

"The Night Mage. Small woman in a black robe. Where is she?" I thunder.

He closes his eyes as I yell.

"I don't know who you're talking about!" he says.

I don't believe him. For all I know, he's on Roallac's side too, or else he thinks that I'm out to harm Wren and he's trying to keep me from her.

I toss him aside and leap back over the bar. I take the stairs three at a time and start opening every door. I can hear the innkeeper yelling at me, but I ignore him. My legs and lungs are burning, but I can't stop. All I can think about is getting to Wren.

I throw open the last door. One of the hinges snaps.

The room is empty, just like the others.

What is going on?

I stop, take a deep breath, and try to think.

I focus on our claim, that magic bond that links a Shield to their Mage. It can be our greatest weakness, and our greatest strength. Now that bond is going to help me find Wren. Maybe she just hasn't gotten here yet. Or maybe she's trapped in the tunnels below.

I head back outside, ignoring the innkeeper's angry hollering, and close my eyes. I tilt my face back, feeling Rigrasil's light on my skin, and I listen. Caelus told me he smells snow when he uses the bond to find Mariana, back at Basti before he left us.

I listen for the clear chiming of a silver bell.

What I hear instead is the sharp cry of a bird and the indignant shouting of a woman making her way to the inn as the hawk grabs a cloak off her cart.

Adriana lands with a flourish, swirling the cloak around herself as she shifts. Her hair is all over the place, her face pale.

"Aris, you have to come quick!" she pants. "It's Wren!"

CHAPTER 22
DELPHINE

We walk into the main hall of the palace, Remiel solemnly answering my questions as we go. The palace is beautiful, light and airy and made of golden stone. I had no idea places this big even existed—beyond the warren of the Temple of the God of Night, my exposure to the world was ... well, nonexistent. My head swivels as we walk, taking in the splendor—the red-and-gold tapestries, the gold-framed portraits on the walls. I fire questions at Remiel as rapidly as they come into my mind, not wanting to waste a second of time with an actual real-life spy.

"Do you know where the real Book of Gold is? How did Evanthia get the Book of Bronze? Where was it hiding? Do you know if she has the Book of Silver yet? What's your shift? I bet you're some kind of cat."

Every time he opens his mouth to answer, I throw another question at him. I can't help it—there's so much I want to know.

"How many Shields are here? Do you train here? Is there someone I can learn from while Commander Markos is away? Can you train me? I'm a fast learner."

"Which one of those do you want me to answer first?" he asks, looking at me sidelong.

I decide I like Remiel. He's funny, but not like Rafael is funny. He doesn't make me laugh and roll my eyes. But I can tell he's laughing on the inside.

Before I get a chance to answer, there's a loud boom, like a clap of thunder inside the palace, and the walls and ceiling shake. We've barely made it to the library entrance—Remiel steps in front of me, putting himself in the doorway between me and whatever is out *there.*

There's a crack behind me, and that big glass chandelier in the atrium crashes to the floor, glass shards scattering dozens of feet in every direction. The spelled candles go out, but the beautiful, sparkling chandelier is a mess. My inner dragon cries out at the destruction of such a beautiful thing, even as I begin to panic. Instinctively I grab a piece, a short chain of round crystals connected to a large teardrop one. I stuff it in my pocket.

"What was that?" I ask Remiel, my voice cracking. "An earthquake?"

He responds by drawing two long daggers I didn't even know he was carrying, and shoving me behind him as footsteps pound down the hallway. My throat feels tight—not an earthquake, then.

There's a cloud of dust before us, obscuring whatever is pounding down the hallway toward us. In a moment it parts, giving way to Ismini in her green robe, swiping her hands through the air and settling all the dust down.

Aleka follows, with another Shield I don't know. He's as tall as Aris, and in his arms he carries a small, unconscious woman wearing a black robe, her long brown braid nearly brushing the floor.

"*Wren!*" I howl, and I throw myself at the Shield carrying her. "What have you done to her?"

"Easy," Aleka says, putting up her free hand to stop me. "We were attacked. We got separated. Wren took a blow to the head."

I take a deep breath, my hands clenching into fists. I can *feel* the dragon inside me, begging to be released, to breathe my unquenchable fire onto whoever dared attack Wren, and ...

Wait.

"Where's Aris?" I ask, my voice cracking in panic. I look behind the tall Shield, but he's not there.

"Panos sent him off, thought Wren was taking some secret passage out of the temple with the book."

My heart leaps into my throat.

"The book? You found it!" I cry, clapping my hands.

Remiel takes Wren from the tall Shield and runs down the hallway with her, like she weighs nothing at all. Ismini and I follow, her green robe flapping like a pair of wings out behind her.

"Delphine," Aleka says, putting a hand on my shoulder. She looks directly at me, directly into my eyes. "Wren will be all right. Aris is fine. The book ... Wren must have dropped it during the battle, when she got hit. Rafael went back to look for it with what guards we have left."

Aleka's eyes are warm, reassuring, level. Despite whatever it was she went through out there, despite the dirt and blood all over her, she is as calm as if she were reading me a bedtime story. I guess you don't get to be captain by overreacting to things. I swallow hard and nod.

"All right," I say.

"Good," she says, patting my shoulder. "Now. I need your help. Lot of injured outside. Come on."

I'd rather burn something, but I swallow that impulse—for the moment—and follow Aleka instead.

CHAPTER 23
WREN

My head is aching, and pain shoots through my chest in sharp waves when I try to breathe.

"Steady now," a soothing voice says. "Give me a minute."

I manage to crack open an eyelid, my world spinning and ... blue? The light in the room is blue? How hard did I hit my head? What happened? My thoughts feel heavy, like I'm trying to swim through mud. Something happened ... something important ...

"Panos!" I shout suddenly, sitting bolt upright.

Then I scream, grabbing the right side of my chest. Or I would have screamed, but I can't force any more air into my lungs. Something is crushing me. Crushing my chest and my right shoulder and the side of my face. Something warm trickles down my scalp—blood, I realize.

"Wren! Wren! It's all right," another voice says—Ismini.

I see her face, bathed in blue light, swimming before my eyes.

"Lie down," she says gently, pushing on my shoulders. "Let the healer do her work."

"Panos," I pant.

"I'll get him for you when the healer's done," she says, smoothing the hair back from my face.

"No," I cry, tears running down the side of my face. "Panos. The book. He has the book."

"All right," Ismini says. She takes my hand in her own warm, calloused ones. "You took quite a fall down those stairs, cracked your head and broke a number of ribs. Just let the healers—"

"No!" I cry, struggling to sit up again. "You don't understand! *Panos has the book!*"

Ismini freezes. The healer, a brown-haired woman I don't recognize, inhales sharply and looks at Ismini.

"I didn't fall down those stairs," I manage to gasp.

There's a commotion in the hallway outside, footsteps pounding—and then Aris, running so fast he has to grab the doorway to stop himself. He flings himself into the room, sweaty and out of breath. On his shoulder sits Adriana in hawk form, clinging to the leather straps of his sword harness, looking particularly ruffled.

"I didn't fall," I repeat, looking at Aris, at his sky-blue eyes, wide with worry and anger. "I was pushed."

For a moment, I worry Aris is going to rip the doorframe from the wall.

"You hit your head pretty hard, Mage," the healer says, trying to urge me to lie back down. "Let me get a few of these breaks set. Then you'll feel a lot better."

I shrug her off.

"Aris! Where is Panos?" I ask.

The healer purses her lips but does her best to go about healing me as I sit panting in pain.

Ismini has gone white and sits back in her chair. Maybe I'm not being clear. It's hard to think, with the bolts of pain lancing through me from every part of my body.

"He said he sent you with the book through a passage in the crypt," Aris says, the muscles in his jaw clenching, "that you'd be waiting for me at the Golden Crown. But you weren't there."

I try to shake my head, to answer him, but the healer moves her hands, and a rib snaps back into place. The pain makes me gasp, a white-hot bolt through my body that temporarily banishes any ability to think or speak.

"I haven't seen him since the temple," Ismini says. "I assumed he found another way back." Her eyes are unfocused, like she's looking at something far, far away. I try to focus on her words, to fight back the wave of vomit that threatens to overwhelm me. "There was ... it was just chaos."

Aris makes his way to me, his hands running over the side of my head, my arm, my ribs, where the healer is still trying to work, a blue glow around her hands. She tsks at him.

"Are you all right?" he asks, cupping my face.

Gods, the way he looks at me. If I weren't so panicked and fuzzy-headed, I'd melt.

"Panos has the book!" I repeat. I'll be fine. I've survived worse than this. "He pushed me down the stairs. *He's* the one who betrayed us, who told the Roallacan soldiers where we'd be. It's Panos!"

Aris's face hardens, from the soft look of concern he was showing me to the calm, deadly mask of a Shield.

"Rest, Firefly," he says, smoothing back a curl from my forehead. "We'll find Panos."

His hands clench and unclench at his sides, and he rushes from the room without another word. Adriana lets out a cry and flies after him.

"There has to be an explanation," Ismini whispers, aghast. "I've known Panos for years—he would *never* ..." She can't finish her sentence. Her green eyes are swimming with tears when she looks back up at me.

"He has to know we'll come after him," I say. "How far can one old man go alone?"

"With the help of the Roallacan soldiers who infiltrated Estana? Who knows?" Ismini says, one hand covering her mouth. "With a fast horse, he could be miles from here by now."

"And if he's got the book ..."

"Then I'll bet he's taking it straight to Evanthia."

The healer snaps another rib back into place, and the pain is so immense that my vision goes black at the edges. The blackness advances, and Ismini's voice begins to sound very far away ...

CHAPTER 24
ARIS

I have never been so angry in my *life*.

I don't even remember coming to the King's Messengers, though I must have run here. They have a small headquarters in a wing of the palace. Leo's important messages—or any political ones that need to be handled with caution—all go through the messengers.

"Aris," one of them calls out when I enter. I don't remember his name, but he looks vaguely familiar. He's a tall, thin man, with several detailed maps spread out on a table before him. "Need to send something?"

"I need to catch a traitor," I say, bracing my hands on the table before him. He's wearing plain, simple clothes—they'll be lost when he shifts, anyway—and he jumps to his feet when I speak.

"A traitor?" he asks. He calls some more of his messengers in from an adjoining room. They come in, laughing and talking, but freeze when they see me. Messengers hold a respected position, though not as respected as bonded Shields, like me.

"How can we help?" he asks.

I explain what happened, and how Panos stole the Book of Gold.

"He's likely headed to Roallac," I say, looking at the map the messenger has spread before us, "probably on horseback for now but likely by sea as soon as he can manage it."

We all cluster around the table, and the messengers point out various routes and roads, as well as likely ports.

"Giorgios, Cassandra, Faidra—you three will go north. The rest of you, east to the coast and then straight to Roallac. If you meet any others along the way, go ahead and route them after Panos too, on my orders. We'll find him, Aris. Never fear," the man says—Romanos, I think his name is.

I clasp his hand hard and wish them good hunting. The first three he named head immediately for a small porch at the back of the room, one with a small balcony, and they shift into their bird forms, taking flight and rapidly disappearing from view. The others soon follow. I feel marginally better at having some semblance of a plan—what would Markos do, were he here? Dispatch the messengers? Absolutely. But what else?

When I find Panos, I will kill him—not for stealing the book but for harming Wren. I can feel my Shield magic vibrating through me, looking for an outlet, for something to punch.

Fuck, I think, running a hand through my short hair. *Now what?*

And then it hits me—Panos spoke of passages under the capital, ones that lead outside the gates, which are currently guarded by dozens of Aleka's men, who have strict instructions not to let him pass.

I race to find Tolis. If anyone knows about secret passages here, it's the palace steward.

CHAPTER 25
WREN

It's colder than I remember.

Colder than the mountains in Abelon. Cold that goes all the way down to my bones. My toes start to lose feeling almost immediately. My black robe does little good here, in this between-realms place. At least the pain is subsiding.

"You called?"

His voice is silk and thunder together, rolling across the mountaintop I stand on. I see him from a distance, walking through the night sky like a giant, invisible staircase. If ever a god could be said to saunter, this would be said about him. His black garments mirror my own, but the edges are vague, indistinct, like he's cloaked in pure shadow. His face is as beautiful as I remember, cold and hard as a marble statue.

"What do we do now?" I ask, crossing my arms. I feel something beyond guilt for letting not just one but two *books slip through my fingers. Gods, I am not worthy of the title of Night Mage. Betrayed first by Mariana, and now Panos? How long has Evanthia been planting her Black Water spies in our midst?*

Caladrius regards me as I might regard a small child—with amusement, mostly.

"What do you mean?"

"I mean that the king's most trusted adviser betrayed us—and he's probably headed to Evanthia right now with the Book of Gold. She'll have all three before the winter solstice, and she'll bring Aenon from your realm. So I need you to tell me what to do to fix it!"

"I already told you," he says, pacing, inspecting me. He even lifts my braid, running his fingers over it. I yank it from his grip.

"I can't get all three books, and I'm not sure I want to bring you into our realm, anyway. How would you being here be any better than Aenon?"

He frowns, and the air—if possible—gets even colder.

I wonder briefly if he can kill me here, and if that means I'll also die in my realm.

I take a step back.

"It is not all about you, little pet," he says. "Did you know that Rigrasil was the first of us, the oldest, the strongest?"

I blink. Even my eyes feel cold, like balls of ice. "What's that got to do with it?"

"Everything, pet. He brought forth the elemental gods to aid him—and then me, to balance them all. We only exist in balance together. Aenon cannot be allowed to enter your realm. He would destroy everything just for a chance to be free."

"So ... you want me to bring you over instead? How is that any better?" I ask, frowning.

"Bring me over; don't bring me over—with the books, I can work through you to rectify the imbalance that Aenon and his human have wrought on your world. Together we can restore magic's balance, the way it was always intended to be."

"What upset the balance in the first place?" I ask.

"Aenon," he says. Caladrius's great black owl wings ruffle a little, as much of a shrug as I think he's capable of. "He seduced the mind of the last Roallacan queen and taught her through the Book of Bronze."

"Great," I say, crossing my arms, trying to warm my hands against my chest.

"I can channel my magic through you, little Mage, and help you," he *says. "Give you powers that mortals only dream of. On the solstice, the veil between worlds is thinnest—and on that longest night of the year, my powers are also at their strongest. But you* must *get to the books before Aenon crosses and regains his strength."*

Caladrius locks his hands behind his back, his wings flaring up and out, like he's preparing for flight, or like a bird trying to intimidate a foe.

I consider myself intimidated. I wonder if he can hear my heart stuttering in my chest. He stares at me, unblinking, with eyes as black as night.

"Or," he says, "you can live the rest of your days—which won't be many—knowing that your own cowardice caused the downfall of your entire realm."

I am cast from the vision with a flick of his wrist, his words echoing in my ears. I sit bolt upright, momentarily confused that I'm no longer in pain. Ismini is in a chair at my side and wakes when I do, reaching for my hand immediately. Her gaze is unfocused as she tries to wake up.

"Wren? What's wrong? Are you hurting?" she asks.

"We're in trouble," I manage to choke out.

CHAPTER 26
CAELUS

I have plenty of time to think as I run.

I think about the day I claimed Mariana in the Shield games—I was so proud that day. Aris fought well and bested me. He picked Wren, and Zale laughed. I didn't even know about Wren at the time—Eudoros, my first Mage, had always been a controversial pick. He had an unwavering devotion to the gods, which I admired—until it led him away from our claim and into the priesthood. Head Mage Saroya herself had to dissolve our claim, and the pain of that dissolution still haunts my nightmares.

But after Zale claimed Rubita, and I saw Mariana standing there, a single shaft of sunlight falling upon her, it was like Rigrasil himself whispered to me. I didn't know her well, but I knew better than to ignore my instincts. She was a powerful Water Mage and would boost my own strength tremendously—that alone would restore my honor in the Hall of Shields. I claimed her without a second thought.

But why did I feel such a pull to her then? She agreed to my claim only to salvage her own pride—she'd planned on being picked first, by Aris. She told me as much many times. I assumed it was merely the sting of being rejected by her onetime lover. Still, I had no insight at all into her treachery until the day we found the Book of Silver.

Why did Rigrasil send me to her? The thought consumes me as I run, over miles and miles of the vast plains of Ocron. Why? Did he know she would betray us?

He must have known. The gods may not be able to manifest in our realm like they once did, when they walked our lands like immortal kings and queens, everyone worshipping at their feet, but they can still hear and see things here, glimpses through the veil that separates our worlds.

Your honor was already tenuous after Eudoros left you, I tell myself. *Maybe Rigrasil didn't want to waste an honorable Shield on someone like Mariana.*

Or, I argue, refusing to believe that my god, the Lord of Day, the mightiest of all the gods, would forsake me, *perhaps he knew that only I would be strong enough to go after her. And I am the only one strong enough to do what needs to be done to stop her.*

CHAPTER 27
ARIS

"If I ever meet this asshole in the mortal realm, he and I are going to have a discussion," I say. "Panos too."

I grab Wren around the waist and pull her into my lap, my arms looped around her middle. She grabs them like she's drowning. I bend to place a kiss on the side of her neck, giving her reassuring sounds and stroking her back as she tells us what happened. Her voice shakes at times—and when she looks back at me, her green eyes are shining with tears. Blood from her fall still cakes the side of her face in rust-colored splotches, mats her hair over her temple. The healer assured us that she'd healed Wren's injuries—but just looking at the aftermath gets my own blood boiling.

"I'm sorry Ismini didn't catch Panos in the passages," Wren says quietly.

I sigh—Panos is as slippery as an eel. Tolis and Ismini have thoroughly explored the passages under the palace but haven't seen so much as a trace of him.

"So ... we head to Roallac?" Rafael asks, slumping in his chair. "And just hope we catch Panos and Mariana before they get there?

And somehow get Wren to Soltaire for the solstice, because 'Caladrius says so'? I don't like it."

"I don't know if I trust Caladrius," Wren says quietly.

I squeeze her gently. "I don't trust him either," I say. "But whether or not you trust him, the fact remains that soon Evanthia will have the power she needs to bring Aenon through the veil."

"Do we have horses?" Wren asks.

I shrug and look to Rafael, who nods.

"Three fleet steeds, ready to go at a moment's notice. Aleka gave me some coin too, in case we need to hire a boat at the strait."

"All right," Wren says, settling now that she has a plan. "We have to catch Panos. Once we get the book back, we can figure out what to do about Caladrius, and the other two books."

"That's assuming that Caelus hasn't caught Mariana yet," Rafael says.

I snort. "If he had, he'd have sent word."

I don't want to give voice to the dark thoughts in my head—that Caelus may be an excellent swordsman and an honorable man, going after his Mage, but Mariana is a talented Water Mage, and a sneaky bitch on top of that. She probably had a boat waiting in Abelon for after she stole the Book of Silver—with her talent, that boat will probably reach Roallac far quicker than Caelus can, even if Leo's navy is patrolling the northern sea.

Too bad Markos took most of the Shields north with him to march on Soltaire, the capital of the stinking Snake Island. A phalanx of Shields could have hunted Panos down in hours. But I couldn't go alone and leave Wren, and she can't keep up on horseback. And like all the *hells* am I bringing Delphine into this mess, no matter how much she begs.

"The *entire* Roallacan army is between us and that fortress," Rafael reminds her. "Not to mention Ocron's."

"Commander Markos and Head Mage Iraklis will help us," Wren says confidently. "They probably have all kinds of information on ways to get into Soltaire if we need to."

I nod. Now we're talking. Military strategy. This I can do.

"Markos will have had his scouts fly ahead, mapping out every inch of that island," I say, frowning. "In the marsh in Aclines, the Earth Mages were able to dry out great roads of dirt through the muck, or raise up stones to do it. It was slow going, but they could do it. Aclines didn't have Water Mages trying to fight back, though." I cross my arms. "We need to get to Markos and Iraklis first. As fast as possible."

Rafael agrees. "We can tell them Caladrius gave Wren a vision and told her she needs to be present at the solstice there. Just be vague on the details."

"We don't *have* any details," I mutter.

"They've been sent messages about the Book of Gold, and Panos," Wren says with a tired sigh. "I can't imagine he'll be able to get through them to the capital, even if he makes it to Roallac before us."

"So Markos, Iraklis, and the army will all be headed to Soltaire to challenge Evanthia and rescue King Leonidas. Can they win?" Rafael asks.

I consider it and shake my head. "We don't know a lot about their forces, but they've got Evanthia, who's reported to be a powerful Mage, plus Mariana and now Panos. Those three alone could hold off the army until the solstice, and once Aenon arrives, no one stands a chance."

I hug Wren around her shoulders, and she lays her head on my chest. I'm proud of her. No matter what comes our way, I'll be at her side.

"What about Estana?" Wren says after a moment.

The temple is a mess, and the soldiers of Roallac melted back into the crowds like they'd never been there at all. The Wind Mages who can do interrogations—and there aren't many of them left—have started their investigation, but likely there are dozens more Roallacan sympathizers hiding inside the city wall.

"Aleka and Ismini can sort that out," I say. "We need to head to Roallac."

Wren doesn't like it, leaving our friends behind. I don't like it either, but my duty is to Wren first, not the country. It's the first law of the Shields. I can feel my fingernails turning into claws, ready for a fight.

Wren looks out the window at the setting sun.

"We should leave soon," she murmurs. "Travel at night, when we're less likely to be spotted."

Rafael stands, balls up his red robe unceremoniously, and stuffs it into a bag he brought with him, ready to go.

Without it, he looks surprisingly ... ordinary, despite his scars. I can't disguise my height or strength, but without his robe, Rafael could be anyone.

"I'm leaving mine on," Wren says, crossing her arms.

I know better than to argue. I'll have to leave Caelus's weapons behind. I know Aleka will care for them as though they were her own.

"Let's go hunting," I say.

What's the worst that could happen?

We're about two days out when the first disaster strikes.

We take the fastest roads to the north, ones we assume Panos might have taken. We ask every traveler we pass along the way, but no one has seen him. Our horses, at least, are as fast as Rafael promised, and we are making good time.

The Black Strait covers over half of Ocron's eastern coast, and every town we pass along the way is ready for attack. Gates are closed, archers and sentries posted on every turret, patrols of armed guards stopping us every half hour to make sure we aren't Black

Water spies. It gets old quickly. At first Wren explains carefully who we are and why we're traveling at night.

It isn't until she unleashes her night magic that they believe us and let us continue. After the first few, she just starts with her magic whenever we're approached, and the patrols go on their way without a fuss.

Wren keeps quiet, but her anxiety is nearly palpable. Animals frequently keep us company—flights of silent owls gliding alongside us, chittering squirrels calling to us from the treetops in the small copses we pass through, glowing eyes flashing at us from the grasses. I spy a fox watching us a few times, his bushy red tail disappearing as soon as I catch sight of him, and for a while, a small pack of wolves joins us. This makes the horses really nervous, and Wren has to take a couple of deep breaths before she calms down enough for them to dissipate.

We're just laying out our bedrolls for the day, so Wren and Rafael can grab a few hours of sleep, when the earthquake hits. It's a slow, rolling, shuddery thing that lasts about a minute. We're on the plains, so we're not really worried about getting injured—but a massive crack forms in the ground about a hundred feet in front of us, splitting the rock below, forming a thirty-foot-wide crevasse that disappears into blackness below. It takes us half a day to ride around it.

The third morning, the tornado strikes. It was a gray night, cold with drizzly rain. I spy our fox friend once, but no other animals. Wren has her robe pulled so tightly around her that I can't see so much as a stray curl. The hood is pulled down hard around her head, and she was silent most of the night.

And then there's a sound like thunder and screaming all at once, the sky turning a strange, sickly color. The horses prance and threaten to bolt. Rafael's rears, nearly unseating him, but he's an expert horseman. I'm convinced Wren would have been thrown and trampled if not for her magic—the horse stays nearly motionless. There's a tremendous pressure in my ears, and the clouds overhead begin to swirl. Wren starts glowing, her own magic lighting up the black storm boiling overhead.

Lighting up the funnel-shaped cloud bearing down on us.

I dismount, grabbing the reins of our horses, looking for somewhere we can wait this storm out—but it came on too fast. We're in the middle of one of Ocron's famous grassy plains, without so much as a ditch to hide in.

Wren must realize this about the same time I do. On horseback, she throws her hands up, green light streaming from her as her mouth moves. I can't hear the words she's using—all I can hear is the funnel cloud, gobbling up clods of earth and grass and stone as it goes. It's got to be a half mile wide—a city killer.

It's got to be close to dawn. Rafael dismounts to help me hold the horses, using one hand to shade his eyes from the debris that's starting to whip past us. Green light is flowing from Wren into the storm, like wool onto a spindle.

And then the spindle slows.

And then it stops.

It reverses, unwinding, wobbling in its course, which was headed straight for us.

Rafael and I hold our breath. Wren frowns, then throws her hands out again, demanding that this force of nature submit to her will.

It unravels, debris settling out around it, like a top that's tired of spinning.

Wren doesn't lower her hands, doesn't stop glaring at the storm until it has vanished.

The sky overhead clears.

And then she topples from her horse, unconscious.

CHAPTER 28
WREN

I wake up slowly, in a way that is starting to feel familiar when I overextend my magic. My head clears quickly, or at least more quickly than last time, so I can only hope I haven't been asleep for too long. If stopping a tornado isn't enough to make me go gray, I wonder what is.

I'm warm and comfortable and lying on something soft—too soft to be the ground—and I smell a wood fire burning, clean soap, and warm bread.

When I'm finally able to pry my eyes open, the first thing I see is Aris.

He is clean, his face newly shaven, his short hair damp. He's wearing the black clothing of a Shield, but in a far finer fabric than I've seen him in before. He must read the question on my face—he reaches out a hand, smoothing it across my brow, moving a strand of hair away from my eyes.

"You only slept a few hours this time," he says, smiling. "After you stopped the tornado. Gods, you're incredible."

"I've never actually seen a tornado before," I mutter, sitting up, wiping the sleep from my eyes. Well, other than the one I made when I was first brought to the School. I shudder at the memory.

"They're not common," Aris admits. "Neither are earthquakes."

It takes a moment for the implication to settle in, and I blink at him for a second.

"You think this is the gods? Cephus and Helene, trying to stop us?"

"Either that, or it's another manifestation of how erratic magic has gotten with Evanthia messing around with it," he says. "Rafael's not sure. He sent a messenger to Ismini."

I nod, absorbing this, and take a look around the room. It's fine, nearly as fine as the rooms in the palace in Estana, though the stone is light gray instead of golden, and the furnishings are blue and silver instead of red and gold. It's tastefully done—the coverlet on the bed is heavily embroidered blue silk, and the sheets I lie on are nearly as soft as the silk itself.

"Where are we?" I ask, frowning. I've never been in an inn as nice as this. We couldn't have traveled far in the few hours I've been asleep. We have to be close to where we planned to cross.

"We're in Raverra," Aris explains. "Home of Lord Timon Antenor and his daughter, Lady Orothea."

The name sounds vaguely familiar.

"Why are we here?" I ask. We didn't discuss stopping at Raverra. We were close to the crossing—we should have been at the shore by now.

"You passed out," Aris says slowly. "I didn't know how long you'd be out for. It was days last time."

I sit up, rubbing the sleep from my face. *There's no way we're going to catch Panos now, not since I delayed things.*

"All right," I decide. "I've slept long enough. Let's get going."

I swing my legs over the side of the bed to where Aris is sitting in an overstuffed blue chair, one leg crossed at the knee. And I realize I'm wearing a gauzy ... thing. A dress, but sheerer and finer than any I've ever owned. Heat rushes to my face.

"What am I wearing?" I ask, plucking the fabric and pulling it away from my body. Gods, I can see *everything* through this. It covers me from neck to ankles to wrists and should be quite modest, except it seems to be made out of wisps of fog and lace. I promptly grab the blanket and attempt to cover myself. Aris raises an eyebrow, smirking. "And where are my clothes?"

"I changed you. Couldn't get road dirt on the bed—Lady Orothea's order," he says innocently.

"*You changed me?*" It comes out in a squeak.

"Well, I wasn't about to let anyone else do it," he says, amused. "I've seen your body before."

"Yes, but ..." I trail off, fuming. "This barely even counts as clothing!"

"Would you prefer I left you naked?"

"Gods ... wait, is that for me?" I ask, eyes landing on a neat pile of brown and green fabric on the chair next to his.

"Nope," Aris says, snatching the clothes and promptly holding them as far away from me as possible.

I glare at him. He grins back at me. If it were night, I'd be glowing with fury.

"Come and get them," he taunts. He's enjoying this far too much.

He's saved from my murderous thoughts by a knock on the door. A servant pokes her head in, smiling but averting her eyes when she sees I'm awake.

"Miss, sir. Lady Orothea asks if you would please join her for breakfast, downstairs in the great hall, in ten minutes," she says. Then she ducks back out.

Aris sighs dramatically.

Relieved, I get up, holding my hand out for the clothing he's offering me.

He promptly grabs my hand, pulling me into his lap, where he plants a kiss on my lips before burying his face in the skin between my neck and shoulder.

"Gods, I hate it when you do that," he whispers. His lips tickle my skin, sending shivers down my spine.

"Do what?" I ask, pulling back.

He's gazing up at me with his blue, blue eyes, all playfulness for the moment gone.

"Fall asleep like that," he says, brushing a curl back from my face. "I never know if you'll wake up again."

I smile, reaching up and grasping his face between my hands.

"You're not getting rid of me that easily," I say, and I kiss him back.

We're late for breakfast.

The clothing that Lady Orothea kindly left for me is very fine, a dress of warm dark green wool that ties up the back and is embroidered with swirls in a darker green thread. There are warm leather boots and a fine brown overcoat of what must be velvet—not practical at all for our travels, but in the cool stone castle, I feel warm and cozy. It hit me while I was dressing that I was clean—my hair too—and Aris admitted he'd had one of the servants help him wash my curls.

"Don't worry. I handled the sponge bathing myself," he said, kissing my flaming cheeks.

The castle of Raverra is unlike the golden palace of Estana—not as fine, and architecturally very different. It is made of a cool, light gray stone, with smooth marble floors. Aris seems to know where he is going—we descend the stairs and go down another long hallway in the interior of the castle, which then opens to the great hall.

It's a beautiful hall, tall enough to nearly hold my lighthouse and so long that I can't hear the people talking at the other end. There is a long table on a slightly raised dais, and more tables down the length of the hall. It's so big that it needs three massive fireplaces to keep it warm. Overhead there are blue banners with a black raven, with a larger red-and-gold flag of Ocron at the end. The giant stones in the wall to our right seem to have shifted and cracked with the earthquake—an elderly Earth Mage works, sweat dotting his face, to level the stone. The crack disappears before our eyes.

Rafael's already at the table on the dais, talking earnestly with the lady across from him. He's clean too, and he's shaved, his golden-brown hair trimmed neatly to his shoulders. The woman with him is stunning, with a kind of delicate beauty. Her shining black hair is left in loose waves, and her eyes are a deep blue that matches her gown. She smiles when she sees us approach and gets up to come greet us. She's barely my height.

"Night Mage, Aris," she says, and she gives me a hug. "I'm so pleased to see you well. Are you hungry? Come, sit by me." She grabs my arm and steers me toward the table.

Aris follows us, amused.

At the head of the table sits an elderly man, his eyes distant and unseeing, his food untouched. His hair is long and white, combed neatly, and he wears a blue cape lined with white fur tucked in close around him.

"My father, Lord Antenor," she says as we approach him. She drops into a small curtsy, so I attempt to do the same, only wobbling slightly.

The man doesn't respond to us at all.

"He hasn't been the same since the plague a few years back," she whispers to me. "I'm not even sure he hears me most of the time. He can't move at all on his left side, but sometimes he'll squeeze my hand." The sadness in her voice is profound, but she squares her shoulders and marches me to my seat.

Aris sits on my other side, and from the other end of the hall, a familiar figure approaches.

"Rigrasil's balls, look at what the cat dragged in," Adriana says, pulling out the chair next to Rafael and helping herself to the goblet before her. She's wearing fine woolen pants and a loose shirt she's left scandalously untied at the neck, her dark hair pulled back.

She studies her brother. Her eyes are the mirror image of Aris's.

"What in all the hells did you do to your hair?" she asks. She looks at me accusingly, one sculpted eyebrow raised.

I shrug, trying not to smile. I've gotten used to his shorter look.

"Cousin, I'm so glad you could join us before you leave," Lady Orothea purrs, patting Adriana's arm.

"Cousin?" I ask, looking at Aris. I don't know why I didn't see it before—of course they're related. Her eyes are darker than his, her skin much fairer, but I can easily see the resemblance. She looks like a more delicate version of Adriana.

"We're related on our mother's side," Adriana says, reaching across the table and grabbing a pastry.

My stomach grumbles—they *do* look delicious. Lady Orothea hears, grins at me, and starts piling food onto my plate.

"It's a far simpler meal than I would have liked to offer," she says, though soon my plate has vanished beneath piles of sliced fruit, cured meats, and sweet, delicate pastries. "Being so close to Roallac, we're sending whatever aid we can, of course. Food, supplies, soldiers. I myself am no warrior." She chuckles. "But there is much I *can* do. Adriana is often back and forth between the Ocronian camp and here, bringing me lists of what is needed, and we arrange transport across the Black Strait."

"Can you get us across the strait, then?" I ask before I bite down on a flaky pastry.

Aris sips his goblet—ash water, of course—in between making faces at his sister.

"I can," Lady Orothea says, smoothing her hands across her skirts. "The Ocronian navy ended up going far around the east of the island, landing and then marching across. That's a cumbersome way to get supplies to them, though, so we've been searching for ways across the blockade that Roallac has set up. Between their ships, Mages, and traps, it's not been easy."

"I didn't think you were welcome in Roallac, brother," Adriana teases. She's rocked her chair onto the back two legs, one slim, booted foot planted against the edge of the table. "Not after you thrashed Evanthia's heir."

"He had too much to drink and made some unwelcome advances when he came to visit Estana a few years back," Aris whispers to me. The story sounds vaguely familiar. "I assure you, I was lenient."

"He couldn't walk for a year, I heard," Adriana says, letting her chair slam back down. "Even with their healers."

"Then I hope he's learned his lesson," Aris snaps back.

"But you *can* get us across?" I ask Lady Orothea again, putting a hand on Aris's arm—besides, none of us are technically welcome in Roallac at this point.

She nods. "I can. For a price," she says sweetly.

I look at Rafael, who carries what money we collected before leaving Estana. He shrugs.

"What is your price?" Aris asks, ignoring his sister, who tries to kick him under the table. He reaches down, catching her foot in his hand, and yanks. She is pulled from her chair, landing on her backside.

Rafael runs a hand across his face.

"Honestly, they're not much better than they were as children," Lady Orothea confides to me with a grin. "But let me be blunt." She clears her throat before squaring her shoulders again and turning to face me directly. "I want King Leonidas, and I want the crown."

Adriana splutters into her ash water.

"All right," I say, not entirely sure how I can help with that.

"I need to know—are you two lovers?" she asks.

Adriana chokes on her drink this time, coughing and pounding her chest with a fist. Rafael pats her on the back—he's not doing a very good job hiding the grin on his face.

"*What?*" I squeak, face heating.

"You and the king. I remember seeing you there, at the ball," Lady Orothea says.

And that's when it hits me. I *do* remember her, from Estana, one of many beautiful women there vying for Leo's attention. Specifically, I remember the dozens of glittering sapphires she was wearing —jewels that are now conspicuously absent. In fact, she wears none at all, save for a small silver raven pin on her collar. The war between Roallac and Ocron must be draining her lands more than I realized.

"No, I mean ... Aris and I, we ... no. No," I say.

Aris grabs my hand under the table, giving it a squeeze.

"Good," she says, like it's a simple business transaction. "Then I'm sure in exchange for supplies, a guide, and safe passage across the strait, I can count on your support."

"You want me to ask the king to marry you?" I ask, brows coming together.

"I've been running Raverra for years," she says, casting a sad glance toward her father, who seems completely oblivious to our conversation. "And I've known Leo since we were children. I'm smart, accomplished, and determined. I'll be a good queen to him."

"I see," I say, though I really don't.

"Ambitious for the daughter of a small lord," Rafael comments, like we're haggling over Leo's future.

Lady Orothea smiles beautifully at him. "Yes. And with the endorsement of the Night Mage, the country will be begging King Leonidas to marry me."

She makes me sound like some sort of hero, when all I've done is bring destruction and death wherever I go. I don't think I've got nearly the influence with the country that she thinks I have.

"I will write a formal letter in your support," I say carefully. "And when we rescue the king, I'll be sure to let him know how helpful you've been."

When we rescue Leo. Gods, I hope he's all right. I think of him shivering in some snake-infested dungeon while I sit here, negotiating a marriage on his behalf while warm and well fed. The fluffy pastry turns to lead in my stomach.

"Do you love him?" Rafael asks. His hands are folded on the table, his face serious. Rafael, ever the romantic.

But Lady Orothea's face goes wistful for a moment, her eyes softening. "Have you met him? Who doesn't?"

CHAPTER 29
ARIS

My cousin has always been the ambitious sort—but queen, that's a new one. Growing up, she always wanted to be the best. Each time we saw her, which wasn't all that often, she'd challenge us to games, to sword battles, to foot races. She usually lost the physical challenges—which honestly isn't fair, going up against Shields—but she kept trying.

Seeing Wren blush and feeling her squeeze my hand when Orothea asked if she'd slept with the king, though—I know her heart belongs to me. I can feel my chest swelling with pride.

Adriana coughs into her hand across the table, eyeing me. Adriana is a cynic. Wren is weighing her options—her friendship with Leo, which is not for sale, versus getting some help from Orothea.

And Rafael asks if she's in *love*.

We work out the logistics for a while—Orothea will have one of Leo's men meet us on the way to the shore, north of here, where they've been able to cross before without getting caught. She offers us horses for the trip, as well as supplies. She's as good as her word, and then some.

She must *really* want to be queen.

Adriana leaves shortly after breakfast, winging her way back to the Ocronian army camp in the Roallacan swamp. The king's man, Orothea says, will be able to lead us there.

I wonder if Leo will forgive us, once we rescue him and end this.

After Rafael heads to his room to catch a few hours of sleep, I drift back down the halls, mostly oblivious to the finery around me. I've never much cared for it—Orothea's mother and mine were sisters. If Orothea becomes queen, then when her father dies, this castle will fall to my family—specifically, my oldest brother, Spyridon. I can't imagine he'd want the job. It would probably end up with Lukas, or Myron.

Me? I'd sooner sleep in a whole bedroll full of snakes for a year than be stuck in a cage like this, however fine.

Ismini has gotten a letter back to us, though. I have the paper rolled in my hand. She seems to think that the erratic weather patterns are a result of Evanthia's meddling, of two books being brought together, and not a direct assault from the other gods. Which is good, I guess, though it means Caelus has failed. One meddlesome god right now is enough. I don't want to think about what's going to happen if Evanthia gets the third book—we've been delayed so long, and the King's Messengers haven't seen so much as a trace of him, that I'm starting to lose hope.

I'm still pondering the implications of this, and Orothea's ambitions, when I reach our room, opening the door and shutting it behind me absently.

The room is dark, the curtains drawn. It's a single room with an attached bathroom, and that's it. A small, intimate space. There are spelled candles around the room, casting it in a golden glow.

And in the middle is Wren, waiting for me.

Wearing the sheer white nightdress, and nothing underneath.

My mouth goes dry. I can see every glorious inch of her, and for a moment my breath catches.

"Hi," she says, clasping her hands before her.

I wait a moment, not sure if she understands all that she's offering. It's like putting a feast before a starving man.

"We have a few hours before we get back on the road," she says, taking a tentative step toward me. "I thought ... maybe I've slept enough for a while."

Gods.

I close the space between us to nuzzle the side of her face, breathe her in, and the scent of the lavender soap she likes. I take her face between my hands, expecting her to look nervous.

She looks up at me, her jade eyes half-lidded, a small smile curling the corner of her lips. I can't stop myself from running my thumb across them.

"We do this, Firefly, and there's no going back," I say. My voice sounds thick, harsh in the quiet space between us.

She looks up at me, and the look in her jade eyes nearly ends me. Despite everything, she looks at me with trust, with hope. And with desire.

"We don't know what will happen in Soltaire," she whispers. "And I don't want to have any more regrets."

Dum vivimus, vivamus.

CHAPTER 30
WREN

I wake up warm—and naked—to Rafael pounding on our door. There's a sheet draped across us, but the rest of the bedding and pillows have ended up on the floor.

"Sun's set, lovebirds. Let's go!"

I yawn, and Aris's arm around my middle tightens. He nuzzles against my back, purring. I'm not sure what I'm supposed to be feeling—but there's no regret. Just peace, like we were always meant to fit together. And a kind of delicious soreness.

And a goofy grin I can't keep off my face.

"Ten minutes!" Aris yells back.

I turn and look up at him, still caged in his arms. "Ten minutes?" I ask, arching an eyebrow.

He grins and rolls on top of me, kissing me soundly.

"And I'll make every one of them count, Firefly," he whispers against my lips.

It's a lot longer than ten minutes before we get out of Raverra and back on the road north. Rafael is dramatic about it, of course.

"You heard us?" I squeak.

He nods grimly. "Pretty sure half of Ocron did. Maybe Roallac too," he says thoughtfully. "Just promise me that if you two want to pounce on each other again, you'll give me a heads-up so I can make myself scarce for a while."

Heat rushes to my cheeks. I'm grateful Aris and I are riding different horses—he protested, but honestly, I was worried we wouldn't be able to keep our hands off each other otherwise. When I explained this, he shrugged but reluctantly helped me onto my own mount.

Lady Orothea has given us three fine, fast horses, and I urge mine into a gallop to avoid talking anymore. Animals here are scarce—the occasional raven, a few rabbits, and once I catch the flash of a fox's eyes, but otherwise, we are alone out here. Rafael and Aris shout in challenge and chase after me. It's a glorious ride, though cold. I've layered my new brown coat under my black robe, and I'm warm enough. The occasional groves of trees we've been passing thin out, until there's just mossy, rocky ground around us for miles. Not even Spit is this desolate.

As we go, there is evidence of the earthquake—some houses have lost their roofs, and there's another wide split in the earth to the left of the road, where the far side has been shoved up nearly ten feet. Ismini's letter mentioned that perhaps the imbalance of magic we've been seeing for years—the prevalence of monsters in the west, Shields like Tekton and Delphine, the decrease in Mages being born—is due to Evanthia's meddling with the Book of Bronze. Her mother was quite a zealot of Aenon, apparently, so maybe she's had the book for a long time. It is a sobering thought, what the books can do.

Another night of riding—Rafael goes on an extended patrol of the area when we camp for the day—and we reach Chanet Forest, a narrow, wide band of trees where Lady Orothea said we were to meet her guide. It comprises mostly medium-sized, hardy pine trees, and the scent of their sap permeates the air. Rafael whistles one of his tunes as we ride, and Aris joins in, drumming out the beat against his thighs and saddle.

I don't think it's the scenery that has Aris in such a good mood.

Then again, I'm humming right along with Rafael.

It's around midnight when we enter a small clearing in the forest. Rafael's eyes alight upon the well-worn lyre leaning against a tree, obviously placed with care. Next to it sits a man with pale, freckled skin, carefully turning the pages of a book, a small campfire at his feet. Though his mouth is scowling, his hazel eyes glitter as they take us in. He leaps up with the athletic grace I realize now comes with the god of day's magic. Though a little shorter than Aris and more compact in build, he is obviously a Shield, though I can see no swords or other weapons nearby. He wears nondescript clothing, well worn, in shades of brown.

Aris growls. Rafael stands transfixed, his mouth slightly agape.

"Your hair looks like fire," Rafael breathes—and it's true. While cut short on the sides, the man's bright red curls glitter in the firelight like flames themselves.

The man himself glowers, bright eyes raking over Rafael from head to toe, before arching one eyebrow and turning to me. I don't think it's the proximity to the fire that's making Rafael's cheeks flush, though that's a thought I keep to myself.

"Took you long enough," the man says.

"Who are you?" Aris asks.

I vaguely recognize him from Estana—after the attack, when I was recovering. He was with Delphine.

"Remiel Pateriadis. Shield and King's Librarian," he says, crossing his arms again. "I've been sent to meet you. Lady Orothea requested a guide. I was on my way north anyway, so Aleka sent me word to meet you."

"You're from Estana?" I ask, my heart leaping into my throat. "Is

Aleka all right, then? What about Delphine, and Ismini, and everyone else?"

"They're fine," he assures me, raising a hand. "Delphine is safe. She's practically stuck to Aleka. Ismini, Tolis, and the palace staff are unhurt. There were some casualties in the Temple District, but the Wind Mages' interrogations are underway. The Roallacan soldiers will not stay hidden for long."

"And you are ... a librarian? One of King Leonidas's librarian-spies?" I ask, eyebrows furrowing.

"A gatherer of information," Remiel explains.

"I've never heard of you," Aris says. His hands are loose at his sides, the posture deceptively unperturbed. He's not going for his swords, his obvious weapons. Remiel can't know that Aris has knives poised at his belt and can launch them with a mere flick of his fingers.

"Wouldn't be a very good spy if you had," Remiel retorts. "Head Mage Iraklis and Commander Markos have been sent word that you're coming. I'm to take you to the camp."

"So what's your shift, then? Something sneaky? A weasel?" Aris asks, smirking, still goading the man.

There's some sort of hierarchy within the Shields—the larger predators, like Aris and his tiger form, seem to look down on the hawks and smaller ones. I once joked about Aris being a rat, before I knew his actual shifted form, and he found that particularly offensive.

"I'm a fox, actually," Remiel says.

"Yes, yes, you are," Rafael says, blatantly looking him over. "But what's that got to do with anything?"

I stifle a laugh, having to disguise it—poorly—as a cough.

Remiel's eyes flash as he glances at Rafael, then back at Aris. "Night Mage, you have my permission to use your magic on me, if you want to confirm that I am telling you the truth." There's a warmth in his tone, a kind of easy charisma—the kind of voice that could have a person spilling their secrets to him if they weren't careful. It belies the careful mask he's wearing.

"How do you know I can do that?" I ask. It's a talent only the strongest Wind Mages have, and I've only used it twice. I'd like to never, ever do it again.

Aris shoots me a glance, and I feel it burning my skin like a lightning bolt.

"Spy," Remiel reminds us in a bored tone. "Go on. Ask me."

"A dangerous offer," I say. "What if I ask you to spill all your darkest secrets?"

"King Leonidas trusts you to save him, to save *us*. I'll have to trust you not to abuse your power," he says, like it's not a big deal.

I could ask him to kill himself—and he would. I have that power now. Remiel knows the immense trust he's giving me, offering me freely, and he does not hesitate.

That's enough for me. I can't bring myself to put another person through what I did to Aris.

"I'll take you at your word," I say.

"Until you give her a reason not to trust you. Then, you die," Aris adds.

Remiel raises an eyebrow.

"In the meantime," Rafael interjects, clapping his hands together. "Do you know how to play that lyre?"

We travel a little longer that night, until the sun is well above the horizon and I'm nodding off in my saddle. Remiel—Remy, as Aris has taken to calling him, mostly because it seems to annoy him—takes us to an abandoned cabin tucked into a hillside. It's old and dusty, but I don't care, because there's a real straw mattress on the bed, and I collapse into it gratefully. Rafael falls dramatically at my side, getting a chuckle from Aris. Rafael is warm, his fire magic making him a comfortable bedmate even as he sleeps. Aris and Remiel chat quietly by the fireplace, catching up about mutual acquaintances until I fall asleep, my head pillowed on Rafael's shoulder.

I wake to the soft sound of music, delicate strings being plucked with skillful fingers, and Rafael's voice, pitched low, singing along.

In a faraway land, a story unfolds
Of a princess fair and a soldier so bold.
Oh, hear my ballad, of two lovers' romance.
The soldier and the princess, a love beyond chance.

I've heard him whistle the silly tune before, but sung softly in the fading afternoon sunlight, their two heads bent together before the fire, it takes on a different character altogether.

We leave the cabin around nightfall. Remiel agrees with us moving at night, when my magic is awake, and he seems to know the surrounding country well. Our horses follow his lead across grassy plains. At times, the ground rises up in rocky outcroppings, and we have to go around, sometimes for a long time. Some of the stone structures are simply boulders; others appear to have been purposely placed in long barrier-like arrangements.

"There used to be a community of Earth Mages here. They're long gone, but some of their caves are still usable. There's one a few more miles north of here where we can camp tonight. Then on to the temple of the water god tomorrow."

"Aenon's temple?" I ask Aris, surprised.

He shrugs. "We're near Roallac. Water magic is highly prized in this corner of the country. The temple's been abandoned for ages, though."

I'm glad Remiel mentions stopping in a cave—the clouds are thick overhead, obscuring the moonlight and making our way treacherous. Rafael's got a spelled lantern, which he has given to

Remiel, riding at the head of our party, and I keep a green glow around my hands. Both make us easily visible in the darkness, but what choice do we have? We can't risk the horses breaking a leg or throwing one of us.

Remiel calls out that we're about two more miles from the campsite, and my aching legs are protesting. All I can think about is Aris massaging them, and other things.

Then the storm hits.

When the first flash of lightning flares overhead, lighting up the whole plain as bright as day, I see a look of concern on Remiel's face.

"Come on!" he shouts, and he spurs his horse faster, heedless of the rocky terrain.

We chase after him, our horses' feet stumbling and clattering over the broken ground as we go. I hold on tight to my mare's saddle, at risk of being pitched off.

Another flash of lightning, this one cracking the sky and striking a tall mound of boulders to our right. The rock glows red and splits down the middle from the force of the strike.

Aris rides at my side, his mouth a tight line.

And then there's another flash, a streak of light and heat directly into the grasses before us.

I've been through enough storms at my lighthouse to know that lightning always seeks the highest point, the quickest route to the ground. My great-grandfather knew it too, and he installed a metal cap on the peak of the roof with a long metal wire leading to the ground. The lightning would hit the metal and pass harmlessly into the rock around us.

This lightning ignores those rules, disregarding the mounds of rock and copses of trees around us to strike the ground in front of us instead.

If I was in doubt that Evanthia had a second book, and that magic was *really* beginning to unravel, I'm not doubting anymore.

CHAPTER 31
ARIS

A lightning bolt strikes the ground, just a few feet ahead of Remy. His horse rears—I'll give him credit; he's a good horseman—and brings the rest of us to an abrupt halt.

The rocky ground where the lightning has hit is dry—no rain is falling yet from the heavy black clouds overhead. The grasses go up in flame immediately, and the fire races to encircle us at an unnatural speed.

Rafael kicks his horse to angle himself ahead of Remy, his scarred hands outstretched. He commands the flames before him to go out, but the ones to the left of us rage on, spreading outward. Wren mimics Rafael, but she's having a hard time controlling her horse at the same time, despite her usual affinity with animals. I reach out and grab her reins to pull her mare's head down, keeping her close to me. The mare jostles against us, hard, and the green light around Wren sputters.

"Where's this cave?" Rafael shouts over his shoulder.

Remy points at a large rock formation—a small hill, really—about a mile away, breaking the landscape.

And it's already surrounded by flames.

Black smoke is starting to billow up around us, making the air thick and the horses afraid. I've got my hands full trying to control both my stallion and Wren's mare—she keeps trying, fighting the flames, trusting me to keep her safe. The flames to the left of me glow green and die out, but there's still a wall of flames between us and the safety of the stone cave.

Wren's mare finally rears, and it's all I can do to haul her head back down. Wren isn't the horseman Remy is, and she begins to slide down the horse's back, her magic going out, her eyes wide and panicked. We're close enough that I manage to grab her arm, slowing her fall and yanking her out of the way of the mare's deadly hooves.

The mare bolts, back the way we came. I'd go after her, but the wildfire has a mind of its own and has cut us off.

I readjust my grip on Wren's wrist and pull her up into the saddle ahead of me, nearly dislocating her shoulder in the process—I'll ask her forgiveness later. I wrap one arm around her middle, pulling her tightly against me, leaving her hands free to work her magic.

"Follow me!" Rafael takes the lead, one hand guiding his horse and the other held before him, palm out, commanding the fire before us to listen to him.

Ahead of him, a charred path opens, walls of flame to either side, close enough that my legs are blistering. Our horses—probably trained by Nestor, though I'm loath to admit it—follow Rafael's without hesitation, bolting over the smoking ground. Rafael's red robe flares around him as he forces the fire to obey—there's a reason Dimitra picked him, over all the Mages of their year. Others might be stronger, but no one has the control that Rafael does, though it was hard-won.

As we get closer to the rocky mound Remiel pointed out, I can't see a cave, or anything besides smooth boulders stacked on top of each other like so many children's toys.

"There!" Remiel shouts, pointing.

Rafael just turns his horse and heads in that direction, too focused to speak. I hold Wren tightly against me, her green light surrounding us as she pushes back the flames that dare escape Rafael's command.

Rafael's horse disappears behind a boulder, then Remy's—there's a hidden entrance there, and when I urge my mount behind it, I see we're in a snug, smooth cave, large enough for a small herd of horses. It's stone, and once we're all inside, Rafael releases his hold on the fire. A wall of flames surges around the entrance, like a frustrated beast trying to catch cornered prey, but it can't come inside.

Rafael runs a trembling hand through his hair. "Well, that was fun." He huffs a laugh.

Remiel dismounts, his hair dark with sweat, curls wild, and grabs the reins of Rafael's horse. "I've never seen anything like that," he says, awestruck, glancing from the cave entrance up to Rafael.

Rafael's face is red and sweating, but he's grinning back down at Remiel.

I look away. The tension between those two is practically palpable.

Wren dismounts, rubbing her shoulder—I'll massage it for her later—and we take stock of the cave. There's a bucket and a small trough for the horses, though both are empty. Finally the skies open up, and rain puts out the flames. Wren is able to use some of her magic to coax the water into our containers, and we're all able to at least clear the soot from our throats. The horses are covered in ash, with singed tails. We're a sorry sight, but we're safe from the fire and the raging storm.

"Let's get some rest," I say after a while, and I help lay out our bedrolls.

Wren snuggles up against me in the dark, and we both fall asleep to the sound of the rain.

CHAPTER 32
WREN

We reach the temple ruins around sunset. We rode as far as a farm about a mile from here, where we stabled the horses with a farmer on Leo's payroll, who promised us he'd take good care of them.

We walked the rest of the way, which wasn't hard. There is no road, but the landscape is barren, and Remiel seemed sure of the way. The temple, the only structure of note for miles, is visible shortly into our walk.

The roof is long gone, the pediment fallen, and most of the pillars are no longer whole. Pieces of them are scattered across the rocky ground like tombstones. Aenon's temple, as one would expect, ends mere feet from the water. There is a wide staircase carved right into the rocky shore, the steps leading down and down into the water. We all take turns jumping in, rinsing the ash and sweat off. I think of the tide pools around my lighthouse, the way I'd just float there, in the clean salt water, watching the seabirds overhead. The brackish, muddy water of the Black Strait could never compare. It's not as good as a real bath, but it's at least an improvement.

"There's a little mooring around this side," Remiel says, nodding toward the left. "We keep a boat stashed there, behind the rocks, for crossings like this. With all of us rowing tonight, we should make it easily before anyone spots us."

"You won't need the oars," I say. "I can speed us along much faster." If I can push *The James*, a rowboat should be a snap.

Remiel raises an eyebrow but doesn't comment. He just makes himself busy organizing our packs and supplies in the shadow of the temple ruins while we wait for the cover of darkness. We haven't seen any Roallacan ships patrolling this afternoon yet, but that doesn't mean they aren't out there.

I head to the shore, walking down until I'm just a single step above the water. I sit down, watching the waves for a bit. I hear birds calling, and a splash somewhere that must be a fish jumping. I take my knife and stab the waves that threaten to splash my boots, imagining each one has Aenon's face.

"Not the most efficient way to go about fighting the god of water," Rafael says, sitting down by my side.

I grin, shoving my shoulder against his. "Yeah, but it makes me feel better."

We sit in silence for a while, watching a few birds wheel and dive. There's clearly something on his mind. He looks at me and opens his mouth, like he wants to say something, before changing his mind and ripping up blades of grass to throw into the water instead. I take a guess.

"I'm glad we have Remiel to guide us," I say.

Rafael looks up at me sharply, his warm brown eyes wide. "Yeah, me too," he says, going back to ripping grass. Some of it is dry, and as he picks it up, he sets it on fire with a whispered word, letting the little sparks drift on the breeze out to sea.

"You want me to ask him if he's got a lover back home, waiting for him?" I ask quietly.

Rafael doesn't meet my eyes again. He just lets out a long, slow breath.

"He doesn't," he says at last. "I was going to ask him ... Well, he told me first."

I nod, waiting for him to continue. He sets some more grass on fire, letting the embers extinguish themselves in the strait, drifting like little fireflies.

"Seems silly, doesn't it?" he says. "We're on our way into the middle of a war between our countries and possibly one with a god on their side, and I want to know if he likes me." His face turns red, and he won't meet my eyes.

"Aris told me once that facing death regularly is what made him cling to life so fiercely," I say. "That every moment is a chance that might not come again."

Rafael nods and burns some more grass.

"I've just been through so much lately, you know? I'm the guy that always falls fast, and *always* falls hard, but between losing Dimitra and then Mariana, I'm just not sure if ..."

"If there's anything left for anyone else?" I prompt.

Rafael swallows and nods, looking out over the water.

"I think you have a big heart, and a great capacity for love, Raf," I say after a moment, chewing my lip. "Opening up again after being hurt, that must take an incredible amount of courage."

"Or maybe stupidity," he says, running a hand through his hair and leaning back. "I'm not even sure he likes me."

"He does," I say, giving him a sly grin. "I've seen him looking at you. He does. I'm sure of it. But one of you is going to have to be brave enough to make the first move."

He considers this, and we watch a shooting star arc across the sky, and listen to the waves lapping gently on the rocky shore. While it's a far cry from the tumultuous seas around Spit, the smell of salt in the air still reminds me of it, and I take some comfort in that.

"I hope, someday, that I can find what you and Aris have," Rafael says quietly.

I hear movement in the grasses behind us, an intentional rustle.

Aris is there, and he wants me to know it. If he didn't, I wouldn't have heard a thing.

"I mean, Aris *is* the most handsome, the strongest, most impressive Shield in a generation—and he even shaved his head for me. Any woman would consider herself lucky to spend a single moment with him," I say, trying to keep a straight face.

"I heard that," Aris says, emerging from the dark and sitting by me, a smirk on his handsome face. His eyes are twin sapphires, twinkling with amusement. "You didn't even mention my speed, my endurance, my expertise with a gladius ..."

"Your humility," Rafael and I chorus, laughing.

Aris shrugs. "It's not bragging if it's true," he says, though he's smiling too.

For a moment, this little bit of laughter is a bright spot in our journey.

"Well then," Rafael says after a moment. He stands and dusts his hands off on his robe, then straightens the collar. "If you'll excuse me. I'd like to go have some words with Remiel."

"Good night, Raf," I say.

Aris quirks an eyebrow but nods his farewell.

Rafael straightens his shoulders and heads off into the grasses.

Aris moves then, draping an arm around me, pulling me into his side. I snuggle into him, glad of his warmth, the solid strength of him. He smells of sunshine and leather and metal, and I breathe it in, like a tonic to steady my nerves.

Together we watch the light fade from the sky, until overhead is only darkness and stars.

CHAPTER 33
CAELUS

For ten days now, I have been in pursuit of my Mage, following her scent, the smell of snow on the breeze, across the plains of Ocron. I barely stop to eat, and only because my body demands it. I stop to sleep twice and am woken both times by a pounding of my heart, a ringing in my ears, which tell me, *Go onward.*

I keep up a steady stream of prayer to Rigrasil as I run. *Rigrasil, mightiest of the gods, father of Shields, may Dimitra find peace and honor at your side. May you keep me safe until my battle is won. May the light of the Silver Flame shine upon us all.*

On the eleventh day, I smell a small pack of Ocronian soldiers along the Black Strait. I only shift when I am close to them. I can imagine how they see me—thin, dirty, my hair wild, a beard starting on my face.

And yet I approach them with my head held high, for I am under divine command. The first law of the Shields: *Protect your Mage—above country, blood, and all else.* And the second: *The bond between you shall be as strong as the roots of the mountains and shall never fail.* My Mage has betrayed her country and has betrayed me. There is no greater dishonor in the world to us, not even brother turning against brother—and it is my job to see it undone.

"Friends," I call, raising a hand.

One of them sees me approaching, naked as we all are after a shift, and hurries to bring me clothing.

"I am Caelus Lazardis, a Shield of Ocron. My Mage has crossed the Black Strait without me, and I would meet her there. I have a strong back—can I exchange a turn at your oars for passage?"

The laziness of men is something easily manipulated. They let me borrow clothing for the trip—I'll just lose it and return it to them when I shift back in Roallac—and also give me useful information. Shield Commander Markos and Head Mage Iraklis have a camp in Roallac, a short run from our landing site. I need information on the lay of the land, so that's where I need to start. They will help me in my quest—they must. The Law of the Shields demands it. The third rule: *Your fellow Shields shall be closer to you than your own flesh and blood. Any evil committed against them is made against Rigrasil himself.*

But no one can right the wrong that Mariana has done except me.

I am ready.

CHAPTER 34
ARIS

The moon is half-full overhead, and the sky is so clear that the far shore is still nearly visible. Remy has pulled the small wooden boat out—it's barely big enough for the four of us, and I'm more than a little concerned one rogue wave will swamp us. He and Rafael are quiet, seemingly avoiding each other.

We start to load up our supplies when Remy spots a ship coming around the far bend. It's a small sailing ship, maybe half the size of *The James*, with dark sails. As it comes closer, we see a black snake in a circle, eating its tail, on the white flag.

We flatten ourselves against the stone steps and remain as quiet as possible. Sound carries over water, and when Rafael's foot dislodges a small rock that clatters and splashes down the steps, we all collectively hold our breath.

But the ship doesn't stop. It just makes its way, slowly, through the middle of the strait.

"Is it true that Water Mages can walk on water?" Wren asks softly.

Remy nods. "Some say under it too."

"Great," she mutters.

She burrows herself into my side, and when I wrap my arm around her, she sighs contentedly. It's cold with the sun down, and if that's the excuse I'm going to use for holding on to her, so be it.

The ship doesn't leave until after midnight. For a while, I thought it might drop anchor and spend the night—had it heard or seen us somehow?—but then it moved on. We climb into the small boat, crouching down low. Wren and I sit in the back, and Remy points us in the right direction from the front.

Wren whispers, and the rowboat surges ahead, throwing Remy and Rafael back into us and nearly capsizing the boat. The boat stops abruptly, throwing a wave over Rafael.

He mutters, "*Dry.*"

A hot wind blows across him, rippling the edges of his robe, and within seconds he is dry again. It looks like Remy considers asking him to do the same for him, but he bites his tongue and turns away, water dripping from his hair. Rafael turns red and doesn't say anything. I try hard not to roll my eyes.

"Sorry," Wren says, and she blows a wisp of hair back from her eyes. "I've only tried this with a large ship. Let me try again."

I take her hand, and she nods, taking a deep breath. She whispers again, and the boat begins to move forward, slowly, then faster as the waves before us are smoothed and the boat pulled along by her magic. There is a faint green glow along the undersurface of the boat—I can only hope that it's dim enough not to make us a beacon. We scan the horizon as Wren zips us along, but there are no more ships. We're at one of the narrowest parts of the Black Strait—Remy referred to it as the Waist—and with Wren's magic, we cross in less than an hour.

As we approach the Roallacan shore, a structure emerges from the trees. There's no real coast to speak of—just swamp. The building looks to have been a lighthouse or watchtower at one time, but the top has crumbled off. Now it is barely a handful of feet taller than the trees.

Remy points toward it, and Wren turns the boat slightly to oblige.

"The Iron Needle," Remy whispers. "An old outpost. Roallac hasn't used it in decades."

He grabs hold of a low-hanging branch and pulls himself out of the boat gracefully. The man has impressive upper body strength—I'll give him that. I notice Rafael noticing too.

Remy grabs the nose of our little boat and pulls it deeper into the swamp, walking along knobby roots as we go. He ties it under a large tree with wide, drooping branches, and we get out. After walking just a few feet, balancing along the tree roots, I completely lose sight of it.

We make camp on the first floor of the Iron Needle. Rafael makes a small fire—we've got three standing walls, so the fire is mostly hidden. Plus, it's fucking cold sitting on the stones. Wren snuggles up against me, and before I can even lay out our bedrolls, she's asleep on my shoulder.

We approach the Ocronian army just before midday. One moment, we're hacking our way through the swamp, soaked to the knee—or in Wren's case, to the hip, though water rolls right off that robe of hers—and the next, the trees clear, and we're faced with rows of neatly pitched tents. I've never really wanted to be a part of the army—I don't historically do well with authority. I like being on my own with my Mage.

There's too much politics in the army.

Wren sidles up to me, uncomfortable with the sudden rush of noise. Remy leads the way confidently, so we follow. He leads us past a few rows of tents, the big ones, that eight of us could sleep in. It's a well-organized camp, orderly. I recognize a few of the Shields and Mages we pass and nod when they call out to me. We get a lot of stares—mostly Wren does—but no one approaches us, and generally the noise dies down as we pass.

Wren slips her hand into mine.

In the center of the camp, we find a cleared area, and the large officers' tent. It's just like the way they trained us. It strikes me that perhaps Ocron has been preparing for something like this for longer than I initially thought.

There's a shout from inside the officers' tent, voices raised and angry. Remy heads right toward it without breaking his stride, without so much as a nod to the Shields guarding the entrance.

They don't stop him, though. He pushes aside the canvas flaps, holding them like a courtier for Wren and Rafael.

He lets them smack me in the face.

The inside of the tent is lit with spelled torches that emit light but little heat and no smoke. Around a rough table in the center of the room are a handful of men and women looking at a map of what appears to be Roallac.

Most of it looks blank.

The group stops shouting at each other to look at us, blinking owlishly, unsure of what our presence signifies.

An older man breaks first, a tired smile on his weathered face. He looks to have aged a hundred years since I saw him last—and he was old then.

"Aris. Mage Wren. Good to see you both," Shield Commander Markos Drusus says, clapping a paw on my shoulder. His jowls are unshaved, his uniform taut around the middle.

It is a strange thing to see one's heroes age.

From the strength of his grip on my shoulder and the fire in his eyes, though, I would wager he could still best me in the arena.

"You too," Wren says quietly, giving him a shy smile.

"What did you do to your hair?" Markos asks, a smile curling his lips. "Rafael burn it off again?"

Rafael coughs into his hand to smother a laugh. It doesn't work. Remy must find this highly amusing—he's as expressive as a stone most of the time, but a hint of a smile touches his face. I run a hand over my head self-consciously. I start to wonder if the healers can regrow my hair for me.

The rest of the group starts muttering. Only one other steps forward to greet us—a middle-aged man with shaggy brown hair, brown eyes, and sun-browned skin. He wears a green Mage's robe, and I swear the earth trembles beneath his feet as he walks, his power at odds with the welcoming smile on his face, showing even white teeth.

"Mage Wren. I'm so pleased to meet you at last. I am Iraklis," he says, leaving off his title, something his predecessor never did. I think I like him already.

"Shield Aris. Mage Rafael. You are all well, I hope."

Rafael nods, and I shrug.

"As well as can be expected," I say.

He smiles at me, round spectacles flashing in the torchlight, like we're old friends.

"Good, good. Lady Orothea sent word that you were on the way. I'm so glad Remiel was able to bring you so quickly. I'm particularly pleased you are here, Shield Aris."

I stand a little straighter.

Then he turns and beckons another Shield from the far side of the table. He's as tall and ugly-looking as I remember.

"After all, your brother Lukas has been such an asset," Iraklis says.

The man must not realize that Lukas and I aren't exactly on good terms—and he greets me pretty much as I expect.

With a cocky grin, and a fist to my nose.

CHAPTER 35
WREN

Aris dodges the blow with astonishing speed, even for him, simultaneously landing a punch to the other Shield's stomach.

His brother—Lukas?—somehow swings his momentum from Aris's blow, landing a solid fist to my Shield's unprotected side. Aris grunts but throws an arm around Lukas's neck, securing him in a headlock. Watching them fight is strange—they are brothers, but they are nearly twins in their black Shield clothes. Lukas wears his hair long, like Aris did, and he's a little taller, his eyes deep brown-black where Aris's are blue, but otherwise, the resemblance is uncanny.

Iraklis sighs, like these two warriors doing their best to beat the snot out of each other in the middle of his tent isn't more than an inconvenience. He whispers, and the ground beneath us rises up to form hands of soil around the feet of our sparring Shields and yank them apart.

I run a hand over my face. This is not exactly the kind of introduction I hoped to have to the Ocronian army, or the new Head

Mage. Aris is panting, a little blood trickling from the corner of his mouth.

Lukas smirks harder, if that were possible, his long hair mussed and eyes glittering with challenge.

"Good to see you, little brother," he says. Even his voice is like Aris's, though the taunting tone he uses reminds me more of Nestor or Spyridon. Iraklis waves his finger, and the dirt holding them back settles back into just regular dirt.

"Wish I could say the same," Aris says, straightening his collar.

Lukas rolls his eyes—which then land on me.

"Well, what do we have here?" he says, sauntering over to me now that the earthen shackles have released him. He's several inches taller even than Aris, with the same kind of radiating charisma that no doubt has drawn its fair share of women to him.

"Night Mage Verena Harker," I say, extending my hand for him to shake formally.

His eyes never blink, never leave mine. A smirk still curls his dangerous mouth.

He takes my hand and brings it to his lips. The contact is scorching.

And then he is knocked sideways when Aris's fist connects with his jaw.

"I had hoped they were past this," a man says, sighing.

Aris and Lukas are sitting on opposite ends of a bench—Lukas holding a bit of cloth to his cut lip, Aris crossing his arms and glowering.

The man speaking is not much taller than me, with the dark skin of the people from the Isles. His scalp is shaved smooth, his eyes dark and lined with long lashes. His robe is red.

"I'm Arion," he says, extending a hand for me to shake. "Lukas's

Mage. You'll find there's a good reason that the Valorius Shields stay far away from each other."

I think back to Spyridon and the greeting he gave us.

"So I've noticed," I say, giving Arion a smile.

He crosses his arms, staring at Lukas in admonition. "You'll also find," he says conspiratorially, lowering his voice a little, but not so low that Aris and Lukas can't hear us, "that trying to make sure your Shield behaves is infinitely harder with the Valorius line."

"So I've noticed," I repeat, shooting Aris a glance.

He raises one eyebrow at me.

We've been banished from the officers' tent until Aris and Lukas can cool down. I feel embarrassed, but honestly, everyone else is acting like this was an expected greeting from the two of them. Iraklis looked at them like a pair of misbehaving children and sent them to sit and "think about what they've done" for a bit.

Rafael and Remiel remain inside the tent—where I should be, I think, scuffing the ground irritably with my boot. *I'm* not the one who punched a high-ranking Shield of the king's army.

"You'll want to put some ice on that," I say, nodding at the bruise on Lukas's jaw.

He touches it gingerly, giving me a wink. "Don't worry your pretty head about me, Verena."

Aris snarls. "Her name is *Wren*."

"Your Shield hasn't forgiven me for sleeping with his last woman," Lukas whispers, chuckling.

Aris shoots him a dark look, half getting up from the edge of the bench he's sitting on.

"If you're talking about Dimitra," I say, putting a hand on Aris's chest and glaring at him while I speak to Lukas, "she's dead."

The muscles along Aris's jaw clench, but he doesn't speak.

I hear a low whistle behind me.

"I'm ... sorry to hear that," Lukas says, with more civility than I would have thought possible for a Valorius. He runs a hand through his hair, blowing out a breath. "She was one of a kind. Sure could use her help now."

"I take it you haven't secured Panos yet," Aris says accusingly.

"We weren't the ones who lost him in the first place. What does that make now? *Two* books you've let slip through your hands, little brother?"

"Closer than you've been to any of them," Aris replies easily, though I can feel his muscles clench under my hand, which still rests on his arm, gently restraining him.

"So no word on Panos at all?" I ask, looking at Arion, since Aris and Lukas seem to be unable to do much besides snap at each other at the moment.

He shrugs. "Not so much as a whisper," he says, frowning. "I've heard rumor that these Water Mages can slip through the swamp unseen, but we've got Earth Mages who haven't felt a single tremor, Wind Mages who haven't caught a scent or sound of him. It's unnatural."

"Are you sure he even came this way?" Lukas asks, taunting Aris.

I grimace.

"He's a Water Mage who has the Book of Gold in his possession," Aris reasons. "He actively tried to kill my Mage, so he's no friend of Ocron. And if he's not here, I'll hunt him to the end of the world."

"We both will," I promise him. "But he *has* to be here."

"Well, now that you're here," Arion says gently, as if talking down to a child, "Markos will want a debriefing. Better let him and Head Mage Iraklis handle this."

"Yes," Lukas says. He looks Aris over and clicks his tongue as if finding him lacking in some regard. "Your time away has made you soft."

I snort—there's not a soft place on Aris, not a single muscle he hasn't toned, not an ounce of spare flesh. The man is a living weapon —as am I, in a different way. I stand up straighter, indignant, still barely reaching Lukas's collarbone. I wonder if I can coax some snakes into his bedroll, the way I did with Mariana once.

Aris's hands clench again at his sides, ready to fly.

"Since it doesn't appear we'll be ready to go back into that tent anytime soon—Arion, can you tell us, please, what else is going on?" I ask, attempting to be the levelheaded one in the group for once.

Arion looks to his Shield and shrugs. He's leaning on a stack of wooden crates, taking bites out of an apple as he watches us, like we're his entertainment.

"Not much to tell," he says, spitting out a seed. It lands at Aris's feet. "We battled hardest for the crossing of the Black Strait. Not only can their Water Mages fortify the hulls of their ships, but the bastards can actually walk on water too, and under it—they'd come up under our ships and just punch holes in the bottoms, or send mists of some acidic gas across. Lukas got the brunt of that one, until Lenna—one of the Wind Mages—figured it out and blew it back across at them."

Lukas shrugs. "My face wasn't as pretty a week ago as it is now, sweetheart," he says, winking at me.

I roll my eyes. "How'd you get past them?" I hear a commotion inside the tent, but it's muffled. There's only canvas between us, so there has to be some kind of spell on it that prevents eavesdropping.

Clever. And frustrating.

"We've got our own Water Mages," Arion reminds me. "And there's a shark Shield, from south of Basti, of all places—massive guy. Anyway, he finally shows up and tears through the water walkers like they were ... I dunno, minnows or something. Had a little too much fun, if you ask me. Limbs and guts were drifting past us for days."

"Stiggur's brother?" I murmur to Aris.

He nods. "Has to be. Shark shields aren't that common." He straightens.

Neither of us particularly wants to dwell on *The James* and the problems that unfolded on that journey—Aris holds my eyes for a moment, then clears his throat and continues.

"So you made it across the Black Strait. Now what? You've made camp? Planting a garden next? Shall we invite Roallac to tea?" Aris crosses his arms.

Arion shrugs.

"It's hard to get through swamp, as you well know," Lukas says gravely.

Aris's face pales a little—his first Mage, Stefan, was killed in swamps like this, where the danger lurked behind the trees instead of facing them head-on, in a Shield's preferred method of battle.

"Soltaire is a fortress city, surrounded by canals that change with the tides, and I imagine at the queen's whim," Arion admits. "We're having our Earth Mages make us roads through, but it's slow. We'll be there days after the solstice at this rate."

"That's too long," Aris says, looking down at me. If Panos gets there, then we have to get there too.

Lukas looks up, a glint in his dark eyes. "Why?" he asks. "Do you have a better plan?"

"No," I say quickly—too quickly, as it turns out.

Lukas raises an eyebrow at me.

I swallow and attempt to redirect him. Our plan was a vague, simple thing—get to Roallac, find out from Markos and Iraklis how to infiltrate Soltaire, get in, get the books, stop Evanthia.

"Can you show us where the messenger tent is?" I ask. "I'd like to ... send a letter to Ismini, let her know we've arrived." In reality, I just want to get away from Lukas. Something about him has me on edge—he reminds me of a snake himself, beautiful and charming, but quick to anger and deadly when called for. Aris has a casual arrogance, a sense of playfulness that his brother lacks. Lukas reminds me more and more of Nestor, and that's not a memory I enjoy reliving.

"I can show you," Arion says, and we stand—but then the muffled sounds inside the tent become a roar, the silencing spell broken.

CHAPTER 36
ARIS

Remy and Rafael emerge from the tent and tell Lukas and Arion that they're to take us to yet *another* tent to clean up and get some rest.

I don't need rest. I need to punch the smirk off Lukas's face, but when Wren puts a hand on my arm, I clench my teeth and go with her instead.

"You can set down your things, and I'll show you where you can eat," Remy says.

"Do you think we'll be here long?" Wren whispers to me. "Should we stay and help them, or go on our own?"

I cover her hand with mine.

"Come on, Rafael," I urge. "Stop holding out on us. What was going on in that tent?"

He gives me a cheeky grin. "Pretty boring stuff. Better leave it to us grown-ups."

"Raf," I warn.

Wren rolls her eyes.

"Numbers, mostly. Numbers of soldiers, and Shields. Days of

rations that are left if Lady Orothea's next shipment doesn't come soon. Miles to the capital. They've been using some of the small Shields as spies—the birds, weasels, those guys."

"No white tigers," Wren says, shoving her shoulder against me playfully.

I grunt in agreement. I would stand out too much here.

"They've got a pretty good idea of the layout of the city, even the vault in the palace where Evanthia keeps all her treasures. Apparently, not all the spies made it back from that one—she has it guarded by snakes," Rafael says with a shiver.

A female voice breaks the stillness. "How in the hells did *they* get here so fast? Didn't you just tell me they were in Aeturnus?" It is a harsh voice, dripping with scorn. A voice like Nestor's.

Two Shields stand before us in the narrow alley between rows of canvas tents, a tall, broad woman berating another, slighter woman.

"Adriana!" Wren cries, throwing herself at my sister, like she hasn't just seen her a few days ago.

"Aenon's salt, Wren. I can't breathe," Adriana says, but she's smiling and thumps my Mage on the back. "I see you made it to Roallac. Brother. Good to see you too." She gives me a nod. Her eyes are troubled, and she glances at the woman at her side, who also wears the black leather of a Shield.

"Right. Good to see you, *brother*," the woman says, her arms crossed. She's taller than I remember, probably close to six feet now, and nearly as broad as I am. Her dark hair is pulled back tightly, her black eyes glaring at me.

Rea. Fuck.

"What are *you* doing here?" I ask, frowning.

She's just a first-year, just eighteen. She should be at the School of the Silver Flame, learning sword drills from Vasilis—not in the middle of a war.

Wren glances between us, confused.

I sigh. "Wren, this is Rea, my other little sister. Rea, this is the Night Mage. Now what the *fuck* are you doing here?"

Rea looks down her nose at Wren, who frowns. Rea probably has at least fifty pounds on her, all of it muscle, and more than six inches of height as well. She looks more like a female version of Nestor than I remember.

"*I* am here because a whole lot of Shields got killed at Soltaire, and Commander Markos needs all the help he can get," she snaps. "Why are *you* here?"

"You should be back at the school," I say. I'm going to have to talk to Markos about this. I know he must be desperate for Shields, but to call up first-years, who are barely months into their official training, and unclaimed?

"Why? Because I'm a woman?" Rea says, arching a dark eyebrow. "I'm not as strong as you? I've changed a lot since you last saw me."

"Because you're a *first-year*. Gods, Rea," I say, rubbing a hand across my scalp.

Wren and Adriana are talking quietly, though both keep glancing at us. I decide I'd rather talk to Adriana too.

"I thought you'd be in Raverra," I say.

Adriana nods, unsmiling. "I go back and forth quite a bit. Those of the King's Messengers that are left are all based out of this camp now. One of the benefits of being a flying Shield—the Roallacan idiots don't know to look at the skies. Daniil—you remember him?—is scouting Soltaire nearly every day. He's been able to give us detailed maps of the whole place, and accurate counts of their soldiers, Mages, and weapons. Roallac has been planning this for a while, Aris."

Rea keeps glaring at Wren, like a lion eyeing its next meal. Wren glares back.

"I've got to get back to my training," Rea says after a moment. She tosses her head and stalks off. I guess that's as much of a goodbye as I'm going to get.

"She's still mad, you know. About Nestor," Adriana whispers.

"Obviously," I grunt.

Adriana elbows me in the gut. “Lukas is keeping an eye on her. I’ve got to get back to Raverra with another list of supplies we need.”

“Right. Well,” I say, hands on hips, looking at my little sister. “Be safe.”

“I love you too, Aris,” she says with a wink and a punch to my arm. “See you after the war.”

CHAPTER 37
WREN

It's a cold, damp, stinking morning, and we've stolen a boat from the Ocronian army.

It was Aris's idea, of course, though Rafael quickly agreed with his plan. They debated asking Remiel to come for a while—Aris wasn't sure he could be trusted not to rat us out to Commander Markos, but Rafael wasn't leaving without him.

We've decided to go off on our own—to get a little way away from the camp, to talk about our plans to get to Soltaire without the entire army eavesdropping on us. Mostly Rea, I suspect.

"We should stay with the army," Rafael argues again. "They have every messenger Shield out looking for Panos. Maybe he hasn't gotten here yet."

"But Evanthia will kill King Leonidas if he *doesn't* make it," I remind him. "And Ocron might lose the blessing of the god of day."

"Might," Aris reminds me. "Didn't Caladrius say the blessing would continue, even if King Leonidas's line ended?"

"Well, Caladrius wants me to come here too," I argue.

"So what's the blessing tied to, then, if not the royal line?" Rafael asks, frowning. He picks up a small brown snake by the tail and removes him from the boat.

"Do you trust him?" Remiel asks, dipping the oars into the black water of the Roallacan swamp. "The god of night, I mean."

"Does it matter?" I say.

I think of the night of the ball, when Leo gifted me that golden gown and danced with me like I was someone worthy of the attention of a king, like I was no longer that small girl from a backwater town. I can't stand to think of him imprisoned in this awful place.

Aris and I exchange a wordless glance. He shrugs.

Aris and Remiel take turns at the oars, while Rafael and I do our best to steer the little boat up a narrow creek and around knobby cypress trees, their knees sticking up under the water like hands, waiting to grab us. The water is murky brown and still, and it is littered with dead limbs, clumps of moss dripping down from the trees, and old leaves. Here and there a fish splashes, but otherwise, the place is eerily silent. The trees nearly touch overhead, blocking out most of the light. I swear I see Roallacan soldiers behind every fallen log.

For an hour, we pass nothing but vegetation and the occasional frog—or snake. No wonder Roallac is known as Snake Island. They drip from the branches like rain, in browns and greens and blacks, their forked tongues tasting the air as we pass. They don't bother us, but they look like they could. We pass one lazy monster, as thick around as my waist, coiled on himself like so many loops of dark rope, his head bigger across than mine. I have no doubt he could swallow me whole, and the idea makes me shift back a little in the rowboat, closer to Aris. I'm not afraid of them, exactly, but they don't behave the way I expect them to. Animals usually like me, listen to me. These look like they want to eat me as a snack. I wonder if Queen Evanthia's influence has something to do with that, her magic poisoning everything.

"I don't like this place," I mumble, pulling my robe tighter around me.

"I don't like Rea being here," Aris says, shredding a leaf into bits and tossing them over the side. He's been distracted all day, thinking about his sister. "She should be at the school."

"Markos is desperate," Rafael says, blowing a strand of hair off his face. "Roallac is well fortified and has more resources than we gave them credit for."

"They'll be slaughtered," Aris says, smacking the side of the boat with his fist. "Sending untrained Shields out against Black Water Witches? I may not like my sister, but I have no wish to see her dead."

We sit in silence for a long time.

"We could end it, you know," I say into the humid air of the swamp. "If we can get just one other book, and rescue the king. This war will be over. No more Shields—or Mages, or anyone—have to die. We'll just ... put it in the king's vault, and no one needs to ever use it, ever again."

For a moment, no one speaks. It's a foolish wish, a naive one, but no one says so aloud. I feel heat tracking up my neck anyway. I am no child. I cannot afford to believe in miracles.

"We need to get a look at the maps Daniil has made," Aris says, perking up. "There have got to be drains, or something we can use to get in."

Rafael murmurs something about crawling through a sewer being even less pleasant than the stench of the swamp, and he removes yet another snake from our boat.

"A fox would not be that suspicious in a place like this," Remiel says, frowning. "I could get inside and find a door to let you all in."

"I am *not* letting you into that place alone!" Rafael says, surprisingly loud. He flushes, then looks stubbornly over the bow of the boat, not meeting anyone's gaze.

When Aris suggests we turn around and go back to the camp, Rafael only grunts in agreement.

The nose of the boat hits another snag. I can't tell if we've dead-ended again or if somehow we can push past this one. It seems to be another large fallen limb, like so many we've passed. The men are clearly uncomfortable with the idea of Markos sending students like Rea into battle—though Rea looked pretty tough to me. Rafael peers over the tree branch in our way.

"It looks clear past this," Rafael says quietly. As he stands, he rocks the boat a little, sending ripples out across the water. We haven't seen any signs of Roallacan Mages or soldiers, but that doesn't mean they aren't here, watching and listening.

"Remiel, come help me move this," Rafael says.

Remiel passes off the oars to Aris and stands in the front by Rafael.

"Sit back with me," Aris says, pulling me close. "Better balance in the boat this way."

"Right," I say, giving him a sly grin.

He responds by pulling me closer and planting a kiss on top of my head, where the hair has gone all frizzy from the dank air. Rafael has discarded his robe again, which is bundled up inside one of our packs. The red is just too visible across the dark murk here—at least my black is somewhat camouflaging. Rafael and Remiel work on the fallen limb for a moment, before Remiel freezes.

"Come and look at this." He gestures to Aris.

Aris sighs, handing me the oars. "Don't drop those overboard."

I snort in reply, and he moves to help Remiel, skirting around Rafael, who comes back to stand by me. Aris peers over Remiel's shoulder. Remiel's freckled face is pale, his lips a pressed line as he analyzes something at the base of the wood.

"It's been cut," Aris says. He whirls back around to look at me, casting me an alarmed glance.

My heart leaps into my throat. *Cut?*

"Someone blocked this path on purpose?" I whisper. "They don't want us going this way?"

"That's one possibility," Remiel says, and he draws his throwing knives.

Aris draws his swords, scanning the swamp for any sign of an ambush.

There is no sound except the croaking of the frogs, the whisper of wind through the treetops.

There's another sound, like the buzzing of a mosquito, growing louder—until an arrow of ice comes out of nowhere. It would have gone right through Remiel's chest, but somehow he heard it coming, and his Shield muscles reacted faster than I could blink to move him out of the way.

The arrow thuds into the dead tree limb, burying itself nearly entirely before melting away.

"DOWN!" Aris roars—but with the oars in my lap and three tall men standing around me in this small boat, I don't really have anywhere to go, no way to hide myself, small as I am, below the low gunwale.

From our left come more ice arrows, a volley of them, as a dozen Mages in dull-colored robes emerge from the trees. Rafael has his flames out in an instant, melting the arrows before they have a chance to reach us. Remiel throws his knives calmly, precisely—and every time he does, a Mage falls.

Aris leans back to give Rafael more room—with his swords drawn, he's good in close combat, but not for these enemies at a distance. As he moves, he knocks against me, and the oars fall from my hands. They're heavy, unwieldy, and the movement sends them overboard, where they float in the brown water, bobbing to the surface.

I cry out and reach for them, leaning over the gunwale as far as I can. I manage to snag one and hand it back to Aris before reaching for the other. Fortunately, they are on the opposite side of the boat from the arrows.

Fortunate, or well planned.

As I lean over the gunwale, one hand outstretched, the other clutching at the slippery wood of our boat, the water beneath me seems to boil. The oar floats nearly beyond my reach, but I can just touch it with the tips of my fingers. I hope whatever is churning the water isn't some god-sent beast, like the kraken. Perhaps a crocodile. Gods, not that *that's* any better.

The water under my outstretched arm parts suddenly in a circle, like the gaping of some giant mouth, and from inside it, two hands reach out to grab my wrists and pull me from the boat.

For a moment, there's another grasp around my ankles, and I am suspended between them, my breastbone scraping the gunwale. Aris has me as whatever monster from the depths tries to drag me from him. Remiel turns, flinging a knife down into the watery pit—there's a howl of rage, and one of the hands lets go—

To be replaced by two more, grabbing my elbows. I am struggling, screaming, crying, desperately trying to get back into the boat, to a place of relative safety.

I turn, looking at Aris, locking eyes with him. He is my Shield, and he will not let me go. I know that beyond a shadow of a doubt. I just have to get myself free of these water wraiths. My wrists ache, and I'm sure my shoulders are dislocating, but I try to keep scratching, keep pulling.

Rafael shouts.

Two arrows of ice sprout from Aris's chest, blood blooming across his shirt like gruesome flowers. His mouth drops open in shock. His grip on my ankles falters.

I scream as he falls, the sound tearing from my throat. My last glimpse of him is his form silhouetted against the trees, head thrown back, the cords of his neck straining as he roars.

Aris lets me go.

CHAPTER 38
DELPHINE

Ismini has been writing to Aris. I scribble a few lines on her latest letter, letting him know that I'm all right and that I fully expect him to return quickly so he can train me like he promised. I feel anxious that he and Wren and Rafael are gone, anxious in a way I've never felt before. Uncle Tekton never goes *anywhere*, so I never really had to feel his absence.

I feel it now.

I write to him too. At least I know he's safe where he is.

Aleka brings me along with her to most of her meetings and things. I like it most when we get to go watch the Shields practice in one of the courtyards. I eye their swords and glittering knives, but Aleka won't let me do more than just touch them. The meetings she has to go to are a lot less fun—but she does insist I come with her, which is nice. I like to watch the old men's faces turn red when she puts them in their place. Otherwise, the meetings are pretty boring—a lot of numbers regarding supplies and troops. I honestly spend most of them daydreaming about when I get my own swords.

Aleka also makes me run a lot. We run down the main road of Estana. We run along the wall around the Golden City. We run back to the palace at night. She rarely lets me out of her sight. Since I'm a Shield, and so I need less sleep, she keeps me with her all night too. We spend some time in the library, which Tolis has had fixed up, reading about the history of Shields. Well, that's what she makes *me* read. I have no idea what she's reading, but I suspect it's dirty, judging by the pink on her cheeks.

It's nice, feeling wanted, but when it's quiet, and Aleka finally gives me a moment's peace … I find myself thinking about my friends, headed north to fight the Snake Queen. I *know* that Markos knows about me—so why won't he let me come too? I heard he's letting the students from the school go. I'm not that much younger than any of them. Besides, none of *them* are dragons.

I wonder what Aris would do, were he in my place.

CHAPTER 39
WREN

There are hands on me, everywhere, and I am surrounded by blue lights and murky water. We're in some kind of tunnel beneath the surface, the water held back by invisible magic. I vaguely remember Remiel saying that the Roallacan Water Mages can walk beneath the water, but I didn't really consider they could build passages like this. Balls of blue light are strung along the corridor, illuminating the brown water. I can see mats of vegetation and schools of tiny baitfish swirling around us, and even some long, sinister shapes that I can't identify.

For a moment I am frozen, paralyzed, my heart pounding as I wait to turn gray. Will it happen all at once? It did for Saroya. Or will it be a slower thing, if Aris is still holding on somehow as his life's blood slowly leaves his body?

Gods, not even Aris can survive two arrows to the heart.

And I'm not dead yet, or even gray—and these bastards took Aris from me. Is he dead? He can't be. He *can't*.

I start to thrash. I flail, kick and scratch and bite anything I can reach. I'm able to pry the knife from my boot, and I stab aimlessly, mostly catching fabric but a few times scoring flesh. There are too many Mages around me—I am able to sink my knife into the wrist of one, but with a howl, he wrenches away, taking my knife with him.

Lashes of water grab my hands and feet, securing me to the floor, spreading me out like a starfish. I buck and I rage and I cry, but the shackles won't budge.

A figure looms over me. I catch a grin of white teeth in a dark face just as I feel a blow to the side of my head.

And it all goes black.

CHAPTER 40
WREN

I wake up in a cage.

Wait a minute. That's not right.

My vision blurs, and I have to rub my eyes for a few seconds to get the specks of mud out of them before I can clearly see where I am.

My initial impression was right—I *am* in a cage. A giant birdcage, the bars of which curve to a dome overhead. It's just tall enough for me to stand in, in the center, and I sway as I move and grab the bars for support.

I can't tell if it's my throbbing headache making me wobbly or this cage being set in the back of a cart drawn by four horses. We're walking slowly through the swamp, a team of Water Mages ahead of us pushing the swamp water out of the way, making a road where there was none. I glance over my shoulder—a few feet behind, the water splashes back into place, leaving only fading ripples to show where we've been. A guard walks on either side of my cart, and a few more walk up front or ride with the driver. They're quiet, maybe tired from the long day. I must have been unconscious for at least several hours.

Overhead, the moon glimmers through the trees, filtering its silver light down through the darkness.

Idiots, I think. I take stock of the situation—I'm not gray, so Aris has to be alive. He *has* to be. I'd know if he were dead, wouldn't I? I know the strength of our Shield-Mage claim has been questioned before—since I'm not an elemental Mage, our bond might not be the same.

No, I tell myself. *He's always been able to hear you. You would know if he were dead. He will find you, no matter what.*

Regardless, these assholes need to be reminded who they're dealing with. I allow a small smirk to touch my lips—I will unleash all the hells on these bastards. I bring my hands up, centering myself, reaching for that pulsating orb of darkness in my core.

I stumble, like the cart has hit a stone or something, only it hasn't.

There's nothing there. In my core. *There's no magic there.*

"What in all the hells?" I whisper.

One of the guards walking alongside has finally noticed I'm awake and calls over to his partner on the opposite side.

"What a pretty little bird you are," they taunt, sneers on their faces. They wear little armor and carry bows and knives—not much room to swing a sword in this swamp. On their chest is emblazoned the black snake eating its own tail.

"What have you done to me?" I yell, reaching again and again inside me, each time finding *nothing*. Is this because they hit my head too hard? I have some sort of injury preventing me from reaching my magic?

"Starsteel, Night Mage," one of them crows, reaching over the wooden cart rails and tapping against the metal of my cage. "A country's ransom's worth."

Starsteel. I've never heard of it—but I take a closer look at my prison. The bars are barely a hand's width apart—small as I am, there's still no way I'd be able to fit through them. The bars extend down to a shining floor, made of the same silvery metal as the bars.

That's when it hits me.

This is the same metal that the manacles were made out of, the ones that are used to bind troublesome magic after being placed on a Mage's wrist. They tried it with two manacles on me at the School of the Silver Flame—it didn't work well.

But a *cage*? A whole fucking *cage*? I thought this metal was hard to find, that manacles weren't even made anymore, because no one had found more of the silvery metal they were made of.

Looks like I was wrong.

I run a finger down one of the bars, feeling its cold, metallic bite, just like the manacles.

I want to cry.

I stick my arm out of the cage, see if I can summon something, anything, with my fingers outside the metal.

Nope.

I grip the bars, rattling them in frustration.

"Where are you taking me?" I ask the guards.

They huff.

"Where do you think?" one of them snarls. "The queen had this metal dragged special from the ocean just for you, pretty bird."

All right. My Shield is wounded—I can't believe he's dead ... I *can't*—and I have no idea about Rafael or Remiel. And Adriana and Rea and the rest? They're loyal to Markos. Would Markos send them after me? He has to, right?

Right?

I grab the starsteel bars of my prison and pull. I pulled three-hundred-pound casks of whale oil up a lighthouse for *years*. I can bend some puny metal bars.

But the bars do not yield, and eventually, with the laughter and insults from the guards ringing in my ears, I lie down and curl up under my robe, hoping that the magic imbued in its black silk remains. I wrap my fingers around the green crystal around my neck, rubbing the smooth facets absently. I think back to when Aris gave it to me—we were putting on an act, so he could track the would-be kidnappers trailing us. The look in his eyes, though, was one I'll never forget. There was no act, not with him. Not with us.

I will not give in to despair. I *cannot*. Aris wouldn't cry, were he in this situation. He'd probably goad the guards into coming closer and then smack their heads together.

I reach for my knife—only it's gone. I vaguely remember embedding it in someone's arm before being knocked unconscious.

Gods, my head hurts. And my chest, where it rubbed the boat. And my shoulders. *Gods, everything hurts.*

All right. No knife. No magic. No book. And no Aris.

Fear clenches in my chest, and I feel my heart start to race. I take deep, gulping breaths of air and will the tears in my eyes to stay right where they are.

Don't give them the satisfaction.

And when we reach Soltaire? What will I do then, with no weapon, no plan, and no Shield?

I sob and pull the hood of my robe up over my head.

CHAPTER 41
ARIS

I have never known pain like this before.

It's not just the spears of ice lodged in my chest, a hairbreadth from my heart.

It's not just the way my left lung burns, unable to bring air into my body.

It's the way Wren looked at me, green eyes so wide I could see the white all the way around, as she was taken from me and pulled under the murky black swamp.

Dimly I register the hull of the small boat at my back. The branches overhead block out the blue of Rigrasil's sky. I can hear our claim, Wren's bell clanging through my brain, angry and hurt—though faint, like she's far away, or her strength is fading.

And then—it's gone.

And I can't move. Rafael's hands are over me, his palms glowing, melting the ice so that my body can heal. My Shield magic and his fire magic fight that of the Black Water Witches.

Remy stands over us both, my swords in his hands. He's lost all his knives, each one lodged in the corpse of a Roallacan Mage, but still on they come, relentless as the tides.

I struggle to sit, to breathe, to think—Rafael's hand presses against my chest, and I don't have the strength to stop him. My breath comes faster, my chest feeling like it's caving in. My healing magic is unable to keep up with the damage done to my body.

And Wren. *I can't hear Wren.*

Not again. Not again.

The world fades to black.

CHAPTER 42
WREN

I've lost track of how long I've been in this cage now. Periodically the guards shove food and water through—not enough to calm the growling in my belly, not enough to slake my thirst—just enough to keep me alive and miserable. They don't bother shielding me from the elements either—no tarp over the top when it rains, which it does often in this gods-damned country. The only small mercy I've been granted is that they've let me keep my robe. It does a decent job of keeping me warm and dry and protecting me from vicious jabs from passersby that would have otherwise cut me—though I have no doubt this small kindness on their part is less to keep me comfortable and more to remove doubt in anyone's eyes that I *am* the Night Mage, and I am as helpless as a songbird in a cage. Part of me wants to tear off the robe, throw it off some cliff as we pass, just to piss Queen Evanthia off.

But if I do that, I will lose my one small bit of comfort, this one connection I have to Ocron and the good people there who are counting on me. Ismini. Aleka.

And Leo. When I think of him, my heart aches until I think it will stop completely. After I lost Aris, I longed to go gray, to enter that state of silent numbness, to let my grief consume me. I have to admit to myself that he likely *is* dead—or he would have found me by now. I know it. With every second that passes, my certainty in that grows.

But perhaps—a small, traitorous part of me whispers—our claim was not a *true* claim, that of an elemental Mage and a Shield, because I was not a regular Mage. If I had been an elemental Mage, maybe then the bond between us would have been so strong that I would not have been able to live without him.

Even now, I don't want to.

But I don't have a choice. *He could always hear you through your bond—it was a true claim. You would know if he were dead.*

I'm being carted to the heart of Roallac, a prize for the Snake Queen, one more trophy for her collection. I look up at the sky—night now. I used to love the night, used to count the stars to help me fall asleep. I can name a hundred constellations, used to be able to predict when the silver shoals of sardines would hit the shores around Spit by the phases of the moon in the spring. Used to watch my lighthouse light shine brightly into the darkness, making passage safe through our treacherous waters.

I laugh at the thought of that naive little girl, staring wide-eyed out into the night skies for years on end. I wonder if Caladrius was watching me all that time, if my nocturnal lifestyle drew his attention. I can't think of any other reason he would have picked me.

He should have picked someone like Dimitra. *She* would never have let herself get caught in this stupid, stupid cage.

My eyes prickle, and I flop onto my back, staring up at the bars of my prison, stripes of silver against the black night. Metal that is a little too bright, a little too cold to be silver.

Metal that renders my magic absolutely useless.

There has got to be *something* I can do. So I can't use my magic—I didn't have magic for the first eighteen years of my life, and I managed just fine.

I kick at the bars near the door. They rattle but do not bend. They make a tremendous noise, though, like massive wind chimes.

"None of that," the guard hisses.

There is always at least one of them walking alongside me. At first they mostly jeered at me, insulted me, my ancestors, my country ... anything they could say to get me riled up. Some of them poke me or throw things at me if I start to fall asleep, but some, like the young blond guard walking with me now, are quiet. He never tries to hit me, and if I manage to doze off for a few hours, he never disturbs me.

I kick the bars again, harder. They jangle and vibrate all the way up to where the bars meet overhead.

"What? Do you need to piss or something? You'll have to wait for sunrise," he says.

"Just bored," I say.

"Yeah, well, we'll be at the capital tomorrow. I don't think you'll be bored for long."

A chill runs through me. *Already?*

"I guess I'd better get some sleep, then," I say.

I take my robe off and lie down as best I can, pillowing my head on my arms. I whirl the black silk over me like a fancy blanket, covering my feet. I close my eyes and take long, slow breaths—the guard is keeping his eyes straight ahead, and the creaking of the wagon should conceal some of my efforts. Beyond him, there is nothing but trees and swamp, and the occasional glint of yellow eyes.

I spent years running up and down the stairs of my lighthouse, years cultivating back and leg muscles to help me maneuver the massive barrels of oil, all by myself. Between that and Aris's incessant knife lessons—gods, the thought of him is like an arrow to my chest—I'm much stronger than I look.

I brace my shoulder against one bar and line my feet up on another. Using my shoulder as a brace, I push—slowly, slowly—with my legs, trying to straighten them, to push the bars apart wide enough so that I might be able to slip through. If I can get through tonight, I'll unleash magic enough to blot out all of Roallac. I'll rain lightning and fire and destruction on this island, the likes of which they've never imagined. I will fly to the capital, as Saroya once did, and finish this myself.

The bars begin to creak. The muscles in my thighs are trembling with the effort—and I'm really hoping the darkness and the robe will mask what I'm doing—and my shoulder is beginning to throb from being used as a brace, but I keep going.

I don't have a choice. If I make it to the capital, I'll be in the clutches of the Snake Queen.

I curse the gods and get to work.

The day dawns clear and cold, the sun doing little to warm the air. Frost lines the wagon and my cage, making little patterns on the metal, like beautiful, delicate flowers.

The metal bars have not budged more than an inch, not nearly enough space for me to wiggle through.

The guard with me closes his eyes as the sun caresses his face, like he's happy to see it—and he probably is. *I* would be, in his shoes. He knows that I'm powerless now. I mean, I am powerless in this stupid cage, but now I'm even more so.

I kick the bars hard for good measure, letting out a short roar of frustration as they rattle and do not give.

"Sleep well?" the guard asks. There's a smirk on his stupid face.

I miss Aris. I miss his stupid smirks and his flirting and the way he always, always makes me feel safe. *You just bloom. I'll be your thorns.* And despite everything, my biggest regret is not telling him I love him. I was worried those words would drive him away. Now I'll never get the chance. And I do love him—I think I loved him from the first moment we locked eyes at the coliseum.

I know now, I always will.

Tears streak down my face as the sun glints off a gray stone fortress in the distance.

We've arrived.

And there's nothing I can do.

CHAPTER 43
ARIS

Breathing is hard. Thinking is harder.

When Stefan died, I shifted into my tiger form. I think at the time it was a kind of protection, to save me from the emotions that being human subjected me to. And at the time, I went a little wild.

When I wake, I find myself in my tiger form again, without having consciously shifted to it. And while I'm trying to figure out why I'm in my shifted form, I'm also struggling to breathe, and I can't remember anything of how I got here.

The pain is so immense that I have little concept of where I am going, where I am being dragged. I am briefly aware of being dumped unceremoniously into some kind of cart, and now we wheel along some kind of passageway. Each bump of the stones on the ground sends ripples of agony through my paws. I can remember *nothing* except pain. Even the rise and fall of my chest hurts, and each time I exhale, I worry it might be my last. Mighty Aris, suffocated by his own weakness.

My memories are disjointed. I remember Wren, reaching out for an oar that had slipped from her hands as Rafael, Remy, and I fought the Roallacan Mages. I remember reaching for her as she slipped, remember her screaming—it echoes in my head even now. It is the most terrible thing I've ever heard. I'm still not sure what happened —some beast grabbed her from the water. Maybe a fish. A crocodile.

And then, when I was turned, two arrows punched through my lung, and I let go.

I fucking let go.

Wren. My Wren. *I let her go.*

I don't remember much after that.

Aris Valorius, the Shield who failed to keep *two* Mages safe. One closer to me than my brothers; the other, the light of my life.

But I haven't gone gray. There's that, at least. That small scrap of hope that I cling to. Wren is alive, out there somewhere. I can't hear her, not with this fucking collar around my neck, but I *know* it.

I'm not sure how much time has passed. My body has partially healed the arrow wounds. It's hard to tell, because the collar slows my healing. I've been kept bound, in the dark, so I have no clear picture of the passage of time. I think I sleep sometimes—but then, it's hard to tell what is real and what is a nightmare.

Sometimes I think I hear Wren, hear our bond, and I wake in a panic, my heart racing.

It's always a dream. A hallucination, fueled by desperation.

The guards spit on me through the bars of the cage, laughing.

I can't summon the energy to care. My legacy is in ruins, anyway. I wonder if Lukas and Rea have even noticed that we're gone yet, if anyone has been sent after us. I look to the sky, hoping to see a familiar hawk form flying overhead—but there's nothing, nothing except the glow of Rigrasil's sun.

The cart stops before a portcullis. The men dragging my cart exchange excited whispers. I'm not even chained—I can rip their throats out in the time it takes them to blink.

Or I could, if I didn't have this collar on.

Starsteel, I heard them call it.

The same bright silvery metal that made the manacles that once bound Wren. It's exceedingly rare. Somehow Evanthia has access to some and has wasted it on this collar for me. It blocks my magic—my muscles are atrophic, my fur dull and patchy. My tendons and ligaments are brittle, threatening to snap if I move too fast. I am a decrepit version of myself, frail and useless. I don't even know if I can open my jaw to snap at the assholes who tip back the cart—I fall to the ground, striking my hip and shoulder on the stone.

I hear the crack of bone from both. A fresh burst of pain sears through my skull.

"Ain't much to look at, is he?" one of the guards says.

He laughs and kicks my ribs. They crumple under the weight of his boot like so many shards of glass. A whine escapes me, and he laughs again.

"Shield scum," he says, spitting on me. "Come on. Time to die."

Beyond the grating I hear the roar of a crowd, not unlike the one back at the arena, back at the School of the Silver Flame.

The guards pull the chains at the side of the grating, and the portcullis lifts. The light is blinding after the dark tunnels. The guards attach a pair of leather leashes to my collar and drag me into the arena. I do nothing to help them—my hide is scraped over the stones as we go, until we reach the arena sand, which is soon stained with blood from my shoulder.

By the time we reach our destination, my eyes have adjusted. It's a smaller arena than Ocron's, and made of gray stone. We've stopped before a dais where a woman sits on a black throne—Evanthia. I've never met the Snake Queen before. She has dark hair and eyes, a square jaw, and fair skin. She's enveloped in a huge black dress, yards of fabric draping to either side of her. A black crown sits on her head, topped with a massive sapphire. There is a large object draped in black fabric behind her, and I wonder what sort of torture she has concealed underneath, what kind of game.

"*This* is the best Ocron has to send against me?" she says. Her voice is like the caw of a crow, and it carries across the arena.

People laugh and shout. A few throw things at me—half-eaten

chicken legs, rotten apples. I don't move. I tell myself that I'm conserving my strength, but honestly, I couldn't avoid them if I tried.

"You were right," Evanthia says, turning to the Mage beside her. "I should have sent you with some manacles after all. This whole affair would have been over much sooner."

The Mage beside her is a woman in a blue dress, her white-blond hair braided ornately. Her eyes glitter with contempt when they land on me.

Mariana. I try to bare my teeth, to extend my claws, to do *anything*, but I get no more than a whine from my throat. My own impotence shames me.

"From what you told me about him, I expected more of a challenge," Evanthia sneers.

Mariana's face turns a little red, her hands clenched at her sides.

"Binding Shields and Mages together is such an unnecessary tradition," Evanthia says, loud enough for everyone in the arena to hear. "The Water Mages of Roallac need no such bodyguards."

A cheer of agreement goes up from the crowd.

"What will happen to him?" Mariana asks.

My ribs protest as I inhale a shallow breath, awaiting the answer.

The arena quiets. Evanthia steps forward to rest her hands on the railing and look down on me like I am an insect to be squashed beneath her heel.

"He will die," she says, the words dripping like venom from her tongue.

Great. Really fucking great. If I was wondering whether she held any animosity toward me for having disciplined her heir, whatever his name was, well ... I guess I have my answer.

She straightens, extending her hands to the crowd, a manic grin on her face.

"My people deserve some sport," she says, and the crowd goes wild, shouting and whistling. "Games, to honor our Lord Aenon's coming."

The crowd roars his name, feet pounding on the stone floors.

"Aenon! Aenon!"

"The best of Ocron, against the best of Roallac!" she bellows.

Across the arena, another grating lifts, and a large man steps forward. He's got a flimsy leather shield across his back, two wooden swords crossed over it in shameless mockery of a Shield's gear. His face is smeared with yellow paint, and a lion's mane is draped over his head like a hood.

This man is no warrior. He is big, but fat, any muscle hidden by a thick belly. He is an entertainer.

And I am the entertainment.

Mariana joins Evanthia at the railing, gripping it tightly.

"Don't underestimate him," Mariana hisses at the man.

He approaches me with a rolling saunter—he is a buffoon, but I don't even have the strength to roll my eyes at him. He steps on my tail, and the crowd roars its approval.

"Oops," he says, stepping back, a grin on his stupid face.

My tail is flattened where he stepped on it—it hangs limply as I try to pull it away from him, broken.

"This kitten is no challenge! I expected more!" the man roars. He draws his wooden swords and strikes them against each other, stirring the crowd into a seething mob.

"Take off his collar," Evanthia orders, a manic gleam in her eyes. "It's hardly interesting otherwise."

Mariana looks sharply at her, as if to disagree, but doesn't say anything.

The guards step forward and undo the collar with a click.

Immediately my body changes. The muscles swell, the broken bones begin to knit. My fur becomes glossy and thick.

And I still can't hear her. My Wren. Even with the collar off, I can't hear her. I bragged to Caelus once that I would be able to follow her across the continent by our bond—but what if she's gone somewhere I can't follow?

I stand, my claws digging into the sand, flexing, feeling my strength, my own magic flowing through me, healing me. I will tear this place apart, brick by brick, piece by piece.

And still the crowd roars.

Twice I have heard a crowd sound like that at the school as I waited for my games. Twice I have entered the arena and battled against every single Shield that Ocron could throw at me.

And twice I have emerged victorious.

This time will be no different.

And when I am done, when I get out of here, I *will* find my Mage, if it is the last thing I do in this world.

I bellow my challenge at Evanthia.

The guard nearest to me flinches, as does Mariana.

Evanthia does not.

"Oh, not as a tiger," she says to me, a wicked smile on her face. "As a man."

I flatten my ears against my skull, glaring at her, baring my teeth. I have no weapons—but as a tiger, I need none. My teeth can break bone; my claws are sharp as any knife.

Evanthia grins, like she was expecting this, and raises a finger. An attendant pulls the black fabric off the object behind her.

It is a cage, like a bird cage but much larger, glittering silvery white under the bright, cold sun.

A cage of starsteel.

And inside, wrapped in her black robe, her hair wild, her face streaked with dirt, is my Mage. Her hands are wrapped around the bars of her cage—she's trying to say something, but I can't make out the words.

I shift immediately, landing in a crouch in the sand before Evanthia. My chest aches, seeing her and being unable to get to her. Whatever pain they have inflicted on my Wren, I will give back to them a thousand-fold.

Still. The joy I feel at knowing she's alive, it's second only to the rage in my chest that this snake woman would keep her from me.

"Release her," I say.

Evanthia cackles, one pale hand on her chest, like I'm some courtier who has made an amusing joke.

"You are in no position to make demands," Mariana says.

My fingers dig into the sand.

"Play my game, and I will not kill her today," Evanthia says. "Give us a show. You are to be part of the celebration games as we await the return of my immortal father. And in return, I will not kill her."

"If he dies, she'll go gray," Mariana reminds Evanthia.

The woman flitters her hand in the air, like it is of no consequence.

Father, I realize, stunned. She called Aenon her *father*. I wonder if she means it literally, or if it's just a way to indicate how close she is to the god of water, like she's trying to impress the crowd listening to her.

"It will be amusing, at any rate," she says. "Go on, Shield. And make it ... entertaining." Her black eyes rake over me, slowly, assessing. Since I have shifted back to being a man, I am naked before her, before the crowd, and without any weapons.

If Evanthia hopes to humiliate me by making me fight this fool naked, she'll be disappointed. I stand tall, my body stronger moment after moment. There is not a single inch of my body that I am ashamed of.

I look back at Wren. Her face is pale, her jade eyes fixed on me. The collar caused me immense pain—I can't imagine what she's experiencing, completely surrounded like that. She was able to overcome the manacles before, but this is a thousand-fold more starsteel. I didn't know there was this much of it in the entire world.

"If I win against your fool, Wren will be unharmed. Your word on it!"

"Yes, yes, I promise," Evanthia says.

She sits back into her throne, accepting a goblet from one of her attendants and taking a deep drink. The crowd is silenced. She lifts a finger—

The fool behind me roars, coming at me with his wooden swords.

Distantly I hear Wren scream my name. The crowd goes silent except for the crunch of the fool's sandals on the sand, the panting of his breath as he swings.

I duck under his arm, landing a quick punch to his throat, cutting off his air. He stops, bending double, one wooden sword falling to the ground as he clutches his neck. I roll and grab it, landing on my feet.

The two guards who dragged me into the arena exchange a glance, then draw their own swords.

Each has a pair of gladiuses and leather armor, against me and my shabby wooden blade.

There will be no honor in defeating them, only the chance to live another day, to keep Wren safe, to come up with some kind of plan to get out of this place.

"Here, kitty, kitty," the fool says. He's wheezing, his face red under the smeared paint, and he comes at me when the guards do—two in front, one to my side. Five blades.

I leap to the other side, bringing my blade up. The sword from the nearest guard slices into it neatly—their swords are well honed, which will work to my advantage. I push the wooden blade against his sword until it splits in two lengthwise.

They advance on me again, an untrained mob, blades held high, confident gleams in their eyes.

But now I have two blades.

And now the thin pieces of wood are sharp.

The closest guard, the one who kicked me and spat on me, reaches me first. He wants to be the one to kill me, to claim the glory for himself. There's a confident, crazed gleam in his eyes. I leap out of reach, whirling on him, and dodge between him and the fool—

And bury one of my wooden spears deep into his flank, nearly to the hilt.

He howls and drops to his knees, dark blood seeping from the wound.

He drops his swords into the sand so both hands can clutch at the stake in his side.

I drop and roll, reaching for the hilts as I pass. The other guard sees what I'm trying to do and steps on one of the blades, but I'm able to grab the other.

Now it's one fool with a wooden blade, one guard, and me. In one hand, a metal blade; in the other, a wooden stake.

The fool, it turns out, is not as foolish as the guard. He breaks and runs back into the tunnel he emerged from. I spit in his general direction, then urge the other guard on.

"Come on!" I roar. "Let's get this over with!"

This guard is more cautious. He's lean and weathered, the quiet kind. His partner is still screaming for help on the sandy floor.

None comes.

None will enter this arena until Evanthia allows it.

The guard swings at me with his left hand and jabs with his right. It's a basic pincer maneuver, one I've taught a hundred times.

I lean back, avoiding his blades, and we circle each other, our feet scuffing the sand. The crowd jeers at me.

The man I staked lies still now, his eyes gone glassy. His life's blood soaks into the arena sand.

"End him!" the crowd yells. "Shield scum! *Hordearius!*"

The guard is wary, sweat gleaming on his forehead. He glances toward Evanthia—he doesn't want to be here either.

I glance toward Wren—my Wren, her face pressed against the bars of her cage.

The guard comes at me again.

With my left hand, I parry his sword with my wooden stake. The wood splinters, but I've caught his hand across the hilt, breaking the bones of his fingers.

And with my right hand, I stab him through the chest.

Blood bubbles from his lips, eyes wide, before he drops.

The crowd goes still.

Mariana is furious, her face red and lips tight as she glares at me.

Icicles hang from the railing where she grips it—I have no doubt she'd end me with but a word from her queen. I may be the strongest Shield in a generation, but against a Mage like Mariana, I don't like my chances.

Evanthia stands, starting a slow clap. The crowd picks it up cautiously, a ripple of sound only. Nothing like the cheers that sounded when they thought they'd see me die today.

"Well, little Shield, it seems you will live another day," she says, haughty. She whirls her black skirts as she turns, leaving the dais.

"Come on, then," a guard beckons from the tunnel. He's accompanied by a whole phalanx of armed and armored guards—they pour from the tunnel and surround me, swords drawn.

"Back in you go, kitten," he says, gesturing at the cart. He holds my collar in his hands, too bright in the sunlight.

He wants me to willingly go back into the cart, willingly let him put that device around my neck again? So that I can be tortured and tormented until Evanthia parades me out to perform for her again?

"Put it on," the guard says, advancing. "Or we'll start taking pieces from your pretty Mage. Fingers first, I think."

On the dais, the pair of guards beside Wren grin, one of them drawing a short knife. Wren lets go of the bars, shrinking back to the far side of the cage—but the other guard is there, prodding her with his own blade.

"STOP!"

They all freeze.

For one moment I pause, looking up at Wren, seeing the tears falling from her face. Then I hold my head high, walk to the cart, and get in. If they so much as touch her, I will have my revenge, now or in the afterlife.

I shift. I growl at the sweating man fastening the collar around my neck, memorizing his features—he will be the first to die when this is done.

And then I fall to the floor of the cart, my muscles no longer able to support my weight. My ribs crack under the weight of my body. Clumps of fur fall from my hide like snow.

The cart rumbles off, back into the darkness below the arena.

I have a lot of time to think while I'm stuck in Evanthia's dungeons. I have to conserve my strength.

And my mind wanders, which is a new thing for me.

Boredom. Worse than any physical torture, really. I don't like to just sit and think about things—I like to *do*.

But I sit. And I think about things.

I think about my sire a lot. The only people I'd claim as family are my mother and Adriana—I haven't heard from the rest, except Rea and Lukas, in ages, and I don't care to. We were often pitted against each other, growing up. Nestor trained us like he trained his precious horses—with discipline, and with the whip. His horses were known for their brutality in battle, how they'd shatter skulls with their hooves and tear the skin from men's faces with their teeth, as much weapons as the Shields who rode them.

His children were even worse.

I didn't grow up in a home so much as a training ground. I wonder about Wren sometimes, growing up in a lighthouse with a father who loved her, who loved his work—who was proud of his job and passed on that passion to his daughter.

I lost track of the number of bones I'd broken by the time I was seven. A broken bone was no reason to quit fighting—I fought my brothers with broken fingers, arms, ribs. I fought with a broken right arm, rebroken half a dozen times, since we healed so quickly, until I was finally as good with my left as my right. We would all be *dimachaeri*, two-handed sword wielders, or Nestor would kill us in the process.

I remember crying myself to sleep at night from the pain, trying not to wake my siblings with the sounds. They'd ridicule me the next day if they knew, and Nestor would punish me with more pain, and more, until I grew as immune to it as if I were made of stone. I remember my mother sneaking in to our shared room—a barracks, really—and smoothing the hair back from my forehead when I pretended to be asleep. She was a force of nature herself—a hawk shifter, like Adriana, and a quick, deadly fighter. Nestor frequently boasted of her ancestry, like she was one of his damned horses—a direct descendant of Odall. Sometimes I think he married her for the same reason he planned his stallions' pairings—for strength in the bloodline.

And bearing Rea killed her.

Six children she'd given him, though, he'd boast. A clear indication of Rigrasil's blessing on our family.

Our family. My parents are dead, and my siblings are scattered over the continent. Maybe my father's obsession with our lineage will live on through Lukas or Myron, or maybe Adriana someday. But not me.

I drift off to sleep, my mind still troubled. I dream a hazy dream of what might have been—of me and Wren, partners in our work and in life. Of a lifetime spent together, memorizing every inch of her, knowing every secret, having her trust and her heart. I dream of cubs playing at our feet, of daring deeds done and stories told of old friends during long evenings together. And I want it all—the adventure and the stability. The challenges of a Shield's work and the warmth of Wren's arms. Seeing her master her power, becoming a legend herself—and being there with her every step of the way.

I wake with an ache in my chest and dampness on my cheeks.

CHAPTER 44
WREN

Aris is alive.

Aris is alive!

When I saw him in the arena, standing tall, when Evanthia ripped the cover from my cage—words failed me. I thrust my hand between the bars, though there were hundreds of feet between us, like I could touch him.

He's alive! My Aris is alive!

The joy that flooded me was replaced by dread when Evanthia set her fool on him for the amusement of her mob—but I needn't have worried. There is nothing, *nothing* in this world that could harm my Aris. Not two arrows to the chest, and certainly not a few of her Black Water minions.

I doubt that Queen Evanthia will make such a mistake again. She toys with us both, like a well-fed cat that knows the mice are cornered, biding her time until the solstice.

But he's alive! The world seems a little less bleak, now that I know he's out there. He will never stop fighting for me, nor I for him.

I sit on the floor of my cold starsteel prison, drawing my feet under my robe to keep them warm.

But if Aris has been captured, then maybe Rafael and Remiel have been too. Gods, I can't imagine what she's done to them.

I shiver despite the warmth of my robe.

CHAPTER 45
RAFAEL

I've never been to Roallac before, but I can safely say that I am *not* a fan. It's not that it's not a pretty place—if you like swamps, and snakes, I guess, though what I could see of Soltaire when we were brought it was fairly impressive. But being chained in a cell isn't all that great, especially with the starsteel manacles we wear.

Aris is alive—of that much I am sure. Or he was, the last I saw him, though he'd shifted to his tiger form, which was fun. The guards did not like that at *all.* And that was, what, a day ago now? Two?

I let my head fall back hard against the wall, revisiting the moment over in my mind a thousand times. I had a choice—keep fighting or stop and try to save Aris. We were vastly outnumbered—but I couldn't lose another friend, not after Stefan and Dimitra. I did my best to tend his wound while keeping an eye on the enemy, but I think deep down I knew there was no way we were going to win. I don't know how they caught Remiel—while I was bent over, melting the ice arrows in Aris's chest, someone knocked me over the head. It *still* hurts, and there's blood matted in my hair over my right ear.

Still. We're alive. I'm just not sure how I'm going to get us out of this yet. And I pray to Ignatius that my right ear will stop ringing.

And then there's Remiel. Gods, I can barely stand to look at him. It's my fault he's even here—he should have stayed in the camp when Wren, Aris, and I took off to get some space. But no. I was selfish and asked him to come along. Not that we'd spoken much since that night before we crossed the Waist.

Just thinking of it makes me cringe. I had some sudden burst of boldness after talking to Wren and went in search of my foxy Shield. He was sitting by our packs, the only light that of a small spelled lantern at his feet, casting faint shadows around him. He looked like something out of a dream.

"I need to know something," I asked him.

In retrospect, it was quite the random outburst, but he didn't mind.

He looked at me, his hazel eyes flashing golden in the lantern light, and nodded to a seat on the rocks next to him. "Anything," he said.

I took the seat, a little farther away than he'd indicated, and took a deep breath.

"As a spy, do you know things about just Wren? Or me too?" I asked. It was fairly mortifying.

"I know that your Shield died," he said slowly. "That she was a fierce and noble Shield. And that it was Mariana's love for you that kept you from going gray."

I twisted my fingers together in front of me. How to explain Mariana? Behind that sharp tongue was a determined, passionate woman—I'd been fascinated, thinking I'd gotten through all her layers, that I'd truly known her heart. Even as she'd planned to steal the Book of Silver from us, she had still helped me when Dimitra had died. I could never forgive her, but my emotions regarding her were ... complicated.

"I have a habit of falling for the wrong people, I'm afraid," I said, planning to explain about Mariana.

Remiel inhaled sharply, and I realized that maybe he thought *he* was "wrong people" too, and that I'd totally screwed up any chance I might have with him.

"I hope you'll be more careful in the future," he said stiffly. Then he stood up. "I'm going to check on the others. It's almost time to go."

And I watched him walk away, my tongue frozen, unable to come up with any witty or romantic or even just banal words at all.

And now?

Now, ironically, he's stuck with me. Manacles on a Mage aren't any great inconvenience—they take away my ability to cast magic, but they don't hurt. They're cold, and I'm not thrilled with the chain linking my wrists together, and then linking me to the wall. I have about five feet of chain, barely enough to let me sit without stretching my arms out.

I look over at Remiel—my quiet Remiel, with hair like fire and a singing voice that must have been god-sent.

Manacles on a Shield ... those are torture. The magic of a Shield is deeper somehow, in their bones, strengthening their muscles, making them stronger and faster than the rest of us.

Without it, they wither. Remiel's strong legs look like twigs, his pants falling loosely around him, and they aren't sturdy enough to even support him. His skin is sallow and hanging from his arms, the freckles standing out like bloodstains, and his sparkling eyes are lifeless, dull. Even his hair has lost its luster. From the way he draws each breath, with a rattle and a heave of his thin chest, I can tell he's in immense pain, and I can't stand it.

So while I struggle to think of a plan, some way to escape this stony prison they've thrown us in, I cradle his head in my lap and smooth the hair back from his face, and I hum every sweet or funny song I can think of.

As if watching Remiel tense in pain with every single breath weren't bad enough, as if knowing Wren and Aris are also stuck here somewhere, as if knowing the solstice is coming and there is nothing in this gods-damned world I can do about it, as if all that weren't enough emotional torture—well, in walks Mariana.

She looks like all the hells. Gone is the sassy smile, the saunter, the flirtatious woman I loved. This ... this "woman" is positively feral. Her white-blond hair is braided, but pieces are all over the place, like she's been pulling at it. Her face is thin, her eyes wild. Her full lips are dry, pulled tight over her teeth. I am the one who lost my Mage, but she is the one who seems diminished. This is not the woman I chased, the woman who challenged me and tempted me and had me screaming her name until we both saw stars.

"Mariana," I say tersely. "You look ... well."

"Why are you here?" she asks. Her voice is shriller too.

Gods, what did I ever see in her?

"Your countrymen escorted us here. You tell me," I say.

She grabs the bars of our cell, glaring at Remiel's head in my lap, sneering at him, at the obvious care in my pose. "You've moved on quickly. Have you told him about me?" she says, like she has any claim on me at all.

"Mariana, dear, you are positively unhinged," I say. "And yes, Remiel knows about you. Fortunately, my taste in lovers has improved since we parted."

She *snarls* at me, baring her teeth like a rabid animal.

Remiel's face turns slightly in my lap, his tongue wetting his chapped lips, his throat convulsing like he wants to say something, but he can't. Gods, his pain is like a blade to my chest.

"Was there something you wanted? To gloat, perhaps?" I tear my eyes from his and stare down Mariana, hoping the false arrogance in my tone is convincing.

"Where is Caelus?" she hisses.

Well. That's interesting. Their claim is real, even if the rest of her life has been an act. Given Evanthia's rather public dismissal of Shields as useless—and therefore any Mage who is bound to one as somehow sullied—it must drive both of them completely nuts. The Mage who handed her the Book of Silver is bound to a Shield. I bet Evanthia can't decide if she wants to praise her or denounce her.

"So Evanthia hasn't been able to break your claim, then? How that must chafe you," I say.

She glares at me, the whites of her eyes now tinged red. I wonder when she last slept, or ate.

"Tell me! Or I'll take your handsome Shield apart, piece by piece," she says, eyeing Remiel. She seems thrilled with the idea.

I look down at him, his eyes closed, his forehead scrunched in pain. I can't even tell if he heard her.

"I have no idea," I tell her, smoothing the hair back from his face. I hope she believes me. "He left us in Basti to come find you. I assumed he'd beat us here."

She lets out a shout of frustration, slapping her hands against the bars and pacing.

"Tomorrow Lord Aenon will be brought into this world," she says, pointing a finger at me, the nail filed to a sharp point. "You and your friends are captured. Your army is miles away. *You* should have stayed *away*, Rafael."

"Well, why don't you release me, then, and I'll be on my way?" I ask. It's worth a try.

Her face softens, as if she actually cares about me, and for a moment—just a heartbeat—there is a glimpse of the woman I loved.

Then that woman is gone, and the Black Water Witch is back.

"There's no point. There will be no hiding when Aenon takes his rightful place beside my queen."

She turns to go—and I can't let her, not without knowing something first.

"Wait," I say. I lay Remiel's head down gently on a folded scrap of a blanket and grab the bars of our prison. "If you ever felt anything for me, tell me, are the others here? Are they alive?"

"Wren is held captive in a cage of starsteel," Mariana crows. "Your king is in shackles. And Aris—tomorrow he faces the queen's own hell beast. You should pray to your gods that he dies quickly."

She whirls and walks away, her shoes clacking against the stone.

CHAPTER 46
WREN

Caladrius meets me atop a mountain again, his hair long and black as night, his dark wings folded. I can't use magic in my cage, but somehow magic has found me *nonetheless. Typical.*

"Evanthia is Aenon's daughter?*" I blurt out.*

Caladrius looks at me for a moment, expressionless, before nodding.

I throw my hands in the air. "How am I supposed to beat her? I'm in a cage! *She will have Aenon sitting at her side, his magic in her own veins, and I can only see you in dreams?" It seems grossly unfair. There's no way Caladrius is* my *father ... right?*

"You have two mortal parents," he says, either guessing what I'm about to ask or reading my mind, which is terrifying and which I'd rather not think about further.

"Great. So I have no chance against her. Why did you even choose me? Why do *any of this?" I'm aware I sound like a whiny child, but I don't care. I'm tired, hungry; my back and shoulders ache from this stupid cage, and I watched Aris allow himself to be collared rather than allow harm to come to me. Even here, I can feel tears pricking my eyes.*

Caladrius is amused by me, like a lion might be amused by a mouse that dares bare its teeth at him.

"Your mother asked me to."

I stop.

"What?"

"Your mother. She was drowning, on the winter solstice. Her ship had wrecked on the shoals by your father's lighthouse. She prayed to me *that night—not to Aenon, who had ignored the pleas of her shipmates—to spare her life. In return, she offered me her firstborn. I think she intended to dedicate you as a priestess for my temple when you were old enough. It was the strength of her prayer, little mortal, that allowed my magic to cross realms. And when she landed, she married the first man she found, to make good on that promise. Your mother was an honorable woman."*

"She loved my father," I say firmly. "The sea brought them together. And he loved her, until the day he died."

Caladrius waves a hand, as if such emotions were inconsequential.

"The plague that took her—took them both—is but one manifestation of magic failing in your world. You need to get the books from Evanthia before it dies altogether—and you worry about whether or not your parents loved each other at first sight?"

"Yes!" I say.

I don't have many memories of my mother, and I won't have them tainted by anyone, least of all this arrogant god. In my memory, she is warmth and softness and a pair of dark, smiling eyes. I wonder, if she had lived longer, when she would have told me about the god of night. I wonder if I would have come into my power sooner, like elemental Mages do.

"I believe they did love each other, after a time," Caladrius says softly, his feathers fluffing and rustling a bit, like he feels uncomfortable with the thought. "I found a way to bring my magic into your mortal realm, as did Aenon. As did Rigrasil, far before any of the rest of us. You were all a fail-safe, nothing more. I intended to leave you ... dormant."

"Why didn't you give your magic to man before you all left the mortal realm?" I ask.

"People don't interest me. They generally sleep through the best part of the night. Why would I gift them with my own magic?"

"There it is," I say, shaking my head. Probably as much of an explana-

tion as I'm going to get out of him at this time. The mist swirls around my feet, the cold seeping into my bones. "Well, I am here now. So what do we do? How do I stop Evanthia?"

How do I get to Aris? Is Leo still here, somewhere? Gods, this is too much! Too much for any one person! My chest aches, like when I hold my breath underwater for too long and my lungs start to constrict for air. I wonder if there is even air here, in this between-realm place.

Regardless, I'm on the verge of screaming.

"Great magic has always required great sacrifice," Caladrius says. "It is the way balance has always been maintained in our realms."

Gods, he sounds as insufferably mysterious as Caelus did—though at the thought of Caelus, my heart aches anew. Why can't the gods ever speak plainly?

"So ... what? I need to kill Evanthia?"

"So bloodthirsty, little Night Mage," Caladrius croons. "She has two books in her possession, soon to be three, thanks to your bumbling. She will be stronger many times over when Aenon crosses. I applaud your self-confidence, but I think you might be outmatched."

"So what, then?"

"I don't know yet," Caladrius says slowly. "I'll be able to help you, to some degree, at sundown. And a sacrifice in the presence of the three books, with the intent made clear—that should be enough to send Aenon back."

"Should *be?" I ask.*

He shrugs.

"You and your 'balance,'" I grumble, thinking. So I must sacrifice something that is important to me. Does he mean ...?

"Aris?" I whisper. I don't mean to whisper, but I still hope he hasn't heard me.

Caladrius raises one perfectly arched eyebrow.

"You'd go gray if he died, and I wouldn't be able to channel any of my magic through you. That hardly helps."

I feel relieved, but also frustrated. I need to dig deeper. What could possibly mean more to me than Aris's life?

"So something that means a lot to the person holding the books needs

to be sacrificed, but not my life. That's not all that helpful." Inwardly I am relieved. If I had to give up Aris to save our world from Aenon, I'd do it. He'd want me to do it. Hells, he'd do it himself—and then I'd hate myself for the rest of eternity.

So what is it that is important to me, that I can sacrifice, to balance the immortal scales? My family and my home have already been taken away from me. I have nothing left to lose.

With a sharp stab of pain through my chest, I realize that's not true, and I fall to my knees.

I have a life that I love again.

I have a family.

One I've built—Aris, Rafael, Ismini and Aleka, Tekton and Delphine. What means the most to me?

They do.

I was raised in a lighthouse, kept away from people because the color of my skin made me different. Now my magic makes me different. When animals started coming to me … I thought it would be enough. Their friendship—without expecting anything in return—started cracking something inside me. And when I realized I loved Aris, my shell was shattered, my heart left wide open, and everyone else came flooding in after.

"Hurry up, Night Mage. I haven't got all night."

"You're mean," I say, running a hand over my face. I can't do it. If this is a dream, why do I still feel exhausted?

"And you are un ungrateful mortal," he says, shrugging. "But here we are. If you and I don't balance the world, no one will, and Aenon will not be a benevolent god to your kind."

I look up at him, so close to me now, the white-marble perfection of his face glowing with its own unearthly light.

He knows I've figured it out. I will give everything *to save the people I love. I can make the sacrifice, and I will.*

"You'll have to leave them all behind," he says, more gently than I expect. "I'll do my best to keep your Shield from going gray afterward."

I'm still kneeling on the cold stone, mist now curling around me, like it's a pet trying to offer comfort. I run my fingers through it, feeling numb.

If it is my death that will make this right, if my death from whatever power Caladrius channels through me will save Leo and Ismini and Delphine—and even Aris—then what choice is there, really? I look up at Caladrius, tears blurring my vision. I blink for a moment, letting myself think about all the futures I've envisioned, the ones where Aris and I are together—and as I exhale, I let them go. Caladrius will keep Aris sage. And Rigrasil will not let him go gray, not after all Aris has been through, after what he has done to get us here.

A thought occurs to me.

"You mentioned Rigrasil," I say, proud of how steady my voice sounds despite the cracking inside my heart. "Three children with their power directly descended from the gods. Evanthia. Me. And one of Rigrasil's line. Do you mean a Shield? Someone he's prepared for this, like you have prepared me?"

"Yes," Caladrius says, gesturing toward the edge of the mountain. "Have you not guessed?"

Out of the mist that surrounds us, a shape begins to form. It prowls toward me, eyes glowing like twin blue stars. The tail flicks, sending a swirl of mist spinning.

"Oh, shit."

CHAPTER 47
ARIS

I'm standing on a cloud. Or it looks like a cloud, but it's a firm surface. Like a layer of mist over hard rock. I shuffle my foot forward, feeling for an edge, but the surface extends in all directions from me. Nothing but clouds and endless blue sky above me, and a blazing sun. I'm wearing my Shield dress clothes, all black, with that stiff embroidered jacket with the collar that I hate. Despite the sun, it's fucking cold, and I'm glad for the layers, even if my neck itches.

There is nothing here from horizon to horizon—but in front of me, in the distance, the clouds coalesce into a shape. As it gets closer, I see that it has the figure of a man, though he must be nine feet tall, maybe more. He is tan and blond, wearing a Shield's armor—but gilded. The straps across his chest holding his shield and swords are a kind of flexible golden metal, as are the greaves, leather skirt, and sandals he wears. His chest is bare other than the sword straps, and there's not a single scar on him.

As he gets closer, I see that his eyes are as blue as the sky above us.

As blue as my mother's.

And as blue as mine.

He stops before me and crosses his arms, looking me over from head to toe like I'm a prize horse or something. He walks around me, nodding.

"Like what you see, then?" I ask, irritated. I'm standing before the god of day—*the founder of Shields, the father of the gods, and all I can think is* Why are my eyes the same color? *Is it a reflection of this place, with its wide skies? Sky blue for the god of day?*

My heart stutters in my chest. There's only one explanation that makes any sense. Adriana and I used to joke about how we were the only ones to inherit our mother's blue eyes—and I suddenly realize that Nestor must have come to the same conclusion. Adriana, as a hawk shifter, couldn't bring him the glory he'd always wanted. She'd never fight in the arena, probably never claim a Mage or go into battle. But me? The White Tiger? He was always harder on me than on my brothers and sisters. I assumed he hated me for a while, and then that maybe I impressed him more than they did.

But my mother could trace her heritage back directly to Odall. His Shield magic had been given to him directly by Rigrasil—and something in his strength had been passed on, from generation to generation. Nestor was not harder on me because of hate, or because I was the most promising of his children.

He was harder on me because he wanted to craft me into a Shield worthy of the line of Odall.

I still hate the bastard, but ... maybe I understand him, a little more.

"You'll do," Rigrasil says, breaking me from the whirlwind of thoughts. His voice rumbles across the cloud plain like thunder. "Why do you summon me, son of Odall?"

I drop to one knee. I've never knelt before another in my whole life, not even to Leo. Bowed, perhaps. But not knelt.

He must realize this and he raises an eyebrow, chuckling. The sound makes the clouds under me vibrate.

"Yes?" he asks, stopping his pacing in front of me. He waits, amused.

"I ... need your help," I say. Gods, those words sting like bees on my tongue. "Tell me how to defeat Evanthia, Lord Rigrasil." I do not avert my eyes—I'll kneel before my god, but he's caused me an awful lot of trouble lately. I can't manage to humble myself any further.

"Is that really what you wish to know?" he asks.

I shake my head. There's no point in lying.

"No. I want to know how to save Wren. But I can figure that out on my own. She's being held by mortals, and no mortal can stand against me," I say, now that I realize in my brain what my heart has known all along. "And I want to know if Dimitra is ... if she's ..."

"All answers come with a price," Rigrasil says. He gleams under the bright sun, and honestly, looking at him hurts my eyes, but I do not look away.

"Name it," I say. I will give anything he asks of me.

"Sacrifice is required," he says. "We gods love the mortals we made. Love them so much that we sacrificed our own existence in your mortal realm to give them the gift of magic. Dimitra gave up her life to save yours, an act that has brought her peace and honor in the afterlife. What is it that you love, that you would give up to defeat your enemy?"

Wren.

What I love ... it's Wren.

Fuck.

I ... I can't.

"You can have my life, if you promise that Wren will not go gray," I say. Part of me is relieved to hear that Dimitra has found peace, but most of me is vibrating with rage.

Rigrasil waves a hand, dismissing the idea. "You promised me that once before, remember? When you battled the dragon. I didn't accept it then, and I won't now. No, Aris—mighty, they call you. The White Tiger. It needs to be more*."*

I think back to the family tree that Nestor had me memorize when I was six. "Our line goes all the way back to Odall," he said, his chest puffed up with pride. But when I pointed out that it was not his *line but my mother's, he broke my wrist. A way to build my pain tolerance, he told my mother when she berated him later. But I knew then what it was—shame. It was my mother's line that held the magic of the First Shield, and that was something that Nestor would never be able to have. And it is his flaws, his desires, that run through my veins.*

"Glory," I whisper.

Rigrasil stands before me, studying me intently. What is it that would break me to give up, if not Wren? My legacy. My name, emblazoned in bronze at the school. My name etched on a tomb in the crypt, my deeds listed for generations to learn about. Aris the Mighty. Dragonslayer. *I've inherited Nestor's lust for glory, though the realization makes me sick.*

"I'll give it all up. My legacy. I'll give it all up. Please."

I hate that word. It makes me sound weak—but to Rigrasil, to keep Wren safe? There is no price I won't pay.

"When the time comes, you'll have to make a choice. Die and remain a hero, taking the risk that Wren could go gray—or live and save her and, in doing so, become the villain. You will break the Law of the Shields. And then you, Aris, son of my blood, will betray me."

I open my eyes. Was it a vision? A dream? A hallucination brought on by unending pain?

I groan, playing the conversation over in my head. Which law would I be breaking, anyway? There is only one way I can think of to do it, but I'm not sure what it means. Gods, I wish Caelus were here with me now. He'd know what to do.

As it stands, I puzzle the words over and over in my mind until they run together like bits of overcooked barley.

There is no way out of Evanthia's dungeons. The bars of my cell are thick and well maintained, even if I had the strength to try to bend them. Patrols of guards monitor the halls. I've seen enough of the outside of her swampy citadel to know that the walls are high and thick. I'm not sure even Ismini could knock one down—so my chances of getting rescued? Zero. I'm not prone to being dramatic—

not when it comes to things like this, anyway. And I'm not a pessimist either.

I'm a realist. I know my own strengths and those of my countrymen.

And we are all hopelessly outmatched, god blood or not. I will not despair—I don't know how to. I am the blood of Rigrasil, and I will not give up.

Evanthia comes to my cage the next day. Up close she is beautiful, in a dark and haunted kind of way. I am barely able to open my eyes to look at her. Being stuck in the collar overnight has weakened me to the point where even my heart falters, and I can think of nothing, nothing beyond the pain.

"Take it off," she orders the guards. I hear her voice as if from a very far distance. "I would talk to him."

They rush to reach through the cage bars and grapple with the collar. Once it's off, the pain eases, though not as quickly as it did the day before. My muscles begin to swell, my broken bones to knit. I am starving, parched—but I am alive. I've endured worse. Nothing comes immediately to mind, but I think it's true anyway, and that gives me courage.

"Shift, Shield," she demands. "Let us speak."

One of her attendants brings a polished stool for her, and she sits, regally adjusting her dress. There's a silver snake draped around her neck like a necklace, and I honestly can't tell if it's a cleverly crafted bit of jewelry or a live animal.

I've never liked snakes.

For a moment I stare her down. I don't want to do as she demands—I am not some puppet under her control.

But she has Wren, and Leo, and I dare not put their lives at risk.

I think back to the conversation, or vision, or whatever, when I spoke to Rigrasil. When he told me I'd have a choice—to die and remain a hero, or to live, and for Wren to live, and become the villain.

So how do I become the villain? How do I betray Rigrasil? The question ran through my exhausted brain all night, and I still have no answer.

So I shift, once more naked in the presence of the Snake Queen, and play her game, and bide my time.

"Bring him something to wear," she says, black eyes looking me over. A slight flush stains her pale cheeks. "To have him thus before me is ... distracting."

I give her a wicked grin, grasping the bars, leaning against them and staring her down while the guards rummage around. They find my clothing and toss it to me. I pat the pocket where I stashed my wolf tooth and dragon tooth, and the leather bracelet Delphine gave me—they are still there. I don't dare look at them, don't dare call attention to them, but I feel infinitely better knowing they are with me.

I pull my clothing on, not breaking eye contact with the queen. I don't fool myself for a minute that she couldn't try to have me killed here. Try.

She clears her throat.

"I've prepared a special challenge for you, Shield," she says, suddenly very interested in a speck of dirt beneath one long, pointed fingernail.

"Oh? I'm flattered," I say.

"Don't be," she says, voice sharp. "You are here for entertainment, nothing more. A sacrifice for our Lord Aenon, as is your little 'Night Mage.'"

"If you touch so much as a hair on her head, there will be no force —none of the gods or of man or Mages—that will protect you from me," I snarl.

She gives a small huff of laughter, but she won't meet my eyes. She glances over her shoulder, making sure her guards are there.

"I've heard a lot about you, Shield. From Mariana."

"Is that why you're here? To see for yourself if the rumors are true?"

"I'll admit, I am ... curious," she says. "You did well yesterday."

"I look forward to whatever you've prepared for me today."

"You won't be so smug later," she snaps. "Aren't you going to ask me to free you? Beg me to release your Mage and your king?"

I shrug.

"I have nothing to bargain with," I say truthfully. "Seems to me you've already won."

"Yes," she says smugly.

"Tell me," I say, looking at the collar her guard is holding. "Starsteel. Where did you get it?"

"*That's* what you want to know?" Evanthia says, arching one thin black brow. "My sire is the god of water *himself*, and you want to know about the collar?"

"I'm a Shield. I leave the heavy thinking to the Mages."

One of the guards chokes on a laugh.

"Lord Aenon's realm," she says haughtily. "Stars have fallen from the sky since the dawn of time, and most of them end up in the sea. My people have been collecting it where Aenon guides us."

"And you had a cage built, what, just in case you came across a Mage that a manacle or collar wouldn't work on?" I ask. That kind of mining from the sea, the craftsmanship ... Adriana was right—they've been planning this much longer than we realized. But why did Evanthia want Wren caged? Why not just dead? And myself, for that matter?

"I tell you this, *hordearius*," she spits, like the word has a foul taste in her mouth. "The gods gave of themselves when they gifted man with magic—and that magic must be returned. When my Lord Aenon returns to take his place beside me, the gift of a gods-blessed Mage must be returned. When Aenon drains the life from your Wren's body, when her blood, with its god-given magic combining the elements, soaks into the sand of the arena, Aenon's power will return once more to its full strength, and the world will once more *tremble* at his name."

CHAPTER 48
LEO

I pace the width of the cell—six paces—over and over and over again. I wonder how long it will take to wear a path in the stone of the floor. I recite the ancient words of Ocron's first poets until my throat is aching. I repeat my lineage out loud, back to the first king. I name every province in Ocron, then begin naming every city, town, and village in each province until the guards threaten me. I can't stop—I don't want to forget a single beautiful thing about my country while I'm here. I still hold out hope that my people—my brave, brilliant people—will find a diplomatic way out of this.

And if not, well, hopefully, Iraklis and Markos are on their way.

It's hard to believe this dungeon is part of the vibrant, well-fortified city around me. I was impressed by the city, by the water gardens and ponds and sculptures. Snakes are the subject of most art, being practically deified here.

It is the treatment of the *people* that is appalling. While I understand Evanthia feels she should unite our countries, her prejudices are not ones that I will accept in Ocron.

I blink—I've stopped at the end of my cell, and when I go to turn, I catch sight of a wizened old face. One I've known since childhood.

"I must be dreaming," I mutter.

The man before me is stooped, leaning heavily on a cane, with long gray hair and a longer gray beard. His eyes gleam like two sapphires in the dark. I've never seen him without his long blue robe—he looks smaller without them. Diminished.

"You're not dreaming," he says, a familiar smile tilting up one side of his thin lips.

I grip the bars, leaning my head against them until it hurts. "Am I hallucinating, then?" I have wondered about being poisoned. The Roallacan people seem to take an unhealthy amount of interest in poisons and venoms. "Or have you been captured too?"

Panos, my mentor, chief among the academic Mages of Estana, shakes his head wearily.

"Neither, I am afraid, Leo," he says. He hasn't called me that since I was a child. Ever since I was crowned, he's referred to me by title only. I frown.

"What are you doing here?" I ask. My head aches, my mind turning fitfully, like it is rusty from disuse.

He averts his eyes, focusing on some patch of dirt outside my cell. "You always were my brightest pupil," he muses. "I'm sure you already know the answer."

And I do. If he's here, it's of his own volition. He has betrayed me.

I grip the metal bars of the cell so hard that my hands ache. I scream, rattling them as much as I can—which isn't much, as it's a well-made cell—and push off the bars to pace my cell with renewed fury.

"You are here as Evanthia's guest, then?" I manage to ask through gritted teeth.

He nods, leaning heavily on his cane. "I am."

"Why would she welcome you when she has murdered so many of your brothers?" I ask.

He blanches at this.

"Unless," I realize, pain gripping my chest, "you had more to offer her than they did."

"That was a clever message you sent to your little Wren," Panos says.

I run back to the side of the cell he's on and stick my arm as far through the bars as it will go, trying to grab *something* so I can smash him up against the bars of my cell. *Wren.* He knew about my letter, and the code, which means any hopes I had that perhaps he'd given Evanthia the fake Book of Gold, the one on display in my vault, are dashed.

He's too far away. All I succeed in is looking foolish, before one of the guards brings his javelin down, hard, on my outstretched hand.

I seethe, bringing my injured hand back inside my cell. The fingers all move, so while it hurts, I doubt anything is broken. There is a welt already rising there, and it stings. I clutch it to my chest.

"Evanthia and I are old friends," he says, venturing a little closer now that he knows the limit of my reach. "I'd been looking for the Book of Gold for a long time. Age, it seems, has a way of making you look at things a little differently. My time here is at an end. I plan to go to the afterlife with my head held high, knowing I did all I could to bring my god back to his rightful place."

"You don't think betraying your country will count against you, then? There are special places in the hells for traitors, Panos," I remind him.

I think he turns a shade paler. In this dimly lit place, it's a little hard to tell.

Panos is here, and he's brought Evanthia the Book of Gold. She has everything she needs to bring Aenon to our realm, and there's absolutely nothing I can do about it while stuck in this cell.

"Panos," I whisper, leaning as close as I can. My hand throbs—maybe something *is* broken—but I try to touch him all the same. "Get me out of here. It's not too late to undo this." I've seen Panos conjure mists so thick I couldn't see an inch in front of my face, seen him freeze men solid when a pair of would-be assassins from the Isles tried to kill me as a teenager. This man could incapacitate these guards in the blink of an eye, and we could be out of here before even Evanthia was aware of it.

If I harbored any hope that perhaps my quiet old academic was here to rescue me, it is shattered by the pain I see in his rheumy eyes.

"Leo," he says fondly, laying his hand on my injured one. "*Heal.*"

A gentle blue light passes between our hands, and the pain vanishes. I flex my fingers, finding they have completely healed. How many times has Panos fixed me up over the years? Too many to count. He healed my scraped knees from fighting as a young child. This is the man who spent many sleepless nights poring over ancient texts to try to save my wife and unborn child from the plague. He cried with me at their burial. I counted him among my closest advisers.

And I have no idea who the man before me is at all.

"I have asked the queen for clemency," Panos says. He coughs a few times and clears his throat. "She's agreed to spare your life, but she will not let you go."

"If you're waiting for my thanks, they're not going to come," I say.

"She might still marry you, if I ask," he says.

I snort, incredulous. "I have no desire to be a part of any country where one group of people hold themselves in higher esteem than another, simply because they happened to be born with water magic. You know me better than that."

He gives me a sad smile. "Be well, Leo. And may Aenon have mercy upon you."

CHAPTER 49
ARIS

For this next challenge, Evanthia allows me to keep my clothing. She's even made sure I got something to eat—water and a bowl of some kind of grain-and-vegetable soup. It's like she wants me to be able to put on a good show today.

And I *will* win. Rigrasil's blood runs in my veins. In that bloodline is the strength of all my ancestors. Against a mortal foe, I cannot fail. I've decided that Evanthia doesn't really need to know about my revelation. She might decide that my blood will do for her creepy ritual as well as Wren's, and that Wren is therefore disposable.

I *have* to free Wren and Leo. I will find a way to bring down the Snake Queen. I will have my revenge on Mariana if it takes the last breath of my body to do so. I don't know how yet, but I *will*. The resolve gives me strength.

This time, I am escorted down the corridor by a phalanx of armed guards. They do not attempt to put the collar back on me and do not harm me. As we approach the grated door, one of them even hands me a pair of gladiuses. They are worn, but they are wrapped with fresh leather straps, and the edges are sharp. They were made in

Ocron, with Ocronian steel. I can see Tulliano's mark on the pommels. The guard offers them like he expects me to choose between them—but I take both instead.

Some prefer one blade and a shield, or the javelin. I prefer two swords—twice the offense, not saving anything for defense. Pretty much how I live my life. Or lived it, anyway.

"*Hordearius*," the guard growls, and he spits at my feet.

I consider running him through. I swing the blades, testing their weights. I can't help but wonder who they belonged to. Zale, maybe. My chest tightens at the thought.

The other guard raises the gate, and I step again onto the blinding sand of the arena. The crowd begins to roar, stomping their feet and raising their hands. This time, no one throws anything at me. No one insults me.

This time, I am greeted with cheers. The crowd is ready for entertainment.

And I'd be lying if I said it didn't cause my heart to beat a little faster, my chin to lift a little higher. There is nothing like the thrill of being in an arena.

Evanthia sits on her throne, as before. Behind her, as before, Wren sits in her metal cage. Her hands are wrapped around the bars, her face pressed against them. There is no way for me to get to her—and even if I could, there's no way for me to break the bars. I could see if the guards near her have a key, but I'd be overwhelmed by them before I could even try.

I settle myself to accept my fate. I spend a long moment looking at Wren, memorizing her. And then I look away, not wanting Evanthia to have any idea about how deep my feelings for my Mage actually run.

I look back at Evanthia. Today she wears blue in deepening shades, like the ocean. Her hair is left loose and flows like black water. Her crown is a tall, dark, spiky thing that sparkles in the blazing sun. It looks heavy. There's a giant black snake winding around the top of her throne, lazily rearranging its coils in the sun. She is too far away for me to make out what she's saying to Mariana, who sits straight-backed at her side. Mariana appears pale and gaunt, her lips a thin, flat line. I can't believe I ever found her attractive—right now she has all the sex appeal of a rabid weasel.

It takes me a moment to recognize the aged Mage on Evanthia's other side. Gone is the blue robe that once swamped him almost comically. Now Panos stands beside the Queen of Roallac in the garb of a soldier, the snake symbol eating its tail emblazoned on his chest plate. He stands tall—though ancient, he appears stronger now than he ever has. Was it all a ruse, then? How long has he been planning to betray us, to betray Leo, the boy he helped raise? No wonder he never claimed a Shield—he's been an agent of Roallac all along, maybe for decades.

There's a special hell in the afterlife for traitors like him and Mariana. And it will be my pleasure to send them there.

I wonder briefly where Rafael and Remy are, and the others. Mariana hasn't gone gray, so Caelus must be alive. I know Evanthia isn't strong enough to break a claim, at least not yet. Only a strong Wind Mage, or a chosen Head Mage, has that power. For all that the Mages of Roallac despise Shields, it is ironic that their own Mariana is tied to one, that there is no Mage in Roallac strong enough to undo the immortal bonds of the claim. It must really drive her crazy. The thought makes me smile.

Evanthia raises a hand, and the crowd settles. Around her are rows of men and women in blue—her Water Mages, the infamous Black Water Witches. Most of them have dark hair like her. I'd be surprised if they weren't related. One of them, a boy about Delphine's age, sits near Evanthia's feet—her new heir, then. I wonder briefly what happened to the other one, the one I'd... educated. I shrug, returning my attention to the sand, to the blades in my hands, the kiss of Rigrasil's light on my skin.

Evanthia gestures to a man on the far side of the arena. He raises the portcullis, but from a place behind a short wall, protected from whatever is going to come out of that tunnel.

The arena is silent. A man coughs. My grip tightens on my blades.

The sand beneath my feet begins to shake as something massive makes its way out of the dark tunnel. A quiet hiss fills the air—a collective inhalation of breath from the crowd.

This is no different from any other foe I've battled in the arena back at the school. No different from the other monsters I've faced before.

But as this one emerges, the hissing sound continues—from three wedge-shaped heads with hoods flaring attached to a single, massive body. I'll admit, it is an impressive beast.

A beast with *three* gaping mouths, each with fangs two feet long dripping with venom that sizzles where it strikes the sand, sending up puffs of smoke.

Fuck.

I back up, not taking my eyes off it. It rears up, lifting its three heads from the sand. The rest of its body is still inside the tunnel—gods, how long is this thing? Forty feet? More?

Doesn't matter. You cut the head off a snake, the body dies. It's the same with this beast as it is for the rock vipers and other serpents we have back home.

I glance back at Wren for one more moment, wishing I could touch her. I wish I could have told her what the god of day said to me.

That his magic flows through me, as potent as Aenon's flows through Evanthia.

And before this foe, I will feel no fear.

This one has three heads, though, and I only have two swords, so I'll have to be smart about my attack. I take inventory—I have the clothes I'm wearing, Delphine's leather bracelet around my wrist, Stefan's wolf tooth around my neck, and a long dragon tooth, hanging next to it until I can ask Tulliano to fashion it into a dagger for Dimitra's stele. It's not much of a weapon, though—it's fairly blunt, meant to be wielded by jaws with immense biting power.

There is the arena sand—maybe I can blind the thing long enough to get a sword through its necks.

Overhead a hawk cries, the sound piercing the stillness of the arena.

Like the sound has broken the snake from its trance, it snaps the focus of all six eyes onto me. On the back of each hood, the scales are yellow against the otherwise gray-green body, forming a false eye. The skin of its necks is flared, making them look bigger, wider than they already are.

Which is to say, really, *really* fucking big.

I adjust my grip on the gladiuses, glad that Evanthia gave me at least that much. It looks like all she really wants is to give her people a show, to make sure I don't die in the first thirty seconds of our match.

Well, I don't want to disappoint her.

The snake approaches me slowly, each head dipping in turn, assessing me, wondering how much of a threat I am. It completely ignores the people in the stands—I wonder if Evanthia is somehow controlling this beast. I don't like the idea. Is this another of Aenon's pets, like the kraken? I've never heard of a creature such as this. Caelus would know, I think.

Well, I killed Aenon's last pet, and I'll kill this one too. I don't have a choice. I have to win—I have to live.

I keep moving, running sideways, keeping my back to the wall of the arena. The snake has to keep turning to keep watching me, ensuring that only one of the heads is ever close enough to me to strike.

Eventually, the snake gets tired of playing, of watching.

The head closest to me rears back, hissing, the beast's mighty tail coiling—and it strikes with impossible speed, its scaled face brushing past me, close enough for one fang to graze my arm. A drop of venom burns my skin like acid, numbing my entire left arm instantly. I drop my sword, screaming from the pain—

And with my right arm, I swing my sword high and bring it down on the snake's scaly black neck.

The sword isn't that sharp, but it gets through the muscle and halfway through a vertebra before getting stuck. The snake recoils, the other heads hissing loudly, and the motion helps me rip the neck the rest of the way through. The head lands at my feet, sand melting from the acid blood. My left arm is now useless.

Well, one down, two to go.

I shake my left arm, willing my god-given healing powers to start working. *Come on, Rigrasil—don't let me fail now.* The venom has eaten through my skin, into muscle, which smokes and gleams wetly under the blazing sun. I've had worse injuries, though this one seems to be causing a disproportionate amount of pain.

But enduring pain is one lesson my father taught me well.

I roar at the beast before me, the crowd collectively inhaling in shock.

That's right. A Shield did that. A Shield from Ocron is going to defeat Evanthia's little worm.

The stump of the severed head has stopped bleeding, and the other two heads strike at me with rage, their snouts hitting nothing but sand, their jaws snapping shut on nothing but air.

The fingers in my left hand start to tingle. My other sword lies useless on the sand, now underneath the belly of the beast—but my right is slashing through the air, sending droplets of acidic snake blood like rain across the sandy floor every time I strike.

For a moment the two heads stop, rearing back again, stretching to the sky and hissing so loudly that the people in the stands cover their ears. I roll my left shoulder—the scar there aches, like the wound is fresh, but my fingers are moving again, and soon my elbow too.

A collective gasp from the crowd has me looking back at the snake—

At the bulge forming on the severed neck—

At the scaled skin stretching, something inside roiling—

At not one but *two* heads bursting out of the stump—

Leaving me with not two but *four* snake heads to deal with, all of them focusing their yellow eyes on me.

Seriously, Evanthia.

What—the—fuck.

CHAPTER 50
WREN

When the first snake head hits the sand, my heart leaps into my chest. Aris's left arm hangs by his side, useless, blood dripping from the fingertips. He leaps back, shaking his arm out, never taking his eyes off the beast in front of him. Panos and Mariana roar and cheer along with the crowd, caught up in the moment.

Overhead, a hawk shrieks. Something hard and thin hits the top of my head, bouncing off and landing at my feet. I bite my lip to keep from exclaiming from the shock—my guards' eyes are focused on Aris in the arena, and I don't want to draw their attention. I look up—the hawk wheels again, circling, before heading south, out of view.

I sweep my robe over the object at my feet and sink into a seated position. One of the guards glances at me for a second—let him think I am tired and just sitting to rest. He turns, squaring himself once more to the arena.

I reach between my boots. There is a flat, hard object there, about the size of my palm, like a flat pane of glass. I steal a quick glance down, not wanting to draw attention—the object is roughly diamond-shaped, faceted and glimmering like a black gem with flashes of red.

A dragon scale. *Delphine's* scale.

Is it a sign? Is Delphine bringing help? As much as my heart leaps at the idea, she's just a girl. I don't want her involved in this mess. I don't want her in harm's way. Perhaps the scale is the message itself—harder than any man-made substance, hard enough to turn steel aside.

I grasp the scale and scratch tentatively at the thin sheet of starsteel below me.

It parts like butter. Apparently, dragon scales are sharper than any mortal knife.

"Thanks, Adriana," I whisper.

I tuck the scale into my boot—I'll have to time my escape carefully. It would be best if I could wait for night, when I'd have my magic to aid me. Hope flutters wildly in my chest, even as a cold sweat trickles down my spine.

I can only hope that Aris will last until the sun sets.

And then I will take this whole awful island down.

CHAPTER 51
ARIS

Aenon is really starting to piss me off. I spare a quick glance at Evanthia—she's sitting on her throne, smug. Even Mariana looks a little pleased.

Shit.

All right. One good arm, one sword, four snake heads.

Even for me, those aren't great odds.

I look to the sky—the hawk is gone, and the sun has started to dip below the edge of the arena. I'm not sure what Adriana is planning, and I hope to Rigrasil that she has help, but I need to keep going. I need to keep the attention of the arena on me, on the snake, and I need to not die.

All right.

Cutting the heads of the snake off—bad idea.

But if I can get to its chest ... if the body dies, then the heads have to die. Not even four magic snake heads can survive without a beating heart, or survive exsanguination. I hope.

This snake does not have impenetrable scales like the dragon at Abelon did, like Delphine does. My blade was able to cut right through them. I glance at its chest, about eye level from the ground now that all four heads are weaving through the air.

"Kill him!" Mariana shrieks, her face livid with rage. She's grasping the railing tightly, leaning over.

I hope her fear that I will yet survive this beast is warranted. She knows me better than Evanthia does—I cringe to think of exactly *how* much better—and somehow that gives me confidence. My enemy is worried. Good.

I adjust my grip on the blade with my right hand. My left is weak but functioning. I raise my right arm, looking for a good opportunity. I'll have to time this perfectly.

The snake chases me around the arena. Despite the cold, sweat starts to sting my eyes. One of the heads strikes at me—the jaws snap closed, catching the edge of my shirt on a fang, and it yanks me to my knees as it pulls back before it rips free. The other three heads seize the opportunity, mouths gaping as they coil back ...

In one motion, I heave myself to my feet and arch back, throwing my sword with every ounce of strength I can summon, aiming for the beast's chest, where I hope its fucking heart is beating.

With impossible speed, the snake moves, the blade harmlessly flying past to wedge into the arena wall beyond.

Well, fuck.

A roar of approval goes up from the crowd, cheering for my doom.

The sun slips a little farther below the horizon.

The crowd murmurs, parting a bit on my right.

And a dark figure leaps the arena railing, booted feet hitting the sand hard.

The snake's heads whip one by one from side to side, now faced with this second threat.

The man moves swiftly toward me, a blade in either hand, his yellow eyes flashing.

"Need a hand, brother?" he calls.

Caelus. *Thanks, Rigrasil.*

"It's about time," I call back.

Fuck, I'm glad to see him. First Adriana, now Caelus? I can only hope that means the others are somewhere nearby. I sneak a glance at Wren—she's sitting in her metal cage, all the way on the far side, eyes wide. Evanthia is clutching the arms of her throne and looks royally pissed. Panos looks pale, and I watch him dart away, into the bowels of the arena.

Mariana, I am pleased to see, has gone completely white, frozen like the ice princess she is.

Caelus tosses the hood of his robe back and hands me a gladius.

The snake heads are having a hard time deciding what to do. They want me, but they're also distracted by Caelus, who's shouting and slicing at whichever comes near, staying between me and the snake, giving me a chance to recover.

He makes sure that Mariana sees him, locks eyes with her.

"STOP!" Mariana shrieks.

A ball of water forms around each snake head, coalescing from the humid air—just the same way Mariana killed that troll in the caves, forcing water into its lungs, drowning it on dry land.

If Caelus is bitten—if Caelus is killed—Mariana will go gray.

"I know my Mage," Caelus says, chuckling. He's counted on her desire for self-preservation, and it has paid off, for the moment.

"Now what?" I ask him.

"I was hoping you had a plan," he says.

He's grinning—gods, I don't think I've ever seen him look so alive before. He's lost weight, and a shaggy brown beard has overgrown his face, but he looks possessed, a man on a mission—to regain his honor, or to die trying.

"Stay alive. Kill the snake. Kill Evanthia. Free Wren and Leo and the rest. Not necessarily in that order," I say.

The snake heads are whipping through the air, shaking, rubbing themselves against the walls of the arena, trying to dislodge the water that holds them captive. Its tail whips across the sand, and we leap over it.

"Are Markos and Iraklis with you?" I ask.

"They'll be here soon," Caelus says. The snake heads continue to whip around, and we have to duck and move to avoid getting smacked. "Head Mage Iraklis took down a section of the wall."

There's a commotion in the stands. Evanthia is pointing at Mariana, furious. People are shouting, and then guards are grabbing Mariana, forcing her hands down, one of them clapping a hand across her mouth. I think she bites it—the guard reels back, shaking his hand. Another guard takes his place, and then she disappears beneath the railing.

The orbs of water fall away from the snake's heads, splashing heavily into the arena sand.

Evanthia gets up, hands outstretched, mouth whispering words that I can't make out. A blast of ice shoots from her hands between Caelus and me, and in its path sprouts a wall of blue ice, like the one Mariana made in the dragon's cave, and at least as tall. We are divided from each other now, the arena in two rough halves.

And the snake is on my side.

CHAPTER 52
CAELUS

I've spent the past few days blending in to the Soltaire ungifted population. I'm taller and stronger, but with a little stooping, my wild hair and beard, no one even looked twice at me. I wasn't able to find a way into the palace, though—and Mariana never came out. I could smell her, like the cold wind of winter, tantalizingly close but ever out of reach.

When Queen Evanthia announced the games, I didn't guess that it would be Aris in that arena. He stood proud and tall, and he dispatched her champions with speed. I spent the rest of that night trying to break into the palace dungeon to rescue him and Wren, to no avail.

But it wasn't a total loss. I saw where they kept King Leonidas, and though he appeared worn, he looked healthy enough, thank Rigrasil. I was able to get that information out to Commander Markos via his scouts. And I was able to sneak into a storage room near the cells.

And then, I bided my time, waiting for Aris to be paraded out again. This time, I was waiting for him. This time, I'd smuggled swords for both of us and hidden them under my robe. Since the guards assumed I was ungifted, no one even bothered to search me. I was shoved and spat upon, but so were the rest of the nonmagical men and women here. But I was no threat.

Queen Evanthia's hydra was a surprise. I'd only read a brief mention of the beast in one of Tekton's books, that they were semi-aquatic, as their name suggested, and therefore under the domain of Aenon. No one had seen one in centuries.

What better beast for the Snake Queen to send against mighty Aris than this?

And I leaped to his aid at once. How could I stand before Rigrasil, my head held high, if I did not go to the aid of my brother? The third law of the Shields would be my downfall. I had no doubt, though, that Mariana would not allow this foul beast to kill me.

And now, like the predator I am, I slink back into the shadows.

And I bide my time.

CHAPTER 53
WREN

The sun is setting, but not fast enough. Aris and Caelus have caused a distraction in the arena, getting Mariana and Evanthia and even my guards to focus on them. I scoot to the back of my cage, where it rests against the wall. Under my robe, I wiggle the scale free of my boot and begin to press it against the starsteel at my back.

I don't dare take my eyes off the arena, but I move my hand back and forth in a sawing motion. The edge cuts into my palm, and I can feel the scale grow slick with warm blood, but I keep going. I'll have to cut through at least two bars and hope I can bend them—or I'll have to try to stand and do this again, making four separate cuts through the bars. I'm grateful for once that I am small. I'd have to remove twice as many bars to break Aris out of this cage.

The four-headed snake is chasing Aris around. He's slicing at it, whirling away, dodging and leaping, more on defense than offense. Is it possible he's outmatched? Or is he buying time? The sun has descended to no more than a sliver of light above the horizon. When night falls, the winter solstice will be upon us.

I push harder—the first bar gives, and I scoot a little to the side to work on the second bar. *Come on.* I have to switch hands. My right palm is crisscrossed with thin lines that ooze red, and I wipe it against my robe.

My robe. The robe that Ismini and Panos imbued with every protective spell they could think of.

I wrap my left hand in a fold of the cloth and go to work again. The spelled silk keeps the scale from biting into my palm, so I push harder, faster. I have to get out.

CHAPTER 54
ARIS

I slice at the snake, opening as many wounds as I can, hoping to at least weaken it. I manage to cut off the tip of its tail—which does *not* regrow—and the four heads screech in unison. I can only imagine that they are swearing at me, and I grin despite myself. I am covered in sweat and sand, but I'm still up, still running, still swinging. I can't see Caelus on the other side of the ice wall—I hope he's escaped, disappeared back into the crowd, before Evanthia's guards can grab him.

One of the heads strikes at me, its snout hitting the sand beside me, hard, and coming up bloodied—but not before its fang rakes my back, sending a lightning strike of pain down my spine. My sword flies from my hand, landing in the sand several feet away.

My left leg goes numb from the venom, and I drop to my knees, unable to stand. My back is on fire, the pain so immense I can barely focus.

This is it. I will die before this beast—I look up at Wren, still huddled in the back of her cage, her face flushed. *Gods, she's stunning.*

The last of Rigrasil's golden light glides across her face and winks out, the day done at last.

Evanthia shouts in triumph, her face contorted from her bloodlust.

I grasp my necklace, and the two teeth hanging from it. One is from a massive wolf that attacked Stefan on one of our adventures. He wore it the rest of his life—and I'll wear it the rest of mine.

My fingers cross to the other, larger fang—taken from the dragon at Abelon, the one that killed Dimitra. Well, I'll be joining both of them soon enough. The dragon was the god of fire's final obstacle before ...

My fingers tighten around the tooth.

My sword is useless against this foe. I told myself that no *mortal* enemy could stand against me, not with Rigrasil's blood in my veins.

It would take the magic of a god to defeat a beast like this, I think.

Well, it's as good an idea as any. I can't say that I have a lot of options.

I'll have to be quick. My legs tingle, but they won't move, and my back screams in pain. A thousand possible futures flash through my mind, lives I might have lived—all of them with Wren at my side—and I prepare myself for what I must do. So much for Rigrasil's faith in me.

The body of the snake ripples closer. It knows it has me. It knows it doesn't have long to wait. It takes its time, coming up in front of me, each head vying to be the one closest to me. One comes so close that I can smell its breath, reminiscent of its past victims, of death and decay, of swamps and mud.

The head closest to me snaps at the other three, asserting its dominance. The other heads lower themselves, their hoods dropping in a show of submission. The dominant head weaves from side to side, massive tongue flickering, tasting my scent on the air.

The crowd is silent, waiting to see how Aris Valorius, the Dragonslayer, is killed.

Not without great effort, as it turns out.

The snake head rears back, mouth open wide, a terrible hiss issuing from its jaws.

And then it strikes, faster than the eye can follow. I fall to my side, letting the snake miss me, feeling its fetid breath against my skin as the jaws snap shut on nothing but air.

And as it withdraws to make a second strike, I turn, grasping the dragon tooth with both hands.

And I plunge it deep into the snake's yellow eye.

The eye steams and hisses at the contact, like plunging a red-hot sword into water. The snake rears back, ripping the tooth from my hand and leaving it embedded in the ruined eye.

The yellow eye turns gray, like stone—and ribbons of gray spread out from the eye, turning living black scales to gray rock, turning the face, then the neck, into nothing more than a large garden statue. The other heads shriek, pulling away to distance themselves from the change—but the magic is spreading rapidly. One of the heads bites into the neck of the transforming head, trying to sever it before the stony gangrene can spread.

But it continues anyway, to the distant howls of Evanthia, and in little more than a minute, it is done, and my dragon tooth falls to the ground, smoking.

Aenon's many-headed snake monster is defeated, frozen in agony, eternally entombed in rock.

I test my legs—they're shaky, but they hold me, and every step I take grows more confident. I lift the tooth, still intact, and loop it back onto my necklace, making sure I keep eye contact with Evanthia the whole time. She's furious, her hair streaming all around her, her pale face blotchy with rage. She raises a finger and points to her guards, screeching.

"Bring me the books!"

CHAPTER 55
WREN

I rise to my feet, the scale still firmly clenched in my hands and a fold of my robe.

When Aris defeated the serpent, my heart was beating so fast I thought it might burst from my chest. With every strike of one of those horrible heads, my breath stopped. I don't care about going gray—but I can't live in a world without Aris.

I get to work on the first bar, a cut higher up, so I can hopefully remove this section. I'm not having much luck bending the metal. No one notices me—the queen appears to be quite mad at the death of her pet, and my guards have moved toward her to watch.

Leo is led out in chains. His fine clothes are dirty, his face unshaven and haggard—but he walks upright, if stiffly. My heart aches to see him.

He is followed by Rafael and Remiel, also in chains. Rafael is dirtier than I've ever seen him, his face drawn. Remiel leans heavily against him. Their chains must also be starsteel, for Remiel's steps are weak, and even from here I can tell he looks half-dead. I remember how Aris looked with his collar on—I'm surprised Remiel is able to bring himself to walk at all.

My heart sinks into the pit of my stomach, and my fingers grow cold.

We've failed. Gods, how I've failed. I look to Aris, hoping against hope for some sort of sign, some indication that he has a plan, some way out of this—he looks back at me, eyes steady.

He shakes his head.

And just like that, my heart breaks. I slump to the floor of my cage.

Evanthia has us at her mercy. She has all three books. The sun has set—the solstice is upon us. The veil between our realms is thinned. I am in a cage; Caelus has fled; Aris is spent; and Leo, Rafael, and Remiel are imprisoned.

So I do the only thing I can do. I have one chance left, and I can't wait any longer. I stand back up, the scale gripped tightly in my hand. I press my back against the cage, feeling for the bars. One is hanging by only a sliver, the other has one more cut to go. Then I will get out of here. There will be no quarter given—I will wipe Roallac from the map. Aenon or not, I will *not* give in to despair.

But then a thick hand circles my wrist, tugging hard, twisting until I'm forced to turn or break my own bones. The scale is plucked from my fingers.

"Well, what have we here?" a coarse voice growls. "Trying to cut free of your cage? The queen won't like that, little bird."

I turn and find one of the guards pressing his ugly face against the bars, the sharpened scale glittering like a gem in his scarred fingers. I can't reach the scale—he's too tall, his arms too long.

But I can reach his face.

I punch, hard, the way Aris taught me—and I'm pleasantly surprised to feel the crunch of bone underneath my knuckles as his nose breaks, blood spraying across his face.

"Bitch!" he yells, grabbing for me—but his eyes are watering, his vision poor, and I am too quick.

I reach for the scale, but he tosses it behind him, and I watch helplessly as it clatters down the stone stairs. So I plaster myself against the far edge of my cage, grateful for the moment for its protection, if I cannot be free of it.

He's quickly joined by two other guards, and they waste no time in finding some old spear shafts to lash to the bars I've weakened. They tie the wood to the starsteel with thick, rough rope and then wind chains around that, for good measure. Some part of me is pleased that they think I can break out of this cage—me, the small girl from Spit.

No. I am the Night Mage, the harbinger, and I will be the ruin of Roallac.

Resolve tightens in my gut.

I don't know how, but I *will* get out of this.

By now, Evanthia has descended from her perch to the arena, on the side of the ice wall that keeps Aris from her. He is once more thwarted by a wall of ice, and he hates it. He races from one end to the other, looking for a way around, but a knot of Queen Evanthia's guards has formed at either end.

My Aris is trapped.

Queen Evanthia preens from the arena floor, her court arrayed before her like rays of the sun. Three of them come forth to kneel before her and offer their tributes—

Three books, metallic and glittering, even in the fading daylight.

A fourth courtier comes forth, and all I can do is watch as he presents her with an enameled box.

"The bones of my mother," she shouts, and the crowd hushes, a thousand people focused on what she is about to do.

Aris has been captured, forced to his knees, a mob of guards swarming him, binding him. He roars—I can hear him across the arena—but then he disappears, shielded and guarded by the enemy.

Caladrius, if you can hear me, I am so close. Please.

Evanthia raises her arms. A bolt of blue light flashes from the sky and strikes the man holding the enameled box, leaving nothing but charred, molten sand behind. Evanthia has sacrificed the bones of her own mother—Aenon's lover—to meet the god's requirement, to activate the books. The men holding the books exchange worried glances—I guess they didn't realize their own immolation might be a part of the process.

The books begin to glow. The people holding the books look nervous, pale—but they don't move.

"My Lord Aenon, I summon thee forth from thine immortal prison. Come, and rule Roallac at my side."

A storm gathers overhead. The clouds swirl, and the sky grows black. Blue light suffuses the arena, emanating from Evanthia's hands, like a small blue sun. The light disperses into a hundred smaller stars, which float about the arena and settle like a hundred torches to light the arena. A cold, blue version of the spelled fire Rafael can cast for light without heat, like the blue torches I saw when the Roallacan Mages pulled me into their underwater tunnel.

Lightning and thunder continue overhead, though no rain falls. Evanthia shakes her hands at the sky, swaying as if in a trance. I can't look away, though tears are falling from my eyes, dripping from my chin. A chant goes up from the crowd: "Aenon. Aenon."

For a moment, nothing happens, and I allow myself to dare hope that her ritual had some fatal flaw—then there's a flash of lightning, a crash of thunder so loud that people scream, falling to their knees. The ground quakes, roiling beneath us like waves.

And before Evanthia now stands a massive man, twice her height.

No, not a man.

A god.

His skin is blue, his hair matted and twisted, hanging down his back. His hair and beard are the colors of the sea—shades of green and blue, tangled, dripping. The smell of brine assails me.

Queen Evanthia kneels, and the rest of the arena drops as well, some flat out prostrating themselves before their god.

Aenon, the god of water. He stretches, looking up at the sky—

then he looks at me, a smirk on his handsome face. I feel it like a punch to my gut.

"My lord," Queen Evanthia says, rising.

Aenon extends a hand to her, and she takes it without hesitation, beaming. She kisses a large, rough ring on his finger before releasing it.

"You did well, mortal daughter," he says. He moves past her, his hands flexing. Water coalesces around him, dancing like droplets on a hot pan. The movements of the water seem a little ... erratic. Like maybe Aenon isn't fully in control of his own power yet, or like he's forgotten how to use it here, after so many years.

He looks up at me. What I thought were ropes of seaweed around his neck are actually layers of necklaces, strung with metal beads that clink and chime as he walks. They are entwined with seaweed and barnacles; some of them look older than others, tarnished or blackened with age. A few glimmer more brightly.

It occurs to me then that the beads are not beads.

They are rings.

My hands clench.

The rings that my people, the people of Aclines, have thrown into the sea. It was our tradition, a way to honor the dead by throwing a ring into the sea—usually it was a wedding ring. My people, now part of Ocron, didn't believe in Aenon, or in the other gods. We worshipped the sea, which gave us life on our tenuous rocky coast. The idea that Aenon has our rings in his possession makes me feel sick to my stomach. I want to tear the rings from him, each one, and return them—if not to the sea, then at least back to my former country, where the dead can be properly honored.

Aenon sees me glancing at his collection, and he grins broadly. His teeth are strong and white, though dotted with barnacles and—I cringe—the odd crab that crawls between them. He picks through the necklaces, looking for something in particular. He plucks three rings off with a little puff of magic and extends a hand so I can see them.

Two are achingly familiar, matching iron bands, one large and one small. The third I've never seen before—a silver band set with a green stone. I clutch the amulet I still wear around my neck, the one that Aris gave me, the one that despite everything, I have never taken off. The stones are the same shade. This is the one that Aenon singles out, turning it over in his massive blue palm.

"Of course, you can imagine my initial pleasure at getting this ring—thinking that somehow you'd been killed, and your ring thrown into the sea like your dear parents'. Pity." Aenon closes his fist. In another small puff of light, the rings are back on the cords around his neck. "Of course, we'll make sure you rejoin them soon."

Aris looks at me, clenching his jaw so tightly I wonder if his teeth ache. He doesn't blink, just watches for my reaction.

My ring, Aenon called it. Judging by the look on Aris's face, he bought it for me. My heart seizes, a thousand thoughts flitting through me. I wonder when he threw it into the sea, right into Aenon's clutches. It must have been on *The James*, when he thought I'd betrayed him.

I square my shoulders. I give Aris a nod—his shoulders relax a little, and he gives me a nod back.

One way or another, I will get those rings back. All three of them.

Aenon and Evanthia are talking, gesturing toward my cage. More guards surround me, preparing to move my cage down to the arena floor. Aenon throws his head back and crows with excitement.

"When I take your life's force, my strength will be returned, and I will *destroy* all who stand against me!"

Well, I've been wondering why Evanthia went through all the trouble of making this cage when she could have just killed me. So Aenon needs to kill me, himself, to restore his power? He looks plenty powerful now. I can't imagine what he'll be like when he's at full strength.

Not that I'll be around to see it, I think deliriously.

Well, Aenon will *not* have me. Caladrius said I'd have to let everything go. Was this what he meant? That I need to kill myself before

Aenon can do it? *I'll do all I can to keep Aris from going gray,* he said. I thought he meant channeling his power through me would kill me—but if this is how I save my friends, if this is how magic is mended, then I will see it done. I clench my fists tightly, my resolve firm. I wish I'd held onto Delphine's scale.

Aenon turns, extending his hand to Evanthia for the books. A trio of men holding lyres begin to play, their melody desperately trying to make the mood festive.

The clouds overhead begin to glow golden, like the sun is rising—but the sun has set, and the crowd looks toward the sky with confusion, a murmur rumbling. Is another god joining us, then? Helene or Ignatius?

The clouds glow brighter and then boil, parting—

And they reveal not a god but a black-and-red dragon with great feathered wings, flame already pouring from her mouth.

"Delphine! *No!*" I scream. I scream it again and again until my throat is raw, until my voice breaks, banging my hands desperately on the cage—she *cannot* be here. Against Aenon, not even a dragon stands a chance.

None of us does.

A dozen Water Mages channel their power, and a deluge of water coalesces from the air, streaking toward her—her fire is mostly extinguished before it can reach the crowd. Vapor envelops the arena, fire still pouring from her throat.

Mariana shrieks—she knows who the dragon is. And—I hope—that means that there are others not far behind her.

Delphine whirls, and her fire lands on the wall of ice, reducing it to a cloud of steam, obscuring her outline. She banks hard, dodging shards of ice being flung at her. A few bounce off her stomach, but one punches through the sail of her wing, and her head jerks to the side in pain.

Or so it seems.

She's headed right at me, and her fire is still going. Like in

Abelon, once a dragon's fire is ignited, it burns and burns until the dragon's stores of accelerant are gone.

I grab my robe and pull it over my head, crouching to make myself as small as I can in the bottom of my cage. The heat is immense as Delphine flies past. Under the edge of my robe, I can see the intense light of her flame, the heat rolling through the air trapped with me like a physical force. I try to breathe shallowly, but I can feel the air burning my face. Tears are streaming down my cheeks, and I have to squint to see. I hear the guards beside my cage scream and run.

At my feet, a puddle of molten starsteel begins to form.

My boots are smoking. I try to stand on a corner of my robe, not wanting to lift the edges of it even the slightest bit. The world around me is nothing but smoke and heat.

I hope the spells that Panos and Ismini put into this robe hold—if there's one lesson I learned about dragon fire, it's that it can melt anything.

Even metal.

But not a Mage's robe.

Something heavy drips onto the outside of my robe, but the black silk does not give way. It heats up until I can feel the skin on my back blister, but it does not break.

A blast of water strikes me, tearing the robe from my hands, knocking me over. The Water Mages—Queen Evanthia and Mariana included—are aiming blast after blast at the flames, desperately trying to put them out.

Aenon has raised his hand, sending an uneven tidal wave of water across the arena. The flames hiss and turn to vapor. Another wave of his hand, and the vapor dissipates.

I look up—the sky overhead is clear and scattered with stars, a full moon shining down on us. Delphine is gone, flown away. I am grateful for that.

And there are no more bars of starsteel between me and that

night sky. They stand like so many unattended candles, nothing more than molten nubs around me.

I look up and meet Aris's eyes. He's staring at me, two guards holding either arm to keep him restrained.

I think of what Caladrius said, about the sacrifice I'd need to save the people I love.

And I let everything go.

CHAPTER 56
ARIS

Wren explodes, a flash of jade light rippling from her across the arena. The guards holding me try to shield their eyes—and when they do, I leap with all my might, ripping their hands away. My own hands are tied behind my back, thick rope so tight that I can barely feel my fingers.

Fingers that are now sprouting two-inch claws, which make short work of those ropes.

I roar, rolling my neck, shaking out my left shoulder—I am surrounded by guards, but a Shield is never unarmed. I leave my hands as tiger paws. It is obvious these idiots have never had to deal with a Shield before—a deadly mistake on their part. They are torn between watching Wren, trying to recapture me, and trying to get away from me.

I slash at wrists and knees, necks and groins, aiming for arteries and tendons. I don't need to kill them—just get them out of my way. The animals of Roallac have joined our cause, too—the giant black snake I saw on Evanthia's throne is now squeezing tightly around one of the guards. I can hear his ribs snapping, one by one.

Snakes pour out of every crevice, searching out Roallacan soldiers and biting and squeezing. The Water Mages attempt to wash them away, but Wren's magic, the magic of Caladrius, is more powerful by far, and they keep coming back. Soon men across the arena are screaming, already foaming at the mouth, their bodies bent in spasms.

I spare a glance at Wren—she is levitating, borne on currents of her own magic the way I once saw Saroya fly to Estana. Her eyes are two green stars, and bolts of green lightning circle her in rings of pulsing light. Aenon, Evanthia, and even Mariana are squared off against her. Mariana is sending bolts of ice at her, but they never make it past the lightning barrier. Inexorably Wren makes her way down to the arena floor, floating as lightly as a feather, as unstoppable as an avalanche.

Caelus is soon at my side. I grab a pair of swords from one of the fallen guards—inferior blades, but they'll do. We make our way through the chaos to Rafael and Remy. Rafael points to one of the fallen guards, and Caelus finds the keys to their manacles underneath a large brownish snake.

The snake ignores him completely but rather searches out the nearest Roallacan soldier like a loosed arrow.

Rafael might not be that useful against the Water Mages, but he's pretty damned effective against the nonmagic guards. He is controlled, precise, not dealing out any bolts of his fire magic until he's sure of the target. After a few moments of healing, Remy is just as precise, his blades moving with grim determination. He keeps his back to Rafael's, not going more than a few paces from him.

Four of us, and the snakes, against maybe a hundred guards.

And I have to get to Wren—but there are more guards *and* a fucking water god between me and her, not to mention the Black Water Witches that haven't yet turned and run.

"Any ideas?" I yell to Rafael.

"I'm all out!" he yells back. "Isn't it your turn?" Blood—probably not his—coats his arm and is splashed across one side of his face.

He's panting from the exertion, his blond hair now dark with sweat. He's got to be getting close to burnout by now.

"I have an idea, but none of you are going to like it!" Caelus yells back.

"This is worse than any idea Rafael has had, *ever*," I say. "I won't do it."

We're backed into a corner now, the arena wall at our back and the wall by the portcullis—the one the guard hid behind while unleashing the snake beast—to our side. The stone snake has been toppled by winds from Wren's magical storm, the heads broken off. It ironically provides us some measure of protection, a way to keep the guards from overwhelming us with their sheer numbers.

"You have to," Caelus says, his yellow eyes locked on mine, unblinking. His gray-brown hair whips wildly in the winds.

I think back to the vision-hallucination of Rigrasil, when he said I would betray him, break the Law of the Shields, give up *everything*—

"Unless you can think of a better way. We can get rid of Aenon—then you'll just have to finish Evanthia," Caelus says, his voice even, calm. Resigned.

"It is an honorable plan," Remy says gravely. "But I don't like it."

"Gods, I don't like it either," Rafael says, blasting a line of fire in front of us, creating a temporary barrier that the guards are unwilling to cross. "But there are rules, aren't there? Great magic requires great sacrifice. I can't see another way around it."

"Let's get to the books," Caelus says. His worn face is tired, his skin practically gray already, but he squares his shoulders, adjusts the grip on his swords, and stands tall. He murmurs a prayer to Rigrasil under his breath.

I regret this already, and for once I begin to doubt myself. Can I go through with it? The very idea makes me want to vomit.

Wren is on the far side of the arena, deflecting bolts of magic from Evanthia, Mariana, and even Aenon, who seems genuinely perplexed. Nothing can get through the sphere of green light that Wren has created, though she seems to be mostly on defense. Three against one is a lot, even for my Mage—especially when one of those three is a god.

The four of us race across the arena floor, aiming for Evanthia. Some of the guards chase us and are either cut down by Remy or by blasts of fire from Rafael. Caelus is single-mindedly running, his eyes focused on the books—and just past them, on Mariana, her clothes ripped and stained, her pale hair wild.

The books are at her feet, discarded or at least temporarily forgotten. She turns and sees Caelus, hells-bent on getting to her, the three of us hard on his heels.

Her gaze flicks to the glimmering books, her eyes wide. Remy and Rafael break off from us, keeping back a phalanx of guards.

Mariana stops attacking Wren, turns from Aenon, and scoops the books up just as Caelus reaches her. She glares at him but doesn't speak—she cannot harm him, not without risk to herself.

Caelus reaches her, his hands over hers on the books, his lips still murmuring a prayer to Rigrasil, mightiest of the gods.

I reach him a breath later, put a hand on his shoulder, and murmur my own prayer.

And without hesitation, I run my blade through his heart.

CHAPTER 57
WREN

Mariana's shriek pierces the night like nothing I've ever heard. As close as I am now, on the arena floor, I see the blood dribble from between Caelus's lips. The beatific smile on his face.

I see him fall to his knees, still looking at his Mage.

I see Aris pull his sword out of his friend's chest, the man he called *brother*, and meant it, more than his own blood.

I see a flash of light, the books glowing in gold, bronze, and silver—

The air is sucked from the arena, a great rush of wind and sand converging on the books, a blinding sun forming for one single instant—

And Aenon vanishes, returned to his immortal prison; the requirement for great sacrifice, met.

The books fall from Mariana's hands, hands that are now listless, falling to her sides. Her skin is ashen, her expression blank.

She's gone gray.

And Queen Evanthia is alone on the arena floor.

And my rage, my grief, my pain, so long suppressed, will not be assuaged.

To lose Caelus, after everything we've been through together—and now, when he gave his life to save ours, perhaps to save our world.

I cannot bear it.

The lightning bursts from me, crackling through the air, striking again and again at Evanthia as she hurls her own magic at me, until she crumples, until she is nothing but a charred husk, smoking against the molten sand beneath her.

And I don't stop there. The lightning strays from my command, becoming erratic, striking out at the arena, at the guards, at the Water Mages still trying in vain to attack. Evanthia was not enough. I will tear this island apart, stone by stone.

Evanthia and Aris were born of the gods.

I have become one.

CHAPTER 58
ARIS

I pull my sword from Caelus's chest and lay him down on the blood-soaked sand. His yellow eyes are closed, a smile on his face. I fold his hands over the hole I made through his chest. My vision blurs. I feel Rafael's hand on my shoulder, and Remy's, in wordless communion.

"Safe travels, brother. And thank you," I say, touching my own chest in reverence. His sacrifice has saved us all.

A blinding green flash lights the arena, drawing my attention—Evanthia is gone, now nothing but a smoking ruin of black fabric, a cracked sapphire in a molten mass that was once her crown.

Wren is hovering a few feet off the ground. She's not far from me now—I can be at her side in a heartbeat, have my arms around her.

Or I could, but there's a growing storm around her, the kind that she made before, back at the school.

Only this time it's not a funnel cloud. There's a net of green light in a sphere around her, fifteen or twenty feet across. Her arms are outstretched, green light glowing from her eyes.

"Wren!" I yell—but she doesn't hear me.

Winds rips through the arena, faster and faster, sand flying into our eyes. I try to shield my face with a hand, but the sand tears into the exposed skin, flaying my hand. I swear, but the skin is already knitting back together.

The guards around us are not so lucky. Some of them clutch their faces, moaning. Most of them turn and flee, as fast as they can. The stands are also rapidly emptying. Lightning the color of jade flashes from Wren, fracturing the stone of the arena with every strike. Pieces of rock fly through the air, some weighing a hundred pounds or more. They smash into the sandy arena floor, or sometimes into someone's femur. All I can hear is the howl of the wind and the scream of injured men and women.

"She needs to stop!" Remy shouts. He's at my side, streaks of blood across his face where sand has struck him and the skin already healed. He's shielding Rafael, who's crouched behind him, holding his own Mage robe over his head.

"Why doesn't she stop?" Rafael asks.

Fuck.

Because she can't.

Wren is beyond listening, beyond reason. She can't hear me, or she doesn't care. Water droplets form a glittering veil around her green orb, then sparks of fire, flecks of sand. The orb grows, and the destruction increases.

A lightning bolt hits near my feet, the shock knocking me to my knees. My boots are singed; the sand, turned to black glass. A rock cracks against my skull, and for a moment, everything goes dark and quiet. Hot blood runs down the side of my face, and I am disoriented.

Wren screams, tears running down her cheeks, and a ripple of green energy pulses from her. People across the arena are knocked off their feet. The green wave strikes the arena stands, and the rock begins to crumble, great sections of it coming down, crushing people beneath them.

I have to get to her. I think back to the first time she manifested her magic, that night at the School of the Silver Flame. She was out of control then, though to a much lesser extent—and it was my touch that brought her back, that grounded her.

Another large rock strikes my ankle, and I both hear and feel the bone crack.

Fuck. Again.

I try to put weight on it, but I can't.

So I hop. I hop, and then I crawl, one agonizing inch at a time, each time getting just a little closer to my Mage.

Remy and Rafael have dropped back. Remy can't protect Rafael against the blasts that Wren is dealing out, and she doesn't seem to care who or what she is destroying.

The ground beneath me cracks, a fissure widening by the second. I struggle into a crouch and throw myself over the crevasse, landing on both feet—the injured one protests, but it holds. *Thank you, Rigrasil, for healing magic.*

A wall of sparks strikes me next, burning the skin on one side of my face. I can smell my own skin charring, can see the sinews of my hands exposed—but I press on.

If I don't stop her, she'll overextend herself. She'll go gray. I don't care if she sends this whole fucking island back to Aenon's depths—but I will *not* let *her* go.

I get to the green orb surrounding her. It crackles and zaps against me, leaving little charred spots on my clothes as I push through. My skin feels like a dozen hot knives are being plunged into me all at once, and my breathing becomes fast, shallow, as my ribs are flayed—but I keep going, and my body keeps healing, or trying to.

Inside the sphere, the storm is calm. The air is still, and I fight to keep from groaning as my body tries to heal the damage it just withstood.

"Wren!" I cry. My voice is hoarse from sand, but she doesn't seem to hear me. She doesn't react to my presence at all, just keeps looking beyond me. She has burns like spiderwebs across her cheeks and hands.

And she is crying.

The whites and beautiful jade of her eyes are replaced with green stars. Her mouth is open in a wordless scream of agony as she hovers several inches off the ground. I can't tell if this is her pain manifesting as the storm, or the storm causing her pain—either way, I get her attention the only way I know how.

I reach up and bring her down, my hands applying gentle pressure to her shoulders. She doesn't register the contact at all. She is a conduit now, a monster in her own right.

And the love of my life.

I lean forward and kiss her.

A jolt goes through me, a lightning bolt to my chest, and I feel like my ribs are caving in. My heart pauses its thunderous beating for a second, then two, then three.

I take a deep breath and pull back, my heartbeat pounding again, quickly, making up for lost time. The storm around us has eased. I can hear the roar of blood in my skull and for a moment feel off-balance.

And my Wren is looking up at me.

Wren, with her clear gray-green eyes, dark purple smudged below them. She lifts a trembling hand to my face, like she's not sure I'm real. Blood covers the side of her head and cheek, the skin charred and peeling. Her hands are blackened and cracked, her nail beds ripped and bleeding. Part of her hair has been singed away. Her lips part, chapped and split, and I run my thumb over them as gently as I can.

"Hey, Firefly," I say. "I'm here."

Overhead, the sky is dark and clear.

She gives me a tremulous smile—before her eyes roll back in her head, and she goes limp in my arms.

CHAPTER 59
ARIS

It's a long, *long* trip home to Estana. Leo leaves Rafael and Remy to manage things in Roallac. After Wren's storm cleared, the Ocronian army swarmed into the capital. There was no resistance to the occupation, not when the citizens got the news of Evanthia's fiery demise. Delphine had already flown back to Estana, Adriana told us. I was beyond pissed that she got Delphine involved at all—she is untrained, still a child, though admittedly she'll be a fearsome Shield someday. Adriana flipped her hair over her shoulder, reminding me that Delphine *had* changed the tide of the battle, after all, and freed Wren. They never planned on her doing anything more than melting the cage that Wren was kept in, one that Adriana had noted on one of her spying flights. The rip in her wing, she assured me, had healed well, barely even a scar.

Still. It will be a long time before I forgive Adriana and the others for using Delphine like that, even though she'd wanted to help. I twist her leather bracelet around my wrist, anxious to get back and start training Delphine for real, so that she never, *ever* has to face anything unprepared again. What would have happened to her had Aenon won? There was no doubt in my mind that he would have started ripping pages from the books, eliminating the magic of the Shields more effectively than any manacle. We would have been a race of cripples, Delphine included. And the Mages? None of us really believed he would have let them keep their magic, either. With the balance of the other gods absent, our world would have had no option but to succumb to his power.

I'll get Delphine some swords of her own, I decide. I'll even let her name them.

We place Caelus's body in a cart and cover him with a golden cloak someone stole from Evanthia's closets. Leo rides at the head of the cart, head high, leading a funeral procession fit for a king.

And it seems, despite everything, Roallac is going to be a part of Ocron after all. Funny how that worked out. The books come with us too—kept safe, under constant surveillance. If Leo's used them to speak to the gods, he doesn't say. I, for one, have no interest in ever speaking to or hearing from any of the gods ever again, for as long as I live.

Leo's own flagship sails us down the Golmere River, borne on the tides of his Water Mages. We disembark and find a small army of courtiers and carriages to bring us home. Leo—after some sleep and food—still has a haggard, haunted look about him, but he's regained a little of his charm, a little of his fire. He comes to check on Wren often, his glance lingering on her fondly.

But still, she sleeps. I know how long a Shield can go without food or water, but she's far surpassed that, her body maintained only by magic and probably her own sheer stubbornness. Her body is in a kind of stasis, though I see her heal day by day. The magic has taken its toll on her, marking her with lightning and moonlight.

I pray to Rigrasil like I've never prayed before. Even to Caladrius, if he's listening. I hope Caelus puts in a good word for me with the gods—or at least for Wren. Leo has his staff bring us food and drink, but most of it goes untouched. I sit in vigil with her—no matter how long it takes. If it takes the rest of our mortal lives, I'll wait.

I adjust the green pendant she still wears around her neck,

rubbing my thumb over a facet. Leo's offered me a ridiculous sum of money for my part in his rescue—I don't often care about money, but I have plans for this, for Wren's future, and mine. And I swear to Rigrasil I will buy her every green gem in the Dragon Spine mountains for her if she'll just wake.

After the battle, when I slumped to the floor of Soltaire's arena with Wren in my arms, the dust settling around us, my knee landed on something hard and metallic. Something so small that either Aenon had left behind by accident or, as I chose to believe, Rigrasil had somehow sent back to me on purpose. I keep it in my pocket at all times, and run my fingers over it as I pray.

When we get to Estana, a horse-drawn carriage awaits us, flying banners of red with the gold sun of Estana, and a black flag adorned with a white crescent moon and the roaring outline of a tiger. It marks the carriage as being of equal importance to that of the king—and people shout and cry as we pass. I'd rather ride with the rest of the Shields or even walk than be stuffed into this small space, but I won't leave Wren. She wears her black robe, face calm in sleep.

People throw roses before the carriage—big, fragrant ones, a deep red-violet. Tamdosan roses. Wren's favorite. I grab a couple and lay them on her chest after trimming the thorns off with my knife. The people call for me too. "Dragonslayer!" they cry. I hate the attention—me, who Wren has referred to on multiple occasions as a "great preening peacock." But now it feels hollow. I killed my own brother—and when I look at the faces of the Shields around me, all I can feel is their judgment, their anger. I broke the Law of the Shields, and I will be—at best—stricken from their records, like I never existed. At worst, they could demand my death.

Their insults are nothing I haven't repeated to myself a thousand times. I will never be able to forgive myself either—but in a way, I know that Caelus did, and that is the only thing that makes it all bearable.

Still Wren doesn't wake. The wounds on her face and scalp have scabbed over, resistant to the Water Mages' healing magic and instead healing at their own rate. There is a full moon in a few more days, and I can only hope that Rigrasil's magic will heal her like it did before and bring her back to me. I care nothing for the scars she bears—only that she wakes.

At the palace, I carry her through the halls. People stop and whisper as we pass, though some bow their heads or clutch their hands to their chests. I ignore them, and they stay out of my way. I'm greeted by Tolis in our old rooms. He's had them prepared for Wren, with every comfort he could gather. I've only just laid her on the bed and tucked her in—still sleeping—when the door to the hallway is flung open, the stones quaking under my feet, and I am tackled by Ismini and Aleka.

"Glad to have you back, kitten," Aleka says gruffly, stepping back and punching me on the arm.

I pretend not to notice her wipe her eyes.

Ismini still holds me, one hand to her mouth as she looks down at Wren. "Still asleep? Like last time?" she asks.

"Longer," I say, unable to keep the fatigue from my voice. I run a hand over the scruff collecting on my cheeks.

"Go clean up," Ismini orders, sitting down at Wren's side and taking her small brown hand between her own calloused ones, dirt firmly caked beneath her nails. "I'll stay with her for a bit."

I nod, for two reasons, really. One, I'm way too tired to argue with Ismini, and I'd lose anyway. And two, the bathing room is adjacent to Wren's chambers, so I won't be far—and I stink. So three reasons, I guess. I'm too tired to count.

The three of us sit with her for days on end. The night of the full moon does heal Wren's wounds—the laceration on her scalp closes, and the burn marks on her face become dark and flat.

And still she does not wake.

The country moves on—but I have no interest in it. Leo stops by a few times a day, usually accompanied by a phalanx of courtiers armed with books and papers, and by the court's most ambitious unattached women, armed with tightly laced corsets and doe-eyed expressions. Leo leaves bouquets of flowers, so many that I've started stashing them in Rafael's old room because the smell is giving me a headache. Well-wishers from all over the continent send letters and gifts, which remain unopened in the common room in great piles, like snowdrifts. Orothea and Adriana stop by, usually together. They seem to have become good friends. Adriana tells me that Orothea still aims to be queen someday. I couldn't care less for the gossip, but it is nice having at least one sibling who doesn't hate my guts.

I've heard nothing from Rea, though Adriana tells me she's gone back to the school to complete her training. Lukas has been promoted and is working directly under Markos here in the capital. He aims to be Shield Commander himself someday, she says. I groan—the last thing I need is Lukas as my Commander. And Myron's Mage has had his baby, a boy, so I guess I'm an uncle now. Delphine is insisting on calling me "Uncle Aris" all the time—at first a joke, because Myron's had a son, but I think she likes pretending I'm *her* family, and I find I don't really mind.

Delphine comes to see me and Wren often, though she's been training with Aleka and the other Shields every other available moment she has. Adriana says she's doing well, working hard. I expected no less. She's filling out, starting to gain some of the muscle that all adolescent Shields gain. Delphine says she'd rather train with me, wherever I go, than stay here without us—though I haven't been to the training room once since we got back. Adriana talks a lot about Delphine, and about everything, really, like she's filling up the quiet space in Wren's room. She talks to Wren like she expects her to respond.

I do *not* want to hear Adriana talk about Tekton anymore.

And still Wren does not wake.

Tulliano has returned to Estana from Roallac, on his way back to the school. I send one of the palace servants to get him. Tulliano greets me with a wordless grunt, but his eyes light up when he sees my swords. I've polished them to gleaming—honestly, what else do I have to do?—and he admires them like a parent admiring a newborn baby. He critiques the leather wrapping on the hilts and offers me a few pointers. I've had an idea rattling around in my brain for ages, and I only trust him to see it through. He's still the finest metalsmith I've ever met, and when I tell him what I'd like to do, he straightens immediately.

"It would be my greatest honor," he says, accepting the dragon's tooth from me. As he takes it, I feel a great weight lift from me. "I will have it for you in a few days."

I give him Caelus's swords and shield too. The palace metalsmiths have offered to mount them for me, in accordance with Shield tradition, but I want Tulliano to do it. He forged the swords, like mine, was there for their births—it is only right that he should be there at their end.

"Aris, where in all the hells is your helmet?" he asks.

I shrug and rub the back of my neck, which is suddenly warm. I loved that helmet—it was made like the roaring face of a tiger, a true masterpiece that Tulliano made for me ages ago.

"Um," I say, looking at him. "Abelon? Or Basti, maybe?" I can't really remember when I saw it last.

"Things have a way of coming back to us," he says, reminding me that he's been able to track it down once before, when I lost it in Aclines. He points one big, calloused finger at me. "But I'm not making you another one!"

I meet Tulliano a few days later at the crypts. I haven't left Wren's side in ages—it feels good to be moving, though strange to be without her. I can feel the magic linking us, our claim, like a distant chime only. If she wakes, I have no doubt I'll hear it, loud and clear as a bell—and then nothing will keep me from her.

When Tulliano meets me, I see he's far surpassed my expectations. He's bound the dragon's tooth, which is longer than my hand, to a hilt of shining steel. The grip is wrapped with twisted gold wire, the pommel inlaid with a stone as golden as Dimitra's eyes. I am at a loss for words, and the ornate dagger blurs in my vision. Tulliano lays one massive, calloused palm on my shoulder. His touch is hot, like the fire magic he works with.

I lay the dragon-tooth dagger in front of Dimitra's tomb. There is no body there, not even her ashes—but I know her spirit is there. Her vibrant, indomitable spirit.

"Told you it would make a good weapon," I say, to no one in particular.

Tulliano looks away so I can wipe my eyes and read the inscription on her stele.

Dimitra Gataki
Leopard
Claimed of Rafael Petreius, Fire Mage
Honorable in life and in death.
Her ashes lie scattered in Abelon.

Hers is far from the only empty tomb.

We go next to Caelus's tomb. This part of the Shield crypts is crowded, the group gathered there murmuring and touching their chests in reverence. This is my first time coming to see him. Word of his sacrifice has traveled the country like wildfire, and prayers written on rolled paper are tied all over this section. He'd have liked that.

I look over the rustling crowd to the tomb, around which a hundred spelled candles are glimmering. His shield is mounted above his stele, the swords crossed over it.

I frown, for a moment not trusting my own eyes.

"You said you weren't going to change anything," I say to Tulliano.

His eyes are wide, his ruddy face pale.

"I swear to you, on the name of Ignatius himself, I did no such thing," he says, and his voice trembles.

A man drops to his knees beside us, praying.

The shield and swords are no longer wood and steel and leather, but gold.

Pure, *glowing* gold.

CHAPTER 60
WREN

When I wake, I'm no longer in Roallac, of that much I'm sure. When I fainted, I was in the arena at night, surrounded by sand. I didn't think I'd wake at all.

Now I'm in a comfortable bed, piled high with soft white pillows and fluffy golden blankets. Sunshine streams in through the doorway.

Silhouetted by the light is a shape I'd recognize anywhere, shoulders slumped, hair hanging, hiding his face.

"Aris," I try to say, but my throat barely moves; my voice sounds like nothing more than a croak.

But he hears it.

He leaps to my side, eyes as blue as the sky searching my face, his warm hands caressing my face, reassuring himself that I've come back to him.

I'm confused, though—Aris has short hair. Or ... he did.

"How long ...?" I croak.

He takes my hands in his; mine look frail, weak. White scars branch and trail across both wrists, disappearing under the sleeves of my white nightgown. I've been unconscious long enough for Aris's hair to grow long again, long enough for the wounds on my wrists—I vaguely recall the lightning burning across my skin—to heal and turn into scars, unless they'd been healed by a Water Mage.

"You've been asleep for a while," Aris admits, smiling fondly. The whites of his eyes glimmer. He bends forward, pressing his lips briefly to mine.

"Where are we?" I ask.

"We're back in Estana. It's done. You did it, Wren. It's done."

"We. We did it," I say.

He nods.

I struggle to sit up, surprised by how weak I've become. *Great magic has always required great sacrifice*, Caladrius said. My skin is warm and brown, not gray—but something has leached from me, something taken in repayment for the magic I unleashed that day.

I raise a hand to my face, to brush a strand of hair back—Aris stops me, taking my hand once more in his.

"The lightning scarred you," he explains after a moment. "I don't want you to be afraid when you touch your face."

I've never been particularly vain. I am proud of my hair, which I've always worn long in a braid, in Aclinese tradition. But my skin tone has too long marked me as someone abnormal, someone unbeautiful, to spend too much time concerned about my appearance.

Still.

When Aris looked at me—*looks* at me—I always felt it. I always feel that in his eyes I am beautiful, even when I'm dirty and tired and sweaty.

I look at him, and the smile on his lips. To him, I still *am* beautiful, regardless of what's happened to me.

And that's all that matters.

I nod, and he releases my hands. My fingers shake as they reach up and trace the contours of my face. My whole body feels stiff and weak, my face included—but my fingers trace the whole curve of my chin, my lips, before encountering a thick, waxy scar on my right cheek. It travels and splits, like tree branches—or like a bolt of lightning—up to my right ear and into my hairline at my temple. I can feel that the hair there has been shorn, now only an inch or two long. The hairs there feel wiry, different—so I pluck one, bringing it down so I can see.

The strand is as white as the full moon.

"The scars healed well. And the white streak—well, personally, I think it looks quite dashing. I may dye mine to match," Aris says, his mouth rising on one side.

"Are you ...?" I ask. Is he all right? I have no idea what kind of torture Queen Evanthia may have used on him, what he must have been through. I link my fingers through his, needing his strength, his warmth.

"I'm fine," he tells me, though his eyes turn dark, like the sea. "I'll tell you the whole tale sometime. After we get you back on your feet. And after I ask you a very important question."

He kneels at my bedside and digs something out of his pocket.

He opens his palm to show me three rings—two plain iron bands, one large and one small, and a silver ring set with a small green stone. I have no idea how he got them—I thought surely Aenon had taken them with him, back to the immortal realm. Were they a gift from Rigrasil, perhaps?

I clutch the necklace I still wear, the green crystal matching this ring exactly. He looks up at me. My Aris. We have been through all the hells and back again together—and I realize our journey is just beginning.

He holds up the ring with the green stone.

"Verena Harker, will you marry me?"

LETTER
FROM KING LEONIDAS III OF OCRON TO NIGHT MAGE VERENA HARKER

My dear Wren,

Verena Valorius has a nice ring to it. Congratulations—my gifts will be arriving at Aeturnus shortly. I do hope you find them useful. I wish you had let me throw you both a lavish wedding ceremony in Estana—the people would have loved it. Still, I understand you aren't ready to be seen yet, as you get used to living with the injuries the battle left you with. Please understand that for the rest of my life, I will owe you everything. Whatever you need, whatever you want, will be yours. You have only to ask.

It seems your support of Lady Orothea has won over most of my council—a royal marriage is always more of a political decision than a personal one. She has been my friend since we were children, and I was impressed by her dedication during the Battle of Roallac. She will make a fine queen.

Adriana tells me that you and Aris are settling in quite well at the

Temple of the God of Night. Iraklis has several students already wanting to apply to your new school—Aleka, too, has recommended a few fine young Shields to train there with Aris (not to mention, they all want to meet the young dragon Shield he's training!). Though officially Aris is no longer a Shield of Ocron, he is still a Shield that will inspire a generation (but don't tell him I said that).

Things here in Estana are remarkably busy. The last of the Black Water Witches have stood trial, and most of them are being sent back to Roallac to work on rebuilding their city, and adding infrastructure like roads and—yes—even schools. Don't worry—nothing like the school you and Aris are building, or like the School of the Silver Flame. (Please tell me you've come up with a better name for your school than the Silver Flame. I think we can both agree it's an awful name. How about 'the School of the Great King Leonidas III' or something?) We're permitting them to start training the younger magic students, though, with the idea that they'll transfer to an Ocronian when they come of age, and I think it's going to go a long way to bridging the gap between our cultures. Rafael and Remiel have oversight of these schools, and we are putting Rafael's brain to work developing their curriculum.

We found Panos. Did you know? Dead in the swamp. It seems not even that slippery traitor could outwit the snakes there—though, I'll be honest, I have to wonder if he even intended to. His loss hits me hard, and I fear I may never get over his betrayal. I could use his sound advice these days, though Ismini is doing her best (and she often brings me scones, which helps quite a bit).

Caelus's golden swords and shield have become something of a shrine. I've had to have Aleka station guards there at all times—she's worried they'll be stolen by some zealot. I must say, Rigrasil's temple (and Caladrius's, for that matter) have both gotten a lot busier lately. I considered tearing Aenon's down, but alas, my advisers dissuaded me.

I hope you are well, my little bird, and that life in the mountains pleases you.

. . .

I remain forever your friend,
Leo

THE END

ACKNOWLEDGMENTS

When I started writing books, I was naive enough to think that being an "independent" author meant that I could do everything by myself.

Nothing could be further from the truth.

I would not be here if were not for the love of reading that my parents fostered; without the encouragement and patience and love of my husband, without whom none of this would have ever seen the light of day.

For my amazing editors, Ben and Leonora. You have taught me so much. I am immeasurably grateful for the time and effort you put into polishing these books.

For my artists—Gabrielle, Christin, and Salome, who brought my beautiful covers to life. For Sebastian, my extraordinary (and extraordinarily patient) cartographer. For Chloe, Meghan, Astora, Alex, and Sophia for the outstanding character art.

For the Bad Ass Book Club—your support and encouragement has meant the world to me.

For my incredible social media community—for my alpha readers, Helen and Katelyn; for my beta and ARC readers, who are too numerous to count at this point which is kind of mind-boggling; and for all those who have read and loved Wren and Aris as much as I have.

Thank you.

ABOUT THE AUTHOR

E. M. Leander lives in the American South with her husband, two children, and two fluffy cats. A life-long lover of all things literary, when she's not spending free time with family, she can be found devouring books and coffee in equal measure.

Also by E. M. Leander:

Space Camp:

-The View from Ganymede

-Daughters of Jupiter

Game of Gods:

-Wren and the Tarnished Tiger

-Aris and the Obsidian Door

-The Immortal Scales

www.ingramcontent.com/pod-product-compliance
Lightning Source LLC
Chambersburg PA
CBHW020458310726
48979CB00016B/2706/J

* 9 7 9 8 9 9 0 4 6 6 6 0 9 *